Quiet Water

Heather Rivera

This book is a work of fiction. Names, characters, places, and incidents are either products of the author's imagination or are used fictitiously. Any resemblance to actual events or locales or persons, living or dead, is entirely coincidental.

Copyright © 2013 Heather Rivera
All rights reserved.

ISBN: 1491027215
ISBN-13: 9781491027219

Library of Congress Control Number: 2013913509
CreateSpace Independent Publishing Platform
North Charleston, South Carolina

For Mom and Mark

Acknowledgments

Mom—who participated in my "All things Tess" adventures and provided much needed and invaluable feedback throughout the process.

Mark—my constant soundboard, supporter, and adviser of the male perspective.

Jill Q. Weiss—my editor: for her knowledge, patience, and kindness.

Jeff Michaels—for his guidance and for challenging me.

With immense gratitude for my very supportive first readers who provided much needed feedback and suggestions—Paula Friedman, Lillian Nader, Lesli McCafferty-Meyers, Jo Cornhall.

Dr. Marjorie Miles and her *Writing with Your Inner Dream Muse* class—it was here, in her warm, supportive class, that I first heard Tess' voice.

Leonard Szymczak—for his coaching, guidance and encouragement.

And for the many that cheered me on—Frances Pullin, Rebecca Proud, Edith Hart, Steven Jay Schwartz, Liv Haugland, Jean Noel Bassior, Ryen Schwartz, Debbie Barnett, Paula Marshall, Carol Hubbard, Sean, Seth, Evan, Maegan, and Amber. If I missed someone, I apologize.

Cover Design by Laura Gordon at bookcovermachine@wordpress.com

Website Design by Kris Voelker at http://www.krisvoelkerdesigns.com

www.heatherrivera.com

www.plrinstitute.org

Prologue

The room is silent except for his singing and her quickened breath. He sings aloud as he twirls her around. They enjoy their private dance. He continues his serenade of a familiar tune—making up the words as he goes along.

"You are not singing the proper words," she scolds.

"Oh, did you not hear? They changed the song after learning of your beauty." He tries to look convincing.

She laughs at his antics, but secretly she's pleased that he's singing about her. He sings softer, closer to her ear. Now he's barely audible—only a hum. He reaches to the back of her head and pulls the tortoise shell comb from her hair. Her long, blond hair tumbles down past her shoulders. She throws her head back in abandon as his lips graze her neck.

Thomas' body responds in kind to Kathleen. He dreams of kissing every inch of her delicate frame. He has imagined making love to her many a sleepless night. Soon they will marry and he can relish all the nights of his life caressing, kissing, and exploring the lovely Kathleen. For now, he must wait with unbearable anticipation.

Kathleen is hopelessly in love with this man and she knows he feels the same. She never knew she could be so happy. Thomas is dashing, and such a charmer. Her life with him will be perfect. He'll protect her and care for her needs and she'll make him very happy as his wife, she muses.

Chapter 1

Broken. More broken plates and cups, or worse . . . Damn, there goes the champagne wedding flutes. I curse under my breath and gather myself and the delicate crystal pieces that spill from the overturned box. Shards of china fall between the open steps and rain down on unsuspecting insects living in the grass below.

The stairs get steeper with each box; I'm sure of it. Whose bright idea was it to attempt moving on my own? Oh yeah, mine. It's taken me three trips back and forth from my old home in the San Fernando Valley, with my dinky new car, to an upstairs apartment in Belmont Shore. In retrospect, maybe I shouldn't have turned down Naomi's offer to help me move. But no, not independent Tess, ready to tackle living on my own single-handedly. Yeah, right. Not only my plates are broken, but my spirit. I'll never admit that to anyone. If anyone asks, I'll adamantly deny it. What the hell happened to my life? What happened to all my planning and good intentions?

My life, stored in twelve non-descript boxes, stares at me from the middle of the living room. How is it that the last seventeen years of memories and life can be crammed into such a few cartons? Mementos and tokens collected over time from my married life with Richard and my son, Wade, reduced to this. Will Wade ever start talking to me again? Maybe it's a teenage phase? This whole situation feels unreal, unfair, and downright depressing. And so, the boxes sit there waiting to be unpacked and be, once more, a part of my life. For now they'll stay in a sort of suspended animation. I'm only living off the bare essentials. That's all I can gather the energy for.

I can't stare at those boxes any longer. Maybe some fresh air will do me good.

At the bottom of the stairs I feel the paralysis of my mood set in; I have no energy to walk down the street. The curb seems like the only viable option. I plop down in front of my grey apartment building. I know I can't sit here on the curb forever. I don't have it in me to suck it up right now. My reserves have been depleted. Jeez, I'm a disaster. I look down at my stained yellow tank top and brush away errant strands of brown hair that tickle my nostrils. I redo my ponytail that was haphazardly tied up who knows when. Not that I need to look good for anyone right now, no need even for makeup. I don't give a damn. I can't even muster up that energy.

The heat is oppressive, pressing down upon me, threatening to meld me to the curb. I let it permeate me and push me further down. Time seems to slow to a crawl as I sit here staring at the asphalt.

From somewhere behind me a clacka-clack of metal on metal jars me from ruminating. I turn my head towards the sound.

"Hey there neighbor," a woman calls out as she slams her screen door.

Shit. I can't even be depressed alone.

"Hello," I answer back. Maybe she'll go away now.

"Hangin' on the curb alone? Want company?"

"Uh."

"Thought you could use someone to talk to. I remember when I first moved here I was a freakin' mess." The door slammer plunks down next to me on the curb. "Hot out here today for January, huh? Want a soda?" She hands me a cold can.

"Thanks." If I get up she'll think I'm rude. Now I'm stuck here trying to be neighborly. Can it get any worse?

"I moved here after I found out that Donald, my boyfriend, well ex-boyfriend, was cheatin' on me. We lived in Escondido, had a real nice condo with a pool. I was a real sucker for him even though he treated me like shit. Well this one day I came home from my job and there he was with this girl in my freakin' pool. Can you believe it?"

I take the soda can and rub my forehead with it. "What did you do?" I ask, my interest piqued a little. At least my over-processed blond, collagen-lipped, door-slamming neighbor is a nice distraction from my own mess.

"Well, that's what I'm sayin,' I was a real sucker for him. I should've left right then and there, but hell no. He says to me, 'Give me a kiss woman' and I . . ."

"No. You didn't?"

"Sure did. He ducked his head under the water as I leaned down towards the edge of the pool to give him a kiss and you know what that shit did?" Ms. Slammer stops to take a long swig of cola. "He pops back up and spits a mouthful of pool water in my face."

"No way."

"Oh yeah, him and his girl were cracking up. Funniest thing in the world to them."

"So you left him then?"

"Ah . . . no, not right away. Guess I'm not the sharpest toothpick in the dispenser. Took a while to come to my senses, but then eventually I got fed up. I transferred to the Long Beach office and moved my ass here. Anyway, I could see the 'just became single' vibe coming off you a mile away."

"That obvious, huh?"

"Oh yeah, honey. If you want to talk about it sometime, stop by. Well anyway, I'm Valerie. Valerie Snyder. I prefer Valerie to Val though. I really hate when people call you nicknames. I was named Valerie, not freakin' Val. Sorry. Gets my goat. I live right below you so no wild parties, at least not without me." She elbows my arm holding the soda causing some to splash on my shorts.

"Valerie, huh? I like you already. I hate nicknames too. I'm Tess Whitaker. I wasn't always Tess. I actually created and became Tess when I was seventeen. Jasmine Estrada was my birth name. Now with the name Tess, no one can shorten it."

"That must be some interesting story. Go on." Valerie tucks her hair behind her ear, giving me the "tell me" look.

"Uh. Let's just say that Jasmine was buried along with many other things. I'm really not up to talking about it right now. I'm having enough trouble with today without dredging more painful memories from twenty-one years ago." I pull out the whale-fluke pendant from under my shirt and rub it as I have done for years. It has become my worry stone of sorts.

"Hey. Don't mention it. One day at a time, right? Let's get through this shit-day first."

"Yeah, I'm aware that I'm going to have to get up sometime. But since I don't have any deadlines until next week, I can stay here until then or at least until I get hungry," I chuckle.

"Well at least you're being productive on the curb." She points to the sidewalk.

Between my legs, I've amassed quite a pile of plucked weeds. Guess I've been absentmindedly grooming the parkway of weeds growing between the cracks of the old sidewalk—controlling the weeds outside before I tackle the one inside me.

"Yeah, being productive." I spot a shard of glass in the gutter, pick it up and cut at the fibers of my already demolished cutoffs. "Ever do this?"

"Nah, can't say I have. We didn't have much money growing up. My mom would've beat my ass for tearing up clothes."

"I remember doing this when I was fourteen. A group of us would gather on the curb and smoke and pick holes in our jeans with glass fragments. Oh, we were so cool. My mom would freak when she saw the holes in my jeans. I'd have to come up with some lame excuse since I really couldn't say how they got there. 'It's been like that,' I would tell her and then dive into my room before any further interrogation. Smoking really never worked for me since I couldn't actually inhale without a severe asthma attack. Good thing it didn't stick, since focusing on health and fitness is, or should I say was, my career," I explain.

"Was your career?"

"Yeah, sold my half of the gym. I do some freelance writing too."

"I'm in travel. Book trips for folks. Really great job and I get to work at home. Really helpful when people get stuck on the curb. Hey, why don't I get you something stronger than a soda? Think I have some beer in the fridge. Back in a sec." Valerie gets up and heads towards her apartment.

The sound of Valerie's screen door slamming shut reminds me I'm alone again. I feel sick.

Chapter 2

Maybe I should call Naomi. She's always been a good listener. Naomi Hall and I have been friends since I started the twelfth grade. She allows me to ramble on and on about plans and how I will strategically tackle my goals. She'll graciously listen and motivate me to move from this spot. I can hear her now, "Tess, you are a strong, independent woman. No one can hold you down. Now get your ass up and take control of your life." Next, she would probably start singing any inspirational song she thinks of to get me going. Gotta love her, but Naomi is completely tone deaf and that itself is enough to get me moving. I can't handle her singing, which of course she knows and will use to coerce me to action. I feel a glimmer of hope as I press the speed dial. She'll save the day. I just know it. She has to.

Three rings . . . Four rings . . . Five rings. And then her cheery voicemail begins. I'm sunk. I hang up the phone. I don't want to leave a voicemail and sound completely pathetic. I can hear myself, "Naomi, I don't want to bother you and I know logically that I'm doing the right thing by striking out on my own, but right now I can't recall why I ever thought this was a good idea. My life was fine and now I screwed it all up. My husband is struggling to adjust to the change. Wade won't speak to me. Oh and by the way, I can't even pull up the energy to get up off this damn, hot curb. So, can you help me remember why I'm doing this?" Nah, I can't leave a message like that so I hang up and stay glued to my spot.

Maybe, I'll use this opportunity to take in my new neighborhood. Let's see:
- Pink house across the street
- One-way street with many cars parked on both sides (and space enough for me to plant myself on the curb)
- One guy (grey tank top stretched over beer belly) fixing his blue mustang two doors down with 70s music playing on his radio

- Yappy dog somewhere behind me
- Ocean to the left about two and a half blocks down
- And 2nd Street with the assorted trendy shops and international cuisine one and a half blocks to my right

This would be great if I wasn't so damn depressed. I would love this town. Wait . . . I <u>will</u> love this town—Belmont Shore. That's why I chose it. I love still being in Los Angeles County, but tucked away, close to the ocean in this tiny section of Long Beach, California. I remember coming here as a child with my older brother, Jared. Grandma and Grandpa lived in Cerritos. A visit to them almost always meant Disneyland. What can be better than that to a nine-year-old? I fiddle with the fluke pendant. Old memories come forth as I rub Jared's necklace. I haven't taken it off since he passed away.

"Jared, you were four years older than I," I silently tell him. "I trusted you. Remember when we got to go off on our own in the park! I felt big, grown up, and free.

"I was so excited to go with you. You were the adventurous one. You could make any activity sound intriguing, but you also could be a real pain in the ass. Remember the time you held me down and shoved an open jar of horseradish in my face? I started gagging. My eyes and nose started to water. I thought I would throw up. Finally, mom came into the dining room yelling for you to stop. You relented and freed me. I was never so glad to see mom. I looked up to you, so when you picked on me it was crushing. Horseradish and I never reconciled. The smell still makes me want to vomit. Since you were my idol, all was quickly forgiven and I was once again tagging along with all of your exploits.

"At Disneyland, you told me the park was all mine and I could start anywhere I wanted. You said it was our goal to see it all. Tomorrowland was my first choice to conquer and we took off running through Main Street. After Space Mountain, the Matterhorn, Autopia, and Adventure through Inner Space (which sounded more exciting than it was), we headed to Fantasyland. There we rode Mr. Toad's Wild Ride, Dumbo, skipped over It's a Small World and ended up on Mad Hatter's Tea Cups. As we sat in our cup, I looked up at you and you had that devious look I had come to know so well.

"You warned, 'This will be a ride you won't forget. Better hold on.'

"'Jared, no. I'll tell mom!' I squealed. But you were right, I never did forget it.

"As the ride started, you were already attacking the wheel in the center that controlled our individual cup. We began to spin. We were spinning faster than the other cups and I was thinking that the other riders were jealous of us. At first it was exhilarating. At first I was glad that we got to do this alone. No family overseeing to keep us from having our fun. Yeah, life is so much better when we can do what we want. At least that is what I thought—at first.

"You kept up the frenzied pace on the wheel and I started feeling sick. I yelled for you to stop. I begged you to slow down, but you laughed. Everything got quiet in my head. My vision blurred, then went dark. I felt like I was going to pass out. I tried to tell you again that I was going to be sick, but no sound would come out. I lost my voice. Briefly I wondered if I would ever be able to speak again or if I was going to die. Suddenly, my head flew back. I couldn't hold it up anymore. I don't remember what happened next, but when I looked up the ride operator was shaking me and yelling at you. We were banned from that ride, I think for eternity. The bench looked miles away as I wobbled over to it. After a few minutes I recovered and then I was really pissed. I wasn't going to talk to you anymore as long as I lived, I vowed. Well, that lasted about twenty minutes. Soon we were heading toward the Haunted Mansion and were best buddies again.

"Yes, that was a lovely day except for the tea cup fiasco, but I kept that to myself. It was our little secret. The day ended up with the whole family having dinner in Belmont Shore—now my new home town. We ate at a great Italian restaurant. I can't remember the name, but I do remember that they had this pizza with ground pepperoni. No bite was lacking in pepperoni goodness. I haven't had that great of a pizza since, but I am not sure if my childhood memory is skewed. Maybe that restaurant is still here."

When I'm more energized I'll check out the area and see if I can find it. I will add that to my list:

- Get off curb
- Unpack
- Shower

- Check out beach
- Walk to 2nd Street and check out shops
- Look for ground pepperoni pizza
- Get life together
- Find out who Tess is
- Find love? (Maybe that's pressing my luck)

Valerie returns with a bottle of cold beer for the two of us and sits once again next to me, breaking me from my past memories.

"Thanks for the beer." I tuck my necklace back in my shirt and take the beer from her hand.

"Sure. I see you're making quite a hole in your jeans."

"Yeah, I guess." I should chuck this piece of glass, but it feels comfortable to hold on to it.

"Feeling any better yet?"

"Not sure. Was making a list."

"List?"

"I'm a list maker. It makes me feel like I have some control of things, of life . . ." I wasn't always a list maker. But tragedy has a way of shaking people out of their comfort zones—a myth that tells you that the world is secure and all will be well. It's quite a wake-up call to find out you really have no control of anything. And so, I was determined to exert some control somewhere. I would control me. I thought I constructed the perfect personality and lifestyle. I decided many years ago only to pay attention to the rational part of me and ignore superstition and hocus pocus intuition . . . What happened?

"Ow!" I cry out as I flinch from pain.

"Shit, girlfriend. What ya doin? You're not getting all suicidal on me, are you?" Valerie jumps up in horror.

Blood is trickling down my right leg, dripping off my jeans, and staining the sidewalk burgundy. For a moment, I wonder if I blacked out. Last thing I remember is picking my jeans with the shard of glass and going down memory lane. How and why did I cut my own leg? What the heck was I doing? Have I lost my mind? I honestly don't remember taking the glass to my flesh. That last cut is the deepest and stings something awful. At least it made me come back to the "real" world before I severed something important and vital. I fling the offending glass into the street and use the bottom of my shirt to apply pressure to my wound.

"Damn that smarts!"

"You gonna be okay? You need a doctor?" Valerie's forehead scrunches.

"No. I'm fine. It's not bad." I'm embarrassed my neighbor had to witness my actions. "That's it. Up I go." I stand up with resolve.

My legs are stiff. How long have I been camped out on this curb? An hour? Two? I have no idea. I stretch and shake my right foot and rub my butt to get the feeling back and the blood flowing.

"Well, if you're sure you're okay, I'll leave you to get settled. I'm here if you need me."

"Thanks so much for the drink and company. Sorry you had to meet me like this."

"It's okay. I've been there." Valerie heads back to her place, leaving me at the bottom of the stairs.

Okay, now what? Upstairs to my new and rather bare apartment? Or down the street to the beach? Wait, there's no way I can head to the beach before I clean up. With my disheveled appearance and bloody leg I may frighten the children and dogs of the neighborhood. Up the stairs it is. Shower, here I come.

Chapter 3

The hot water cascades down my body, causing my depression to recede a little. Maybe part of my sadness is washing down the drain with the suds. I try to visualize my fears, tensions, and apathy washing away. I remember reading that somewhere. Something like our thoughts become reality? I'm not sure I believe it, but it never hurts to give it a go.

The water is soothing and my muscles respond. I feel as if I'm starting to relax. Minutes pass and I wonder if I will now be as stuck in the shower as I was on the curb. Looking like a prune from being water-logged is not appealing and then, of course, I'm worried about water conservation. I turn the water off and step out of the shower onto the wet tiles.

Crack! I hear the noise clearly, echoing in my head, before the pain registers. Slipping, falling, I watch the walls and ceiling recede as the floor approaches quickly. I slip on the wet floor. Crimson blood runs down my face. My forehead bears a large gash. My hip and left arm wrenched in awkward positions. I cry out in pain.

With my towel I hastily wipe off the fogged-up mirror. How much damage is there? After the cutting to my leg and now this, I will definitely have some explaining to do to a doctor. Will my forehead need stiches? I assume that's where the blood is originating from.

I peer closely into my reflection and freeze—stunned. Huh? Nothing. There's no blood. Hey, no pain in my arm or hip.

Ohhh dammit!

Not the damn visions again. No. No. NO. I shake my head to clear the image from my mind. Am I seeing the future? Could be, since I don't have a bath mat yet. I hate those stupid visions. I thought I was done with them.

I really need to get a mat though. These tiles are really slippery when they're wet. I probably will fall and crack my head open. And because I was so stubborn and wanted to live independently no one will find me until my body has been rotting for months. Or at least until my editor notices I'm missing when I pass a deadline.

Stop doing this to yourself, I admonish. One moment I think I will be okay and the next I have made my life into a catastrophe. I really need to get a grip. I need to think of something positive. Hmmm. Well, I did get up off the curb, didn't I? Yup, did it without Naomi. I am a strong, independent woman. Got off the curb and showered. Now we're talking. Okay, what can I tackle next? Maybe I should call Richard and see if he is getting on okay and ask how Wade is doing? No. That would be falling into old patterns. Richard needs to take care of Richard and Tess needs to take care of Tess. That's what is best for all of us. Richard needs to learn to be his own person and not be so dependent on me. That wasn't love. I'm not sure what it was, but love it definitely was not.

Wade is just going through teenage angst. He will come around, I try to convince myself. And Wade and Richard get along famously. I was the thorny one in the relationship. I'm the one who seemed to cause friction in the family. They seem to glide well without me around.

No, they'll be fine. Take care of me! Yes, that's what I plan to do. We all agreed that this was for the best. Richard was so understanding and thoughtful, but that's Richard. Good hearted, compassionate, gentle Richard. I'll be the bad guy. I'll take the blame for the failure of our marriage. It's the least I can do since I'm the one that initiated the divorce.

I dry off, but notice that I still feel damp. In fact, my towel felt damp before I started drying off. This humidity, from living so close to the ocean, is going to take a little getting used to. Thirty-eight years in the San Fernando Valley with its dry heat is all I've known. Amazing how only a couple of hours to the south and a little to the west can make such a difference. After bandaging my leg, I throw on some old loose jeans and a favorite olive tank top with my business logo on it. Well, it was my business—"R & T Fitness." Now, Richard's brother, Terrence, owns my portion. So, I guess it will still be "R & T Fitness." Convenient, huh? Terrence always wanted to go into business with Richard, but I "stole" him away and since I'm out of the picture now, it is the perfect opportunity for Terrence to swoop in.

Forget about all that, I tell myself as I lace up my comfy tennis shoes. Then I comb out my wet hair and I'm set. Set for what? As I look around the bare apartment, I don't think I can sit here staring at the nothingness. It is a reminder of the nothingness I feel inside. Maybe I'll take a walk around the neighborhood and check it out? I grab my phone and notice I missed a call from Naomi. Thank God. A friendly connection is definitely what I need right now.

I play her voicemail message on the speaker as I apply a little eye pencil and mascara to make me look alive. Naomi is the dreamer, the romantic. She has wispy, fine, red hair down the length of her back. She has one of those bodies and metabolism that I love to hate. Naomi can eat anything and not gain an ounce. Her body is lithe and graceful and with her fair skin and flowing clothes she gains the attention of men wherever she goes. Hell, if I were into women, I would be into her. She's gorgeous. I, on the other hand, have to fight for my body. I watch every calorie and exercise like mad to stay in shape. I try to convince myself that I hate food and love exercise. Yeah, that works for a couple of weeks. Then I'm fantasizing about gorging on an entire box of cheese crackers where my cheeks are bulging like a chipmunk, but then I get myself a nice large mug of green tea and I'm completely satisfied. Sure I am.

Naomi is jealous of my skin, though. Ha. I tan without any effort, while she with her vampiric complexion burns as the sun rises. A few years ago Naomi got into Wicca and Earth Medicine, whatever that is. Come to think of it that's around when her wardrobe got more, I don't know how to put it . . . flowy? I know she has explained Wicca to me before, but truthfully I'm not as good a listener as she is. I nod my head and try to look interested, but really I'm thinking, "Should I order the skinny latte or go for the calorie laden, delicious tasting, chocolate raspberry one?" as I'm calculating in my head how many calories I've already burned this morning on the elliptical and will that account for the "real deal" drink. I know that is superficial, but when you are in my business, every calorie counts . . . and I should also strive to be a good listener like Naomi.

"Hey Tess," Naomi's voice message plays. "Just wondering how you are settling into your new place? I'm planning on stopping over tomorrow after work. Got you a little housewarming gift and we can catch up.

Love you, talk to you later sweetie." I hit replay and listen again for the company. As I'm playing the message for the third time someone knocks on the door. A real live person, I think. Hurrah!

"Who is it?" I call through the closed door.

"It's June, dear."

"Oh, okay." I open the door for June, my landlady. She seems nice enough, although she doesn't have a clue about fashion sense. Not that I do, but I can match colors and patterns pretty well. June can also talk your ear off if you give her half a chance.

"Dear, you look dreadful. Moving must be so stressful to do on your own."

"Yes, it has been hard," I admit. I still feel bad lying about my intent to be a long-term tenant. I'm so unsure of my life right now. I can barely plan minute to minute, let alone a whole day. And she wants me to make a long-term commitment. I couldn't commit to my marriage. I'm not in any way capable of committing to an apartment.

"You'll get settled soon. It will be nice to have a stable, long-term tenant in this apartment. It's had its share of short termers and I'm tired of that inconsistency."

"Yes. Not to worry. I'm the stable one," I fib.

"Yippee skippee!"

Who says yippee skippee? As June checks out the kitchen, a pang of guilt for lying starts to bubble up. She's too nice to lie to. Maybe I should confess. Tell her that I'm unsure of anything now and that I hope to be a stable tenant. I cannot guarantee anything though. But then I notice her yellowed slip showing beneath her brown polyester skirt and now that's where my attention is focused. Do I tell her? Or pretend I didn't notice? June keeps babbling on and on about who knows what. I pick up a word or two, but I'm too distracted.

". . . lovely weather . . . they play the music too loud . . . husband would rather stay home. I want to travel . . . neighbor downstairs works in travel . . . now don't you try doing your divorce on your own."

Finally, I have had enough and decide to tell her about her slip. "Uh, excuse me."

"One of the tenants here knows someone that can help you with your divorce . . . do you have a good lawyer?" she says, pronouncing lawyer like "lie-yer." "By the bye, I need you to complete the walk-through checklist."

I try again, "June, your slip."

". . . and these broken tiles on the kitchen counter will be fixed, of course."

Oh, never mind. To hell with her slip and fashion sense and talking and with my guilt over lying—serves her right for not listening, I rationalize.

"Tiles?" I reply, realizing my mind has drifted again.

"Jim will be calling you to check out the work that needs to be done in the kitchen."

"Jim?"

"Dear, you are stressed. Were you listening? We discussed this. Jim is the contractor who has been hired to fix the broken tiles."

"Oh, yes . . . Jim. I remember," I reply, but really don't.

"Well, get some rest, dear. If you notice any other problems with the apartment, just give a ring."

I close the door and sit on the floor. How does one short visit feel like it zapped a year off my life? I'm in bad shape. Maybe I'll play Naomi's voice mail again? No. This is ridiculous. You are a strong and independent woman, I remind myself once more. I am going out of this apartment and check out my neighborhood. First, a quick text to Wade. This is my new thing; I text him, he doesn't answer. It's my only connection to my son, this one-way communication. Maybe someday he will forgive me for leaving, or for being a crappy mom, or whatever he blames me for.

Hi sweetie, just checking in to tell you I love you. Hope you r doing well. Ttul

And that is how it goes, over and over. I'll keep trying though. Okay, Tess, let's check out this neighborhood:

- Keys?—Check
- Sunglasses?—Check
- Determination?—Sort of
- Courage?—Nope

And I'm off. First, I'll check out the landing. Hmm, looks promising both directions. Beach or 2nd Street? Or maybe up and down the residential streets. I pull out my necklace and caress it as I walk and talk quietly to Jared.

"Zoning is strange in these older towns. There are apartment buildings in between expensive houses. If I had the money to buy one of these houses, I wouldn't want to be next to an apartment building. Would you? Oh well, I guess I don't have to worry about that any time soon.

"I'm on Dublin Avenue. No, it's not named after Ireland, just the city in California. In fact, all the streets in my new neighborhood are named after California cities. There is Santa Ana, Covina, and Gardena, and so on and so forth."

A couple of blocks down I come to a beautiful house decorated in Mexican tiles and mosaic murals of blue and gold on the walls. I pause to take in its art work. A black lab who lives there, I would suppose he is to guard the house, comes up to the gate to greet me.

"Hello, Boo-Boo," I tell him.

They're all Boo-Boos, until I get to know them and come up with some other made-up name. I'm met with licks and a paw instead of any barking to shoo me away. Instantly, I'm in love.

"Midnight," I decide to call him. I've made my first friend.

Chapter 4

I meander up and down the streets that afternoon, taking it all in. Talking to Jared for company. Behind my sunglasses, I feel hidden and invisible. That's where I want to be right now. My goal was to get a feel for the "vibe" of this town.

"One thing that I notice is all the flip-flops. Flip-flops appear to be the dress code around here no matter what the occasion or weather. Wearing a dress or slacks? Pair it with flip-flops. Shorts or bikini? Flip-flops. Cold and rainy weather? You guessed it—flip-flops."

I come across a very animated man, waving his arms about, talking to another homeowner about tourists driving too fast on the residential streets. The homeowner is being polite, but by his silence and body language, I can tell he only wants to get back to fixing his sprinklers. "Animated Man" looks exactly like a caricature of an old surfer from the 60s. He has the shaggy, sun-bleached hair, Hawaiian shirt, weathered skin—the whole bit. All he needs is the ukulele and surfboard under his arm. Is he for real? I wonder. I want to stare, but I keep my head down and keep moving. I do, however, note the flip-flops on him and the homeowner.

"My energy is low and after only a few blocks I'm worn out. Maybe I'll head to the beach and rest there for a while. The beach is right down the street from me. I never in my wildest dreams thought I would be living so close to the beach, but here I am. Jared, you would love it. Remember, you always wanted to live here, close to the aquarium. You wanted to be a marine biologist. I'm here partly for you." I choke up, clear my throat, and change the subject.

"If I wasn't feeling crappy, I would actually be ecstatic. Now I'm merely bland about it all, like the way I feel about my new white hatchback. Don't get me wrong, I'm not saying my car is bland—merely the color. I would never choose white. I had a beautiful sedan and loved that car. It was a deep and sophisticated grey. I kept it immaculate. It was a sturdy family vehicle that also portrayed a sense of professionalism for a business owner. Richard has a black sports car—very cool, but not the kind of car that I would be comfortable with Wade driving.

"When Richard and I were discussing asset separation, I offered to quit claim the house to Richard so that Wade would not have to change schools and could stay in his home. I remember how difficult it was for me to change schools during high school. And since Wade will be driving soon, I left the sedan for Wade and purchased the hatchback. It's perfect for fitting in tight parking places and maneuvering through the narrow one-way streets. It's the color—white, how plain can I get?

"When I went into the dealer, I was haggard and the salesman could pick that up immediately. I would have to wait for a silver one, he told me. They could have it here sometime next week. I wasn't in the mood to wait. I still had packing to do, apartments to search for, and life to straighten out. Car color choice was not on my list of priorities and so white it was. I didn't even test drive it.

"'Fine, I'll take it,' I declared.

"The salesman looked agog. 'You don't want to take it for a spin first?'

"'Nope,' I said in resignation.

"And so, I made a salesman's day as I paid sticker price. They should always work with those going through drastic life changes—less haggling as we simply don't have the energy for it.

"I remember one time, many years ago, I was driving to our gym and I was rear-ended at a stoplight. I had a bad cold and should have stayed in bed, but no, not suck-it-up Tess; I decided to go to work. After the woman hit my car, I went to assess the damage. Clearly on the back bumper was the impression of her license plate frame and her red paint was transferred to my grey car. She actually wanted to argue with me. I'm at a red light and she plows into the back of me. Okay, maybe plow is not accurate, but it does sound more exciting, doesn't it? Well, anyway, I was plain sick: red nose and eyes, foggy head, you know, the works. With my hands full of used tissue, I stared at her for a moment, and then all I could think of is a nice warm bed and a cup of hot tea. The next thing I did made me wonder about my sanity. I told her 'fine' and walked back to my car and drove away. When I looked in the rearview mirror she was still standing there in disbelief. See, get them when they are sick or in crisis and they'll let you walk all over them. I have allowed people to walk over me many times as a result, hence overpaid, sticker-priced, white hatchback."

I walk across Ocean Blvd. and onto the beach. It's an expansive beach. There is a cement path where people are riding their beach cruisers or jogging along the scenic area. The beach isn't as crowded as I would've imagined. To the right is the Belmont Veterans Memorial Pier and beyond that I can make out the orange smokestacks of the Queen Mary. The aquarium sits next to that. To my left is Naples. Naples is also part of Long Beach. It's known for the upscale homes on tiny canals and waterways. There are even gondolas that can take you around for a romantic cruise up and down the canals. So romantic, and so what I don't need right now.

I plop myself down on the warm sand by lifeguard tower number ten. Immediately, I untie my shoelaces and kick off my shoes and socks. Jeez, how much sand can I accumulate in my shoes after such a short walk on the sand? Now the locals' shoe attire makes more sense to me. Maybe I need flip-flops. "When in Rome or, should I say, Naples," I think to myself. The sand is a soft grey and slightly coarse; I was hoping for something softer and whiter. But it still feels surprisingly good. Mmmm . . . sinking my toes further into the cooler sand beneath helps me to relax. I pick up a stick and aimlessly start drawing squiggles in the smoothed-out beach. So easy to create, destroy, and re-create. If only the creation of my life were this easy.

Out of the corner of my eye, someone is exercising. I look up from my sand drawing and notice that Mr. Lifeguard from tower ten is doing push-ups on his perch. Yum! All tanned and muscled. I'm not sure if he is Hawaiian, Asian, or Latin American. He definitely has it put together nicely. He probably needs to keep in shape in case of an emergency. I look up and down the beach and out at the water. There is only one other person on the beach, except for the joggers and bicyclists passing through, and there's no one in the water. Wonder if I should keep the poor lonely lifeguard company? Where did that come from? Am I lusting over a lifeguard I've barely noticed? Focus. Focus. You're here to get your life together, not to get googly over the first cute guy you see, I remind myself. Take a deep breath. Good. Ahhh, much better. I'll lie down and close my eyes and *"poof"* cute Mr. Lifeguard will disappear from my sight.

"Kathleen. We will always find each other. I promised to take care of you forever. You are my true love . . . never forget that. Kathleen, look at me darling. Do you understand what I am saying? Please answer me. I will find you again. Kathleen . . . Kathleen . . . my love."

I must have fallen asleep and was dreaming. I wake up searching for a blanket because I'm cold, but I'm not in my safe bed. I'm still on the beach. The wind has picked up and has a biting chill to it. Getting up, I shake off the sand from my hair and clothes and walk towards the street. When I reach the curb, I put my shoes back on, sans socks. I only need to make it a couple of blocks home and the socks are embedded with sand. I climb the stairs to my apartment and head to the bathroom. Oh no, I'm sunburnt. This can't be—I never burn. I love to boast to others that I have great skin that tans, but doesn't burn. Terrific—one more irritation to add to my list: even if it's cold outside you can still get sunburned.

At nine p.m., I decide that it is a respectable time to go to sleep. Although by seven-thirty p.m. the exhaustion had really set in and I was nodding off on the couch. I couldn't go to bed then, that would have been too weird and so I struggle, watching the clock until finally the clock clicks over to nine p.m. Thank God, I exclaim. Get ready bed, here I come.

Nine-twenty p.m. Why do I feel wide awake now? I couldn't keep my eyes open on the couch. Maybe I should go back to the couch? I hear something. Boom. Boom. Pop. Pop. Pop. What the heck is that? Off in the distance it sounds like . . . like . . . fireworks? Is that what it is? Where is that coming from? Disneyland? Queen Mary? I hope that doesn't happen every night. Finally around ten p.m. and after the grand finale, it suddenly stops. Silence, glorious silence.

Chapter 5

I wake up with a horrible headache. It feels like I got three hours sleep all night.

"I kept tossing and turning, and then I had that dream again, Jared. I've been having the same dream ever since I can remember. I'm watching the scene as a bystander, but still feel a connection with that woman, Kathleen. Maybe I long for what she is experiencing. The best way I can describe her elation is effervescent. Yeah, that's what it is. She's bubbling over with love. I want that! I have never been good with history so I can't really say what time period it is. It looks to be a long, long time ago. Her blouse has a high collar with long sleeves. Her skirt is also long. She has a small, upturned nose, the way I wish mine was. Her blond hair is pulled up and fixed with a comb. I think it's in America in the early 1900s, but that's as close as I can figure. Kathleen uses old-fashioned language like 'dashing,' something that I would never say. But in this case I would have to agree with her description of Thomas. He is dashing with those piercing blue eyes, dark hair, and firm jaw line. Yes, quite the hunk."

Although I love the dream, I think it's been somewhat of a disservice in my life. This love is what I base all other love on. It has been my measuring stick. And I've never experienced it. Maybe it was the dream that did my marriage in. I always felt that I was performing a duty instead of being in a validating relationship. I tried very hard to stick with it. There was nothing I could point to that would affirm that I should leave. Richard is a good, caring husband, and Wade . . . well, Wade is Wade. He'll grow out of it, I keep telling myself, but when I think back he has always been angry. He was screaming mad when I gave birth to him and it has pretty much been the same all these years.

Actually, the family dynamics are a bit odd, come to think of it. Richard can be needy and dependent around me and then Wade will step in and take charge. And underneath there appears to be a current of animosity towards me. I haven't been able to figure it out. Maybe I spoiled him too much. Isn't that what we modern moms do? With our play dates and multiple classes, sports and the like, I was being the "good" American mother.

At five-thirty a.m., after I was sleeping well, yappy dog started in. That's when I gave up and decided to greet the morning.

"It's a new day!" I declare—time to start fresh in my new life. Let's see what this day has to offer.

Maybe I'll head over to 2nd Street and check out the shops and the restaurants. I wonder if I can find that great pizza place. No, it would be more practical to head to the gym and get that out of the way, then have a nice, healthy, low-calorie lunch. I should use the gym membership I purchased when I moved here, *Belmont Fun and Fitness*.

"Can you believe that name Jared—*fun and fitness*? Who are they kidding? I don't find fitness all that fun, but I would never say that to my clients. Er . . . previous clients. I mean, for heaven's sake, I owned a gym. I always had to promote healthy living and fitness and, of course, how enjoyable working out is. But inside I was trying to get through my workout so I could move on to other more enjoyable things. Exercising was more of a thing I had to do, a step towards something else. What that something else was I don't know, seems like everything in my life was a scripted duty or chore. The only area that gave me pleasure was writing. It seemed to be the only color in my grey life, so when I started writing a couple of articles for magazines on health and fitness I, for once, felt a sense of worth and accomplishment.

"Richard is a much better business person than I am. Get him in that gym and he is a no-nonsense take-control kind of guy, such a contradiction from how he is around me. I'm not good for him. It's like I'm toxic. He doesn't thrive when I'm near. Yes. This divorce is good. It's good for him, the business, and me."

I make a nice mug of green tea and sit out on my balcony. Even though it's southern California and known for the sun, I need a sweatshirt. It's very different from the valley. I'll bet right now, back at the old house, it's ninety degrees. Here it is damp, overcast, and chilly. I lean over the balcony. Can I see the ocean? Nope. Come on, how come I'm only a couple of blocks from the water and still deprived of the view? So close, yet so far. Guess I can always walk down there and check it out. Right now I need to relax and get rid of this headache. I sip the tea and breathe in the clean ocean air, hoping it clears my head. *Breathe in peace, breathe out stress,* I quietly chant. I think I saw that on some yoga program once and guess it stuck with me. Ah, relax. Relax, dammit. Well, maybe a nice hot shower will do the trick.

As I wait for the water to warm up in the shower, I notice how blank my walls are. I'm going to find something festive to put up, I decide. Naomi is coming over tonight and I want to show her that I'm adjusting well, even if most of my stuff is still packed away. At least I can put up something colorful and festive. This is the new Tess. Old Tess would have only chosen muted colors, but I'm ready to step into a brighter world, at least that's what I'm telling myself. Yes, I will head to the shops and find something to liven things up around here. It's a cute apartment. It simply needs some life breathed into it.

The apartment is light and airy with a vaulted ceiling revealing exposed natural wood beams. There is a skylight, too. I have a balcony off my dining room and the kitchen is divided from the living room with a tile counter. There are two bedrooms and one bathroom. The second bedroom is waiting for Wade, if he ever chooses to visit or stay, someday. That is a long shot though, but it's there for him, just in case.

I feel good about my resolution to fix the place up as I step into the steaming shower. Heaven. I'm feeling more peaceful already. Maybe some music around here will help too and I will look for a colorful spread for my bed and maybe some potted plants to cheer up the place. Now I'm on a roll. I can see it all put together—and me, happy and adjusted. Yes. This is all good.

I step out of the shower, feeling uplifted, but that emotion is quickly aborted. My feet slide out from under me and then, as if in slow motion, I start falling. I've lost my balance and slip on the wet tiles. I watch the ceiling and walls move in front of my eyes as I head to the floor. I come to rest on my left side and have wrenched my left arm. I lay breathless on the cold floor. Ohh, I can't move and there's no one to call to help me up. What seems like an hour is probably only minutes. Soon I find that I'm cold, wet, and the pain in my arm is throbbing horribly. Tentatively, I prop myself up on my right side and check out my injuries. I grab the towel off the rack and cover my shivering body with it. Then, grabbing onto the toilet, I heave myself up to sit on the seat. I want to cry. I hurt inside and out.

With my left arm held protectively against my body, I stand up and hurriedly wipe off the steamed-up mirror with my good hand. In my reflection, I assess the damage. It looks like I got an abrasion on my forehead, blood is oozing down my face, and my hip and elbow are red from the blow. How in the world did I get scraped on my forehead? I look down at where I landed, trying to retrace my fall. Then I see it, blood on the shower door handle. I didn't even feel it when it happened, but now the stinging is setting in. Well, so much for my big excursion out. I one-handedly put my sweats back on and huddle on the couch, my hair still dripping wet on my clothes, causing me to be chilled again. I don't care. Guess I should have paid more attention to my stupid warning vision.

I put on a tankini, loose fitting drawstring pants, and a t-shirt; putting on my sneakers is a real struggle. Add flip-flops to my list of things to buy, along with a bath mat! A soak in the hot tub at the gym is what I need to ease my sore muscles. Down the steps and into my car, I start the engine. My left arm is held close to my body as it is still throbbing. If I try to reach my arm straight out I'm greeted with a shooting pain in my elbow. I think I will keep my arm right where it is. I can manage with one arm. I pull up to the *Belmont Fun and Fitness*, brightly adorned with blue awnings. Although the streets are un-crowded at this time of day the gym parking lot is full. I find a tight parking spot in the corner and snap it up. I'm appreciative of having a small car right now. My sedan would've never fit.

I attempt to head straight back to the women's locker room after I show my pass to the front desk staff. The desk attendant blocks my path as she greets me cheerily. She is all of nineteen and way too chipper for this time of the morning.

"Welcome, Mrs. Whitaker. Since this is your first visit to the *Belmont Fun and Fitness Center*, I would like to take this opportunity to show you around and acquaint you with the machinery," Miss Chipper announces.

She must be parroting some manager's instructions on greeting clients. I cannot imagine this girl using the word "acquaint." More accurately it would probably be, "OMG, like, you wanna work out or what?" Okay, I know I'm being very cynical, probably too many years of living in the valley has gotten to me. But, you get the point.

"*Ms.* Whitaker," I correct her and add, "Just making my way to the hot tub today. Maybe another time," I mumble and keep walking.

I can hear Miss Chipper calling out to me. I don't turn back. I'm not in the mood for small talk with the staff. I know all the ins and outs of a gym and could chat up the best of them. No, now I'm an anonymous patron, in my mind willing everyone to leave me alone. I grab a locker close to a wood bench and take off my shirt, pants, and shoes. The hot tub is right off the locker room. Immediately, I notice that it's full. As I step down into the hot, bubbling waters, one woman scoots over to make room for me. The women are watching me as if I am some type of new animal species that they have never come across. I'm not sure if it is due to the way I am hobbling and holding my arm or that they've never seen me before.

Closing my eyes made the lifeguard disappear the other day and so I use the same technique. All gone—just the water, the jets soothing and kneading my wracked body, and my thoughts to torment me. If only I could shut out my thoughts too.

After twenty minutes I feel sufficiently cooked. I climb out of the spa and head back to my locker. I dry off as best as I can with one arm and arrange my dry clothes on the bench. With my good arm I reach down at my waist to pull off my wet tankini top. Okay, I can do this. Up and over my head. But it is wet and tight and ends up stuck on my head with my sore arm up in the air, dangling. This has to be the most embarrassing moment of my life. I'm sitting in a strange locker room in a compromising position. I can't see anything with the tankini top covering my face and my boobs are left hanging out for the entire world, well at least in the women's locker room, to see. I twist and squirm and still can't get my right arm to the correct location that will work the top the rest of the way over my head. After a few minutes of struggling I stop to take a breath. Wait, I hear murmurs close by.

"Help," I call out. Nothing. "I'm stuck," I call out again.

The distinct sound of two women giggling reaches my left ear. Now I'm pissed. With a burst of fierce determination I reach behind my head, grab a large chunk of soaked suit, and pull as I simultaneously drop my left shoulder and twist my head. Out my head pops, free of its neoprene prison. I want to know who was laughing at me and how they could so inconsiderately ignore me when it was obvious I was in a desperate situation, at least to me and my modesty. But they have all gone about their business, as if I'm not here.

I throw my clothes on in haste and stomp out to my car. I peel out of the parking lot and head a few blocks away. Then it hits. My eyes are prickling, tears at the ready. Tears start to flow, blurring my vision, streaming down my cheeks. I pull over to the side of the road since now I'm sobbing heavily. I can't control the tears and the racking sobs.

"I just want to die," I cry out and wail to no one in particular. "I can't go on without him," I announce. "Let me die. Let me have peace. I can't live without him."

It continues and continues and I'm completely at its mercy. Eventually the sobs diminish and my wailing quiets until I'm worn out and tired. My glove box supply of napkins from various fast food restaurants is depleted as I use the last one to blow my nose once more.

A strange feeling arises in me, like a memory from long ago. I remember and then I don't. What was it? I was crying that *I can't go on without him*. Who is him? It wasn't Jared. It was from another place. It felt as if someone else was saying that, not me. I feel confused and strangely peaceful. An image flashes in my mind briefly and then flits away, like a gnat. It's me, but not me. I see me in another time, long ago. I'm crying, "I can't go on without him." The feelings are so real and close to the surface, as if it was yesterday. Yet it was long before my life. I'm reeling from this image, but I know it is accurate, as if I always knew this other life.

"I wonder if it has anything to do with the recurring dream. In that dream, however, the woman is always laughing and she and her lover are dancing and singing. They are happy. I have always loved that dream. It was a fantasy, a dream, right Jared? I notice there is a similarity in the mannerisms of the despondent woman and the dream woman."

Was this woman real? Was she me? Or have I launched off the deep end? A few minutes ago I was at the end of my rope and now I'm curious. Well, curiosity is better than depression, I surmise. I want to understand what happened.

"I've never been interested in the supernatural, past lives, psychic abilities, and the like. It isn't that I haven't had my run-in with the supernatural. You know that very well, Jared. It's just that I'm simply not interested in anything that does not follow a logical path. That's how I've lived my life since I was seventeen.

"All my life I've seen or known little things and have hated it. Remember the time we went to the carnival that came to town? You told me to enter that raffle and I did. It was great in one way because we won tickets to the water park but it also sucked because when they announced my name there was no element of surprise. They pulled my name out of the barrel. However, I'd already 'seen' it in my mind, so when the attendant called my name it was anticlimactic. It ruined the whole event. What good is knowing if it does no good? And so it has been like that my entire life. Mostly I work to ignore it and choose reason over intuition. Although that has not worked out famously for me either.

"I didn't always ignore it. Once when Wade was around three years old I got a clear vision of him walking in front of me from my right to my left, choking on a jelly bean. Not more than thirty seconds later he came walking into the kitchen from my right side of view and, sure enough, he was choking. In this instance, since I already had advance warning, I didn't panic. I immediately smacked him between his shoulder blades and out popped, no other than, a jelly bean. That's the only time I felt this vision thing was useful.

"After what happened with you I vowed never to listen to any intuition and only use reason and logic. I changed my name to Tess and re-created myself. Excluding Wade's jelly bean incident, any psychic mumbo-jumbo was banished from my life. But, if I'm being honest, my slipping out of the shower could've been avoided had I bought a bath mat. In fact, I hate to admit it, but I did get a vision of that too. Okay, maybe this vision thing is not all bad." I cross my arms to feel the whale-fluke tips press between my breasts.

Tonight when Naomi comes over I'm going to discuss this with her and get her opinion. If anyone would be open minded enough to listen to this gibberish it would be her. Somehow for the first time in a long time I feel a sense of curiosity and interest as to what this all means. I have time to explore this part of my past. Since I got a large chunk of money from my portion of the gym and am only freelancing as a writer, there is something to focus on now besides getting through each day. Who knew I would be grateful that I fell and had a mini breakdown?

Chapter 6

I head back to the apartment to clean up. The morning overcast has burned off. My mood is also improving, as if I burned off the overcast in my internal world. The sky is an azure blue, dotted with lacy clouds. The breeze that has been cooled by the Pacific's waves allows some relief from the heat. I'm looking forward to really exploring the shops and restaurants. I change into khaki pants and a black tank top and grab a small, woven, colorful, embroidered backpack I picked up at an open market in Sedona years ago. Although this backpack is something I wouldn't usually wear, as I like earthy colors, I was drawn to it in Sedona. I felt as if I had to have it. The woman from whom I bought it told me she made it by hand. The embroidered design and stitching is remarkable. Not only was it practical, but attractive too. I'm anticipating filling it with treasures from shopping. With a burst of energy and enthusiasm I start down the walk. First stop—visit Midnight, the dog.

As I approach the house where Midnight resides, I can see his black shape rising and falling with each breath. He is sleeping soundly on the red-tiled ground. I don't want to disturb him, but as I near the gate he wakes up as if he has a sixth sense that I am coming to see him. He stretches and gives an audible yawn, then stands to greet me. I reach in to scratch his neck. He tilts his head further into my hand. I can tell he loves my caress as his eyes seem to glaze over. He pushes his head closer to the gate and I lean in and plant a kiss on his muzzle.

"Okay, gotta go. See you soon, Midnight," I tell him.

I weave myself through the back alleys. The alley behind my apartment dumps me in a parking lot for 2nd Street shoppers. As I am making my way through the parking lot, I hear a squawking above my head. In my peripheral vision, I saw a large black bird—a raven perhaps? I turn my head to get a better look and it's gone. I heard it and saw it. It's not possible to disappear so fast. Did I imagine it? I've gotta tell Naomi. This has been an unusual morning.

The street is bustling with activity, alive with people shopping and eating, cars making their way slowly through the traffic, and bicyclists weaving in and out. The sidewalk cafes are already packed with diners. What a different scene from early this morning.

I come across a tiny boutique with eclectic clothing and home decorations. I'm on a mission to brighten up my apartment. Entering the store, I'm greeted by the storekeeper.

"Welcome. Let me know if you need any assistance," the shopkeeper informs me.

"Thanks. Just browsing."

Cute stuff, but pricey. There are wind chimes of all sizes and sounds located in the back corner. Maybe some chimes for the balcony would be nice. It would be pleasant to sit out there and hear the tinkling of music. With the ocean breeze it would probably work well. I try out the assorted chimes, listening for the right sound. I don't know what the right sound is; I'll know it when I hear it.

I try the largest one first, out of curiosity. I've never seen a wind chime that big. Of course, that would look ridiculous on my small balcony. *Bong!* Yikes! Booming and intrusive. A man paying for his purchases turns toward the sound and looks at me. Okay, now I'm embarrassed. More gently this time I try another chime. Nope, then another one. Eww, too tinny. Over and over I play with the chimes and then I test a simple set of chimes. It has a modest, yet elegant, design. The pipes are a burnished copper color and when I strike them together they have a sound that resonates deep inside me. It must have been the way I hit them, but immediately the tune that Thomas sings to Kathleen in my dreams pops into my head. How weird is that?

Well, of course I have to buy these chimes even if they are overpriced. I rationalize that it is all part of my healing journey and that they are meant to be with me. I'm throwing logical Tess out of the equation for the time being. For heaven's sake, I nearly had a breakdown this morning. I deserve some spoiling after that episode. My stomach starts grumbling.

Guess I should feed it, I decide. Across the street I notice a sandwich shop and head that way.

After I order my tuna and avocado sandwich on rye, I choose a seat by the window so I can watch the goings-on outside.

"This is my town. This is where I live. It seems strange. I never thought I would be living here, so close to the beach, Jared. When I was a little girl and upset about something I would picture myself back with our grandparents, visiting this town. It always brought me comfort. I've taken myself here, in my mind, many times over the years. In my mind, however, it wasn't exactly like this. In fact most of what I imagined isn't really here. I created shops, restaurants, and parks that did not actually exist. So it's like I'm coming back to a town I know so well, but still seeing it for the first time. It really is more of a feeling of home. This area has a sense of familiarity and comfort for me."

My food arrives and I dig in. A group of firemen come in and order. I notice that to my left is a fire station. I'm eating with the locals. Well, I can see why. This tuna is delicious. Good Albacore tuna and they don't skimp. I hate when they serve you the cheap tuna. It makes me gag. To my right, in my peripheral vision, brightly colored flags are waving from the awning of the shop next door. The colors are drawing me in. I'm going to check out that place next. Maybe I'll find something perfect to cheer up the white walls of my place.

I finish my meal and head next door. It's a Tibetan store. The shopkeeper looks like she may be Tibetan herself. Her eyes are beautiful: full of happiness, joy, and a deep sense of contentment. My eyes, in contrast, are filled with heaviness from the last few years. I want what she has.

There is incense burning from an altar of some sort. Some type of haunting flute music is playing over the speakers. There are pictures of a monk in mustard-colored robes on the shelf above the cashier's desk, and the entire shop is filled with color. My eyes are dancing from one spot to another. There's so much to take in. It's actually a little overwhelming, yet I'm intrigued.

Not moving from my central spot I survey the entire shop. Miss Joyful Eyes smiles generously and welcomes me to the store.

"Please, please do look around. I am here if you need me," she tells me.

"Thank you," I reply. "What are those colored flags?" pointing outside to the awning.

"Those are Tibetan prayer flags. They are for luck, and good health," she explains. "We have them over there for sale," gesturing over to a long table loaded with packages of rectangular multicolored flags.

I wander over to the table and notice they are reasonably priced. In fact it appears that most of the items in this store are priced low compared to the store I visited earlier. And this stuff is so much cooler, I decide. Drifting from one table and display to another I start collecting items:

- Tibetan prayer flags
- Colorful throw pillows for the couch
- Incense
- Journal

Yeah, a journal. On a small table towards the front of the store are handmade journals. "Fair Trade" it says on the package. They're covered in decorated cloth with symbols. The journal ties close with an attached piece of twine. I chose a turquoise one. But the most interesting thing is the paper. It's handmade paper, too. In fact there are actual leaves and petals embedded in the paper. Journaling will be a great way for me to work through my issues, I conclude. I can't wait to sit at the beach and write.

I plunk my purchases on the counter and Miss Joyful Eyes starts ringing it all up. Again, I glance at the smiling monk. He looks like he's really happy, and peaceful, too. I know I've seen his picture before. However, I can't remember who he is.

Timidly, I ask, "Who's that?" I motion my head above to the photo.

"His Holiness the Dalai Lama, you mean?" she questions.

"Oh, right," I answer.

She continues, "He is the reincarnation of the thirteenth Dalai Lama. The monks recognized this when he was only two years old."

"Reincarnation, how interesting," I reply.

I want to ask more questions, but I feel strange talking to someone I just met about this. I'm sure she doesn't want to get into a conversation with every person who walks into her shop. She's probably only interested in making a sale. I place my new items in my backpack and wish her a nice day.

"Namaste," she calls out to me. Huh?

Last stop before heading home is the drug store two blocks down. Here I pick up some staples for the apartment.

"Yes, a bath mat was one of them. I didn't forget," I tell Jared.

At the last moment, I run back for a pair of flip-flops. Now I'm all set for beach living. The rest of the afternoon I find myself actually enjoying decorating my apartment with the few things I bought. The wind chimes are hung in the west corner of the balcony and are already playing a tune for me, trying to harmonize with the music on my CD player. Native American flute music is playing in the background. The haunting melodies are great for background music when I'm writing.

By the time Naomi is due to come over, I've hung up the blue, green, red, yellow, and white prayer flags on the wall in the living room, arranged the pillows on the couch, unpacked a few necessary items from my boxes, and set up the bathroom. The rest of the boxes I move with some difficulty to the garage, my arm arguing with me the entire time. I have a tiny garage off the alley. It barely fits my car and the boxes. I feel like I want to live with only the essentials. I feel a need, for the time being, to leave my previous life behind. My life, in storage, will be safely waiting for me if and when I choose to revisit it. Exhausted, I stretch out on the couch and start to doze.

Chapter 7

The doorbell ringing startles me from my nap. I jump up as if I were stung by a wasp. My first guest, yay!

"Welcome to my beach abode," I announce to a grinning Naomi, who is bearing gifts.

She looks so put together, with a relaxed confidence. Tonight she is wearing a jade-green flowing skirt with a multicolor floral blouse, and in her hair is a long scarf fashioned like a headband with the long tails trailing down her back. The green really sets off her eyes and goes well with her red hair. I can tell that Naomi notices the brightly colored flags on the wall right away.

"Oh, you're already decorating. That's wonderful," she exclaims as she awkwardly tries to hug me and not smash the gift basket. I carefully hug her back, protecting my injured arm.

"Come in. I'm so happy to see you," I tell her as I take the basket from her hands and place it on the counter.

The basket is filled with pears and apples, nuts and wine. Naomi also thought of wine glasses.

"Got a corkscrew?" Naomi asks as she removes the foil from the wine bottle.

"You're kidding, right? Wait, let me call Valerie."

"Valerie?"

"Yeah, my neighbor. She's a character." I walk over to my landing and notice her door is open. "Hey Valerie," I call down. "Do you have a corkscrew?"

"You betcha," she yells back up.

In moments she's at my front door, corkscrew in hand.

"Thanks so much. Valerie, this is my dear friend Naomi. Naomi, this is Valerie. She saved me the day I moved in."

"Sure did. Don't forget it." Valerie slaps me on the shoulder. "Hey Naomi, nice meeting you."

"So nice to meet you. Thank you for being there for Tess." Naomi takes Valerie's hand in both of hers.

"Yeah, not a big thing. Well, I'll let you two catch up. See ya soon?"

"Thanks Valerie." I close the door behind her.

"Seems nice." Naomi adds.

"She is."

Naomi opens the wine and starts in with positive affirmations on how well I'm adjusting and how the Feng Shui of this apartment is just right and if I place some quartz crystals in the four quadrants it will help to keep the negative energy from entering. I'm nodding and spying the food in the basket. Feng Shui, crystals? This is Naomi's way, so I try to go with the flow. I've not eaten a bite since lunch and feel famished. My eyes land on a large pear resting in the basket.

Naomi is still jabbering, but my mind is focused on the beautiful pear. I pick it up and gently turn the fruit in my hand, holding it up and admiring the varied colors ranging from green to a warm yellow and then finally a rusty orange hue. I deeply inhale the scent of the pear, letting the aroma fill my nasal passages. My tongue can almost taste the sweetness from only its fragrance. I close my eyes as my teeth pierce its delicate skin. It's ripe and juicy as I knew it would be. The juice runs down my chin as the flavor delights my tongue.

As always, the smell and taste combined leave a profound impression on me. Instantly, I'm transported to another place. I'm not sure where I go—simply to a place of senses. It's not so much a scene as it is a feeling—a feeling of peace and serenity. The world I live in fades away and I can't hear anything. My vision narrows as I lose my peripheral sight. There is no fear though, as I have visited this sensation many times over in my life. It's only me and the sensory experience. The external world disappears. If Naomi is still talking I'm unaware of it. All sounds and sights around me have simply faded away.

I take another bite, adding to the experience, deepening it. I'm floating, drifting in my timeless and dreamy world. Colors swirl and music becomes visual. Tunes play and dance in my mind's eye. Tunes of long lost love, laughter and comfort display their colors for me. Each bite adds another instrument and harmonizes to enrich the ensemble.

I try to prolong the experience, but after the pear is gone, so is my secret place and, once again, I am back in the "real world." Bummer. As I return to my living room, I notice that Naomi has gone quiet.

"Where were you?" she asks me.

"Nowhere, just enjoying your gifts. So tell me about your day."

"No, you were definitely somewhere else. You had this faraway look in your eyes and I kept calling you, but you didn't respond. It was like you were in some kind of trance," Naomi replies.

"It was nothing . . ." I start and then reconsider.

Naomi knows how much I love pears and thoughtfully added them to the basket, but I never told her about the out-of-body experience that comes with the package. It's time I start sharing some of myself. That is why I struck out on my own. I wanted to stop burying myself in work, marriage, and parenting. I wasn't me anymore. In fact, I don't know who me is. Is it Jasmine Estrada? Is it Tess Whitaker? Or am I someone else altogether? If I'm trying to figure it out, I should at least be honest with the one person who has been close to me for the last twenty or so years. Right? I decide right then and there to come clean, well, at least about some parts of myself.

"Let's sit and I'll tell you about it," I invite.

We relax on the couch, with our glasses of wine and snacks to keep us fortified, and I proceed to share pieces of my internal world with my dear friend.

"Pears have always had an effect on me. I'm not sure why. It's sorta been my secret escape and I've never told anyone . . . until now," I start.

"Go on. You can talk to me."

"Okay . . . when I bite into a pear the world fades away and I have a . . . strange but amazingly sensual experience."

"Oh, like an out-of-body experience?"

"Maybe that's what it is. I don't know. I know I love it and sometimes wish I could stay there. As soon as the pear is gone so is the experience."

"Wow. I wish I had those. So you only have those sensual paranormal experiences with pears?"

"Well, there are the dreams too."

"Dreams?"

"Yeah. I've been dreaming of this couple from another time period for as long as I can remember."

"Who are they? What time period?"

"Slow down. You're asking me about history? You know I flunked it in high school."

"Oh yes. I remember."

"I can tell you this. They wear old-fashioned clothes and use words I don't use. I think it's here in America."

"Like the turn of the century?"

"Yeah, maybe. Anyway, their names are Kathleen and Thomas."

"Oh. Cool. So what's their story?"

"They are deeply in love with each other. Oh Naomi. It's so romantic watching them dance and caress each other."

"Sounds romantic. So you have out-of-body experiences with pears and romantic dreams of a couple from another time. Looks to be all positive."

"Well, except for the visions."

"You do have a lot to tell me."

I pause, allowing stale air to exit my lungs, taking its leave to find other areas to bog down. An empty space remains in my lungs allowing for fresh air to fill the void. This new air fuels my voice as I relay my visions: the fall in the bathroom, the gym mishap, and resulting meltdown.

When I finish, Naomi is quiet. She reaches for my hand and gives it a little squeeze of reassurance. I feel exhausted, yet relieved. I lifted and heaved away one of the bricks of heaviness from all the years of holding everything in. I feel a little lighter now.

"Kathleen and Thomas, huh? Maybe that was a past life?"

"Come on, Naomi. Past lives, really? Can we come up with an explanation that is more . . . uh, reasonable?"

"You have weird dreams and hear tunes in your head from who-knows-where and have out-of- body experiences from pears and talk to a dead brother." She points to my necklace. "And you think having past lives is unreasonable. Now who is being unreasonable?"

"Okay, good point."

"I'm glad you shared with me. I know that you've been keeping that inside for a long time. And to tell the truth, I'm not surprised or shocked by your tale. I had the feeling that you were more than you showed to the world. Secretly, I'm delighted. Now I can officially introduce you to my metaphysical world. I know you will really benefit and grow and eventually help heal others."

"Whoa. Slow down. I'm still trying not to freak out and now you are scaring me. Let's just go slow. Okay?"

"Sure. Sure. Of course we'll take it slow—one baby step at a time," she says to pacify me, but I can tell she is already scheming and planning. She suddenly sits upright, her eyes are looking up and to the left at some imaginary world in her brain. The wheels are turning in her mind.

Yikes! I've never seen Naomi this excited. It's kind of infectious and I get caught up in her telling me about her latest class in Reiki. This, she explains, is a type of Japanese energy healing. Naomi explains that using this with her aura-reading abilities has really honed her healing skills.

"There's so much more to this world than you can ever imagine. There's Reiki, auras, astral travel, all types of psychic phenomena, and past and future life regression," she goes on to tell me.

"Past life, is that for real?"

"Yes, very real. You should hear about this one woman I watched in a regression. She had this horrible fear of fire and then right up on stage she regressed to a lifetime where she was burned as a witch! Months later she came back to the group and told us that her fear of fire had been completely resolved. Can you believe it?"

"I'm not sure, but it's interesting," I mumble. My mind keeps returning to the dreams and Miss Joyful Eyes telling me about the Dalai Lama being reincarnated and then that weird feeling that something dreadful happened to me before. I had that flash of an image. I said, '*I can't go on without him,*' during the meltdown. What did I mean?

I glance at the clock and notice it's getting late. Naomi is being polite, as always, but I can tell she's tired. She has work in the morning. I'm being selfish keeping her out this late.

"Wow, look at the time. Where did the time fly to? I really should be getting to bed." I lie so Naomi won't feel as if I was wrapping up this evening on her account. She wants to be the good and supportive friend and will suck it up and suffer if she thinks that's what I need.

"Okay, if you're sure you are okay, I'll head home. Call me if you need anything. I'll keep my eye out for interesting classes to help you in your journey," Naomi says as she is gathering up her purse and keys.

"Thank you for listening, really. You don't know how much that means to me, just being open minded and not thinking I'm crazy. I'm very lucky to have you as a friend," I tell her as I hug her.

"Yes, you are," she retorts. I shake my head.

Lying in bed, loosened up from the wine and conversation, I notice my arm is feeling a lot better. Sounds of the night come into my awareness:

- Television playing in Valerie's apartment downstairs
- Yappy dog
- Boom boom from fireworks

Yes, all the usual sounds of my neighborhood. They are actually comforting now and soon after I fall fast asleep.

Chapter 8

Most mornings are the same. My arm has healed from my fall and I've established quite a routine during my short time in Belmont Shore. The mornings usually look something like this — tea on the balcony before the neighborhood wakes; even the wind chimes are still asleep. Then I slip on some sweats and head to the beach.

"This is the quietest stretch of beach I've ever been on in my life, Jared. It's nice to see some areas that have not been mauled by tourists and beachgoers. My piece of sand that I claim is behind and to the right of lifeguard tower ten. From here I have a good view of the water, and the lifeguard as he does his morning exercises. Over to my right is Mr. Tai Chi, doing his, well . . .tai chi.

"Mr. Tai Chi is here consistently. Our own silent club, joined together by time and location. If Mr. Lifeguard is off and the other lifeguard, Mr. California Surfer, is taking his place or if Mr. Tai Chi is not here for some reason, I feel a little lonely, as if our club is not complete. I wonder if they feel the same when I don't come.

"At first I thought Mr. Tai Chi was a homeless man sleeping on the beach. He was so still and always here early in the morning. Looking back, I realize he was meditating. He looks to be close to sixty years old with a balding head and long scraggly beard. He is thin, but fit, and surprisingly flexible. Guess that tai chi is really working. Something about him is intriguing, and I feel a sense of comfort when he is here. I wonder if he found out the secrets of the universe from all that meditating. Maybe I should give meditation a try sometime. Nah. I'll stick to journaling for the time being.

"Journaling seems to be working well, so far. Using the journal I picked up at the Tibetan shop, I have been purging my thoughts, frustrations, and worries onto the beautiful handmade paper. Originally, when I decided to journal, I found it hard to actually make a mark on the paper. It was strange, like I could not deface the work that someone on the other side of the world took the time to put together. And then I thought, if I do write in it, it should be only words of beauty. But that would defeat the whole purpose—to work out my issues. This is absolutely nuts, I thought, and then closed my eyes, took my pen and scribbled hard on the first page. Okay, now that it is defaced, I might as well write my thoughts in it. It was as if I felt that my "stuff" was not good enough to put on paper, my "garbage" should be written on garbage. Had my self-esteem sunk so low that I didn't feel worthy to write out my feelings in a journal meant for that purpose?

"That was what my first entry was about—my issue about writing my issues. After that was out of the way, I moved to other areas of irritation and frustration—such as my relationship with Richard, my relationship, non-existent as it may be, with Wade, my search for something else in life, my loneliness and my desire for love. Love like I've seen in the movies or that I've witnessed in my dreams. I secretly hope that the romantic, sweep you off your feet love does exist. I mean, it did for Kathleen and Thomas. Although I am not sure they're even real or something that my over-active imagination created."

The afternoons vary from walks up and down the streets, writing and editing the latest article, running errands, or taking naps. Sometime close to five p.m., I take my evening jog on the bike path at the beach. I've noticed a few regulars at this time, too. A couple of joggers and rollerbladers, but the majority of the exercise enthusiasts I see are bicyclists. Pretty much the standard fare for bikes is the beach cruiser. A couple of people ride mountain bikes and road bikes, but at least ninety percent have beach cruisers. While jogging up and down and dodging the bikes, it got me to thinking that maybe a bike is what I need. I could explore a wider area. I wouldn't have to worry about parking and I could take another step in acclimating to the beach lifestyle.

With my mind made up I jog back up to 2nd Street and over to the bike shop I spotted a few days ago, just to check it out. I'm usually one to research a purchase to death, but lately I've been more impulsive. Today,

I'm going to put some thought into bicycle shopping. The store is large and stocked full. There are two levels. Right away the smell of rubber hits me. It makes me a little queasy. How can they work with that smell all day? What am I saying? I worked in a sweaty, smelly gym for years.

I'm greeted right away by "Tom," according to his name badge.

"I'm thinking of a bike to use around here," I tell him.

"Okay. What type of use did you have in mind for cycling?" Tom asks.

"What use? Cycling use," I answer. What kind of question is that? From the look on his face it's obvious that he thinks I don't have a clue, which is true, but I'm not going to let him know that.

"Yes, but are you planning on going long distances, on rugged surfaces, or cruising the beach and local areas," Tom tries again.

"Just the area, something like the rest of the bikes I've been seeing in this area."

"Got it. Well, we have beach cruisers or hybrids. If you haven't had a lot of experience on a bike, the hybrid would be more comfortable and we could outfit it with a basket for you to put a few belongings in." Tom points to the hybrid bikes in the corner.

They look similar to the beach cruisers to me and come in cute colors. I like the green one. The only difference I can see is that the handlebars are not as wide.

"This one has seven speeds and hand brakes, whereas the beach cruiser does not have any gears and you pedal backwards to stop," Tom explains.

Okay, there's another difference. "Well, I'm just looking, but can I try one out while I'm here?" I ask.

"Sure, pick one out and I'll pull out a beach cruiser. You can try them both to see what works for you. We'll go out back into the parking lot."

I grab the green one and roll it outside. I climb on and test it out. I haven't ridden since I was a kid, but what they say is right. It's just like riding a bike. It all came back to me and soon I was doing figure eights around the parking lot.

"It feels great," I exclaim.

"Okay, now try the beach cruiser." I get off the hybrid as he is pushing a red cruiser toward me. Right away I notice that it's more difficult to maneuver. The handlebars are so wide it feels like all steering is controlled with my shoulders. In minutes I'm sore and then I forget that there is no hand brake and put my feet down to stop.

"Help!" I yell as my feet are sliding on the ground. Tom runs by my side to steady me before I fall. Well, no contest there, I like the hybrid.

"I'll take the green one," I announce and then realize I don't have any money on me since I came from jogging. "Er, I mean, can you hold it for me until tomorrow?"

"Sure. If you want, I can attach a water bottle holder and basket so it will be ready when you come in the morning."

"That would be great. Can you add a bell too? See you tomorrow and thanks for your help, Tom."

I leave the store, excited about my shiny new bike. Just like when I was a kid, I can't wait until tomorrow to get my bike. I jog home only to find someone standing on my landing. Damn. I forgot the tile guy was coming by to see what needed to be fixed. He looks irritated.

"Jim?" I call out.

"Yes. June did tell you I was coming?"

"Uh. Yes, I'm so sorry. I, uh, got tied up with . . . business," I stammer.

Jim looks me up and down and gives me a puzzled look. I glance down and remember I came from jogging and bike shopping. He is probably wondering what type of business I'm in, looking sweaty and disheveled. Oh, well, he's only here for the kitchen tiles, he can think what he likes.

"I'll show you the area that needs to be repaired." I unlock the front door and guide him over to the kitchen.

Jim closely examines the six broken tiles on the kitchen counter. As he is moving around the room, measuring and jotting notes down on a tiny pad he keeps in his shirt pocket, I watch him. He has rough, large hands. His arms are firm as well as the rest of him. Jim's face is worn from time. Years in the sun, and life taking its toll, I would guess.

"I'm going to have to order these tiles. They look to be from the 70s. If I can't find them, would you be okay with me replacing them with something similar?" he asks, turning toward me for an answer.

I was admiring his firm backside when he turned to speak. Shit. I think I've been caught. I'm sure my face is red, since his eyebrows went up suspiciously.

"Uh, I don't mind, but you probably should check with June, the landlady," I stammer and turn back to the living room and straighten up the room a bit. Need to get some space between me and him. First I'm lusting after the lifeguard, now the tile guy. Next, it will be Tom at the bike shop or pretty much any man I come across. Because I'm suddenly unattached does not mean I need to latch on to the first male I encounter. I need to take my time. Heal first and then I'll see.

Jim packs up his tools and heads to the door.

"I'll check with June and get back with you," he announces as he walks out the door.

"Fine, see you later." I answer with my back to him, busying myself with some dusting. After he leaves, I breathe a sigh of relief and grab myself a glass of wine. I really need to get a grip.

The next morning I start my routine with my tea on the balcony, then throw on my sweats and flip-flops and head to the beach for journaling time. Sure enough, my private club members are there. Mr. Lifeguard is doing sprints up and down the sand. That looks hard. Simple jogging in the uneven sand is a challenge. Mr. Tai Chi is sitting quietly, cross-legged with his eyes closed. He's the picture of serenity. I attempt to emulate his position and close my eyes. Okay, now what? What's he thinking about? Maybe he's chanting or praying. Or maybe there's a sequence of lines he must recite silently to ascend? I would love to ask him, but he might think I'm intruding on his space. I mean, he does come here early when the beach is desolate. He probably doesn't want to bother with some woman with issues. Hell, my issues have issues.

And so I journal about what I think he's doing. Well, it's productive, I tell myself. Maybe I'll discover something about me from writing about someone else. No, I guess that doesn't make sense. I should be writing about my issues.

Journal Entry Feb. 2—What's my real problem? Why am I unhappy? What does my inner self crave?

Well, this is getting way too personal. Let's take a quick peek at what Mr. Lifeguard is doing now. He's not at his tower. I frantically search the beach for him. I want everyone to be in their positions, almost like they need to be there for my benefit and comfort. Crazy, I know.

I whip my head around looking for Mr. Lifeguard and find him behind me, walking with his bag over his shoulder. Whew. Good, going back to his tower. All is well. He catches my eye.

"Looking for me?" he calls out.

"No. No, just . . . ," I start. But, what am I going to say? I can't admit that I was looking for him, or my ludicrous reason. I can't think of any logical answer, so I say nothing else. He walks over to where I'm sitting. He's even better looking close up.

"I see you here almost every morning, thought I'd introduce myself. I'm Jesse," he tells me.

"I'm Tess. Nice to meet you," I answer. "So, you've been doing this lifeguard thing long?"

"Three years, and have you been doing this writing thing long?" Jesse teasingly motions to my journal.

"Oh, the journaling . . . yeah, about three weeks." We both laugh nervously.

"Well, if you ever tire of writing in your book, maybe we can get a coffee sometime. I hear coffee helps the writing process."

"Yeah, I heard that. Sounds like it might be worth a try," I reply as nonchalantly as I can muster.

"Okay, here's my number. I'm free most evenings." Jesse writes his cell phone number on the back of a business card for a kayak rental outfit.

"Thanks."

Jesse strolls casually back to his tower and I sit here bewildered. Did I get asked out on a date? Awesome. I feel weird sitting here now. I feel exposed. I glance over at Mr. Tai Chi and he's looking my way. I smile and give a little wave. He waves back. Okay, this is too much interaction for one morning. I gather my belongings, brush the sand off my butt, and leave the beach. Time to get my bike and I can ride and forget this odd morning. Yay.

Chapter 9

At 9:00 a.m., on the dot, I'm waiting outside the bike store. Hurry up and open. Tom comes up 9:03 a.m. and, finally, unlocks the main door.

"Excited?" he asks.

"Yes, very." I follow Tom past all the racks of bicycle tires to the front desk and there on the side is my beautiful, shiny, green bicycle. It's been adorned with a black basket, bell, and water bottle holder. Tom starts ringing it up.

"Wait," I tell him. Going back through the aisles, I choose a water bottle and bike lock and place them on the counter.

"Okay, now I'm set," I announce.

"Did you want a basket liner?" Tom asks.

"No, I think my backpack will work fine." I place my Sedona bag in the basket and it fits perfectly.

Immediately after leaving the store I'm on my bike and riding up the street. Since I'm not used to riding I pull into the residential area and cruise up and down the side streets. Already, I love it.

"Jared. This is much better than walking. I can still take in the sights, but with the breeze going through my hair it adds to the sensation. It's like I'm flying. There's an unbelievable freedom with cycling. How come I never realized this before? I should've taken up cycling years ago, instead of countless hours inside a musty gym. I could've been outside getting fresh air and exercising with pleasure!"

With my new bike, instead of walking or driving, I'll cycle, I decide. Up and down the streets I ride. I don't seem to tire. It's invigorating. Next I ride over to the beach and try out the bike path. The paved path there is painted with a dividing line. One side is for the joggers/walkers and the other for cyclists. Before I figured it out, I was jogging on the cycling side and was blasted by a bike horn and a few choice words from an oncoming cyclist. I've since learned my lesson. Today I get to go on the "big boy" side and ride with them. Over to Naples and then back to the Belmont pier in such a short time, it's terrific.

I spend a few good hours riding around and start to head home—time to get some work done. Tomorrow I'm going to check out Naples and Seal Beach. And then maybe the next day, head over to Sunset Beach and Huntington Harbour. Now that I have my bike, my excursions are limitless.

The next morning at the beach, it's once again overcast. Today I'm getting damp from the mist. Damn, my hair is going to frizz up in this. I twist my dark hair up in a knot. I plunk down in my spot, my piece of real estate in the sand.

"It's so quiet here; it almost feels like my own private beach. I dub thee *Tess' Beach*," I declare to Jared's pendant. "From my vantage point, I can keep an eye on Mr. Lifeguard . . . er, Jesse. Guess I should use his real name now. I'm so used to creating names that I occasionally let one slip out at the most inopportune times. Like the time when speaking with my next door neighbor in the valley I accidentally referred to the guy at the end of the street as Mr. Dick Do. Well it was Dick Do's fault. One day he was joking around saying he should come to my gym.

"'Hey, I've got a 'dick do' belly,' he said.

"'Huh?' I replied.

"'You know, when your stomach sticks out further than your dick do.'

"'Oh,' is all I could say.

"My neighbor thought it was so funny and told Dick Do about it. Yikes. I'm glad I moved. Don't want to make that mistake here, too."

In the water I've noticed three manmade islands dotted with palm trees. I heard that they are oil drilling facilities that have been camouflaged for aesthetics. Behind me are the restrooms, flagged by tall palm trees. I can hear the gentle surf. This is a bay of some sort since I can see breakwater walls to the right and left of me—not a good area for surfing. Maybe that's why this beach is so quiet and unoccupied. Jesse's surfboard is propped up on the sand, ready and waiting to be used if there is an emergency. A new friend has come to meet me—a seagull. He hops closer, turning his head, hoping I have some food to share.

"Sorry, little feathered friend." I whisper, "Maybe next time."

After a while, I take off and meander through the streets again. I walk slower these days, not in the hurried pace I was accustomed to.

"I actually start noticing details. For instance, Jared, each house here is unique, not like the cookie-cutter house I had in the valley. Not to say that my old house wasn't nice. It was generic. It was practical though. That's me—practical Tess. I chose very carefully. I researched the best schools, in anticipation of having children. Richard and I found a place close to Northridge Hospital and good schools, tucked away on a quiet cul-de-sac. Practical and boring, that's us.

"Even though the lots are small here, the homeowners really make good use of what land they have. There are so many tiny touches and details: a colorful pot, an interesting sign, and the use of color and texture in the plants they choose to make their home a work of art. Each house is fascinating to look at. At times like this I wish I was with someone so we could discuss the use of the plants or what this house would need to create this or that mood. For now I'll walk these streets alone. Maybe Jesse would be interested. Never mind, I can't see that happening."

For my afternoon I'm free to cycle around Naples. I finished my latest article and emailed it to the editor. Now, I'll wait to hear back on the inevitable rewrites. Naples is absolutely adorable, but jeez is it cramped. The streets are so narrow. I'm not sure how cars actually fit. Parking is atrocious. Fortunately, I have my trusty bike. Ms. Glimmer, I'm calling her as her green paint glimmers and shines in the sun. She's a lovely girl, my favorite purchase so far. Here the homes are more upscale than in Belmont Shore. It's a real treat to take a look at the beauty, architecture, and landscaping. It's evident that these folks take pride in their homes. I bet it looks dazzling during the holidays. I make a mental note to visit then.

When I return home it's already getting dark. I don't have lights on Ms. Glimmer, so there will be no night riding for me. Valerie is sitting on her front doorstep as I ride up.

"Hey lady. Settling in?" she calls out.

"Yeah, finally."

"Wanna chat for a bit?" Valerie asks. "Got a bottle of wine in the fridge."

"Sure, that sounds good." I put Ms. Glimmer away and smooth out my windblown hair as best I can.

Valerie's apartment is furnished in, what appears to be, hand-me-down pieces from various decades. My eyes take in a 1960s style worn floral sofa, plaid green chair, fashion and travel magazines strewn around, and chocolates on the table.

"Ooh, chocolate," I say.

"Help yourself, girlfriend. Wine and chocolate. What can be better?" she says. "Well, a man would be good too," Valerie adds.

"Yeah. That's for sure."

Valerie pours us both a glass of Riesling. I perch on the end of her sofa and take a large gulp of the wine. It feels cool and refreshing after the bike ride.

"See you've been bicycling a lot."

"Yeah, it's been great. Love it. You ride?"

"Me, honey? Oh not a chance. I dance for exercise."

"Dancing is great. Funny, after so many years in the gym, I never realized that exercise can be fun. I'm having a great time exploring on the bike." The wine is helping me relax. I settle deeper into her couch and close my eyes for a moment. It feels nice.

"Let me fill that up for you." Valerie pours me another glass. "So your leg healed up okay?" She makes a cutting motion on her thigh. I cringe.

"Yeah, thank you. I want to apologize again for my behavior that first day you met me. It was, as you put it, a 'shit day.'"

"Like I said, I've been there. Felt like dying after Donald, even took some freakin' pills, but we move on. Right?"

"Right."

"So if ya don't mind me prying. What happened? Did your husband cheat on you?"

"No, not Richard."

"Ohh. Beat you, huh?" Valerie's eyes widen.

"Oh, no. No. Nothing like that. Richard is very kind and gentle."

"So you left why?"

I take a deep breath and another swig of wine. How do I explain this?

"Okay," I start. "Richard, that is, my soon to be ex-husband and I split up recently. We owned a gym together but now it's turned over to him."

"Is he all muscular?"

"Why, you interested?"

"No . . . oh no . . ." Valerie actually looks embarrassed.

"I'm just kidding. Yeah, he works out a lot so he's pretty fit, tall and handsome in a boyish sort of way. It wasn't like he was mean or abusive or cheated on me or anything like that. It was just that . . . oh, I don't know . . . something was missing for me. I'm not sure Richard even realized it. One day, I was at a health and fitness seminar and as the seminar was ending I was dreading going home. I thought to myself, I don't want to go home, and this voice inside my head said, 'You don't have to.' Now, normally I would ignore any voice telling me what to do, whether it was good or bad, but this time I listened. And so here I am, a stranger in this town trying to figure it all out—trying to figure out who I am."

"Voices? Cool. Go on. So what ya looking for?"

"Uh. I don't know. I realized I wanted something real. I want real, deep love—like in my dreams. Crazy huh?"

"Wow, you're brave."

"Brave or stupid? I'm not sure which some times. I mean, I loved Richard. However, it was this strange mothering type of love. He always acted dependent and needy and I felt, I guess, compelled to jump in and take care of any situation that arose. It was like I was the caretaker in the family and it was suffocating. And then there is Wade. Wade is our son. He's fifteen. I hate to admit it, but we don't have a good relationship. Actually we never had. He has been angry at me his entire life. I honestly cannot tell you why. I read all the parenting books. I behaved like all the other mothers did. I participated in all the activities he was interested in. Still . . ."

I pause to catch my breath. My eyes are tearing up. I don't know why this is all coming out now, to this woman I just met. Maybe it's the wine or that she already saw me in my worst vulnerable state. We have that connection.

Valerie grabs some toilet paper for my eyes. Her eyes tell me it's safe to continue. So I do.

"Still, Wade gets along great with Richard. Although sometimes it's as if Wade is older than Richard. I don't understand our family. I feel hurt. I feel guilty. I feel like there's more to life than this. And then there are the dreams . . ." I stop again. Guilt bubbles up in me, not so much for leaving Wade, but for not feeling much guilt about it. I stuff that back down. I'm tired and a little embarrassed. I'm sure Valerie doesn't want to hear all my problems.

"Dreams, huh? Your life is sure more interesting than mine."

"I don't know about that. Thank you for being a good listener." I stand and head to the kitchen with my empty wine glass.

"Anytime. Would love to hear about them dreams sometime."

"Yeah. Another day in Tess' soap opera life." I laugh uncomfortably.

Valerie hugs me warmly. "Let's do this again. It was nice having the company."

"Sure. Thanks again." I head upstairs.

After I settle in for the evening, I start planning my next day's tour. My life has become a routine of beach, bike, and exploring. I know I should probably be working more on issues, but I'm enjoying the escape for the moment. I haven't checked in on Richard and Wade for three or four days. Last time I called, Wade was out with friends and Richard appeared to be adjusting okay. He seemed a little resentful on the phone, but sometimes it's hard to tell with him unless I see his face. I start to punch in the number to call him but Naomi rings through. She always seems to know when to call and save me from a guilt trip from Richard.

"Hi, hope you're not busy," she says.

"Nope, just sitting here. What's up?" I leave out the part about almost calling Richard.

"Well, you know how you are interested in metaphysical studies now?" Naomi asks.

"I don't know if interested is the word, but okay?"

"Anyway, I got this flyer in the mail. There's a women's festival in Irvine this weekend. I think we should go. They'll have speakers on a bunch of topics. It'll be great. This will give you an introduction to my world and you might get some answers you're looking for. What do you say?" She's trying to sound upbeat and convincing, but I can tell she is worried I'll shut the door on the idea.

"Um . . . I'm still not sure what questions I have so I don't know how I'm going to get answers, Naomi."

"Oh, come on. It'll be fun. There will be food and vendors, and belly dancing and . . ." Naomi pauses, obviously trying to find the one thing to sway me over. She adds "with music and tambourines and . . ."

I start to laugh. Poor girl, she's trying so hard. "Tambourines? Well, why didn't you say so? I can't miss out on the tambourines," I tease.

"Great. I know you'll love it. I'll pick you up Saturday at eleven. See ya," and she's gone.

What did I agree to? I'm just glad she didn't start singing.

Chapter 10

Today, I headed straight for the coffeehouse first before hitting the beach. I'm craving an onion bagel and coffee. It's been cold out lately. A warm toasted bagel and steaming coffee will warm me as I sit on the cool sand. The bagel has a dual purpose: 1.) I'm hungry and 2.) My seagull friend will probably be ready for breakfast, too.

I plunk down in my spot to find my club members in their locations doing their thing. All is right with this morning. I start breaking off pieces of my bagel and feeding some to the gulls and some to me. Seems like my gull friend told his buddies about me since now I have a whole group gathered for breakfast. The squawking increases in volume causing Mr. Tai Chi to take notice. He smiles at me.

"That's it. I'm going to introduce myself to him. I mean, he seems like a nice guy. I sort of know him. It's not like he is a stranger. He's here almost every morning with me. He must be okay, right Jared?"

Next thing I know my body is standing up. It's almost like I had the thought and my body responded before I could really think it out properly. Okay, now that I'm up, I'm going to walk over and introduce myself. Why am I shaking? Maybe it's because he seems kind of like some spiritual holy man? This is weird. He's simply some guy on the beach. No big deal. Except that he meditates, does tai chi, and looks extremely serene. Yeah, no big deal.

"Hi, my name is Tess. I see you here most days and I felt like I needed to introduce myself."

"Sit down," he says softly.

"Uh, okay, sure, why not. I mean one area of the beach is like another. This is a big beach, isn't it?" I'm rambling.

I sit down and fidget with the zipper pull on my windbreaker. Why is he making me so nervous? Maybe I should leave and find another stretch of beach, far away from him and never have to see him again. He smiles at me. His eyes are blue and deep set, with soft creases around them. Smile lines, I would guess. He reaches towards me with his hand. Instinctively I pull back.

"You have something in your hair, let me get it," he tells me. I look down and, sure enough, I have bits of bagel stuck in my hair. Can this introduction get any worse?

"Oh, shit. Oh sorry, I didn't mean to swear around you," I apologize.

"Don't worry about it. I'm Doug. It's nice to meet you, Tess." He's reassuring, which helps me relax . . . a little.

I'm not sure what to do next. Do I stay a while, say "see you around" or what? Being uncertain, I feel frozen as if I'm waiting for the universe to direct me. This isn't typically how I react, in fact I would never wait for guidance from somewhere out in the cosmos or if I did, I would definitely respond with an opposing move. And so I continue sitting, next to Doug, waiting and not waiting. He is quiet and strangely comforting. We're both sitting looking at the water. There's nothing for me to say right now. I resolve to enjoy the peace.

How long we sit like that I really don't know. But at some point I realize that I have to get on with my day. I break the "spell" that I've been under and start to get up.

"This was really nice," I tell him and do a sort of bow to him. It felt like something I should do, like I have seen in the movies when the Buddhist monks bow out of reverence. That's how I felt. I think I've lost my mind. Doug gives me a curious look.

"See you tomorrow," he tells me. A smile appears on my face. I feel things are turning around for me.

The next morning instead of coveting my usual piece of beach, I sit next to Doug. He's doing his meditation practice and it feels good being there next to him. I wonder if I get any benefit from his meditation with the close proximity. Enlightenment by osmosis — it sounds like the perfect solution for the lazy. After a while, Doug opens his eyes, turns his head and smiles that welcoming smile he gave me yesterday. It's as if he knew this was to be our established routine. He doesn't seem a bit surprised that I showed up again. It's eerie, in a good way.

"So," I begin, "you look really peaceful. Is it from that meditation you do?" I ask more out of a need to fill the silence than a wanting of information. But, the information could be useful anyway, I rationalize.

It takes Doug a while to answer. I'm not sure if he's thinking of how to explain it to a novice. Or if he doesn't want to be bothered with me, or maybe . . .

"It is and it isn't." He interrupts my thought.

"Oh," I say, because how else am I to respond to that cryptic answer? Again, he's quiet. I'm racking my brain trying to come up with something to ask him. Okay, let's try another tactic.

"So, do you want to know anything about me?" I pose.

"If you would like to tell me," he invites.

Well, at least I took that as an invitation. "Uh, I moved here a short time ago, learning about the area. I'm recently single and, uh, I would like to know more about meditation. Maybe it will help me."

Why can't I think of anything else to say? I close my eyes for a moment and a strange quiet comes over me. I look down and then peer up at Doug. Looking through hair that has fallen over my eye, I'm searching for some reassurance that I'm okay.

"About meditation," he starts and adds, "just sit. See you tomorrow." Fluidly, he rises and walks away.

Huh? Just sit? And that's what I do. For the next half hour, I sit.

Chapter 11

That afternoon, I take Ms. Glimmer for a ride through Sunset Beach and Huntington Harbour. I feel like I'm ready to change. "This is the new me!" I yell out to the passing cars. It's a fun ride over the Alamitos Bay, through Seal Beach and down Pacific Coast Highway to Sunset Beach. On the west side of the street is Sunset Beach and on the east side is Huntington Harbour. Sunset Beach looks like an older town with the strange zoning I have noticed in Belmont Shore and Seal Beach, while Huntington Harbour is broken up by manmade channels with uppity-up homes lining the water. Attached to these waterfront homes are slips filled with expensive boats to accessorize their houses. I come across the kayak rental place from the business card Jesse gave me. I still need to call him, making a mental note.

Pacific Coast Highway is peppered with seafood restaurants, tattoo parlors, psychics, and bars. I stop at a fish taco stand to get lunch. Next door is a tattoo shop, the third one I've come across on my ride.

"Maybe I should get a tattoo to commemorate the new Tess. Yeah right, old Tess would never get a tattoo in a million years. Old Tess is a practical, rational woman. Tattoos do not make one irrational, right, Jared? Besides, one tattoo is not extreme. Everyone has them."

I'm excited. It feels dangerous and rebellious and oh so damn good. That's it, after lunch I'm going to get one. Maybe I'll have a beer first, to go with the fish tacos, of course, not to settle my nerves.

My stomach is filled with jumbling butterflies when I push open the door to *Inkblaster's Tattoo Shop*. Garbled, hard rock music is blaring on the speakers. Instantly, I'm greeted by one of the staff. He's covered in tattoos. Which, I guess, is to be expected since he works in a tattoo shop.

"Can I help you?" he asks loudly.

"I was thinking of getting a tattoo," I yell back.

He turns down the music so we can talk without yelling—whew.

"I'm Steve, one of the artists here. Take a look at the portfolios and some of the flash. Let me know if you have any questions."

"Flash?" I ask.

"What you see on the walls." Steve waves his arm around indicating the laminated prints of various tattoo designs adorning the walls. I thought they were for decoration, but now I see that they are there to give customers ideas if they, like me, don't know what they want to permanently place on their body. Actually, come to think of it, it's kind of stupid for me to walk into a tattoo parlor not having a clue about what I want, where to put it, and how big it should be, with it being attached to me until I die. This is a big commitment. Commitments are not something that I'm good at. Maybe this was a bad idea. I feel panicky and grab a photo portfolio of previous tattoo clients and sit down on the waiting area bench.

"Take your time, look through the photos. Think about it," Steve gently tells me.

He probably knows I'm not an old pro at this and can see how nervous I am. He really is very nice. Not anything like I expected. Well, I'm not sure what I expected. Steve has tattoos covering his arms, even on his neck and hands! The abrasive music playing when I walked in, the sound of tattoo machines humming, I guess I expected someone gruffer. Steve is polite and professional. Had it not been for his calm manner I may have walked out already. But, here I sit, turning the pages, trying to find a picture or symbol that means something to me.

I browse through page after page of skulls, flowers, old sailor-type tattoos, tribal bands, and cartoon characters. Nothing strikes me. The skill displayed in the photos looks good, from what I can tell. I really don't have anything to base it on, but the lines are clear and the colors are bright. It's not like I'm planning on doing my whole back or anything, just something little that is special to signify the change I'm going through. I close the portfolio and stand up to examine the flash covering the walls—more of the same.

There is one laminated poster I come across that is filled with symbols. Under the symbol is the definition. Hmm. Maybe that's what I should get. I can get a symbol that represents . . . I scan up and down and spot a few that could work . . . maybe *peace* or *strength* . . . or maybe *love*?

"Those are called *Kanji*. They're Japanese symbols. Very popular tattoos," Steve tells me. I turn around and see he is standing behind the counter now. I wonder how long he's been watching me.

"Oh, thanks."

"You know . . . what I tell people that are getting their first tattoo . . .," he starts. I'm listening fully now. "…is not to pay attention to what others are getting. Not to pay attention to the flash. Pay attention to you. What means something to you—that's what you get."

"Yeah. You're right. Thank you."

I sit back down on the bench. Steve is really quite deep. It's like he read my mind, probably because he's seen many people wander in here in the same state I'm in. I think back to Doug and his words, "Just sit." The cool cinder block wall provides a supportive respite. I ask myself what means something to me: my son, my bike, the beach, Naomi, the list goes on. No, this is something that's special to only me. Something that I'll wear on me all my days. Something that's not so identifiable that others would figure it out. Something that can transport me and help me to remember a special time when I glance at it. I breathe in and out slowly and try to block out the rest of the world. Then I remember the pears that Naomi brought over that night in the housewarming basket-o-goodies.

Pears have always taken me to a special place. That's it. I'm going to get a tattoo of a pear. It's perfect. It's only special to me. No one would know what it meant and I didn't see one pear tattoo in any of the flash or portfolios. It's unique and it's all mine.

I stand up too fast. I'm excited about my choice. Steve jerks his head up.

"Know what you want?" he asks.

"Yeah, I do," I announce.

"Okay, what would you like and where do you want it?"

Where do I want it? Another decision to make? I'm mentally scanning my body. I want to see it, but I want to be able to cover it up if I need to. I look down and rule out areas:

- Breast—sounds painful
- Wrist—too noticeable
- Hip—too intimate
- Ankle—perfect

"I would like a pear tattooed on my right ankle," I decide.

"A pear? Okay, give me fifteen minutes to draw it up and then you can let me know if you like it or need to make any changes." Thankfully he takes my pear idea in stride. He's probably heard and seen it all.

"Sounds good. I'm going to take a short walk."

I head to the beach and walk off some of this nervous energy. Ms. Glimmer is safely chained to the bike rack in front of the tattoo shop. Am I really going to get a tattoo? It's not a Tess thing to do. My mind wanders back to the day I decided to change my name to Tess and re-create myself. Today, I'm doing the same thing. I'm making a new Tess, one that is bold and independent and sports a tattoo. I want to call Naomi and tell her. No. I'll surprise her when I see her Saturday. That's even better.

I glance at my watch and notice that fifteen minutes flew by. At a hurried pace, I head back toward the shop. Okay, here I go. Steve is finishing up the final touches of the drawing when I get back.

"Take a look. Is this what you had in mind?" He hands me the tracing paper sketch. He's a good artist. There's more to this craft than meets the eye. He has drawn a very life-like pear, complete with stem, leaves, and even a water drop on one of the leaves. I'm impressed.

"Exactly what I had in mind. This is great."

While I'm wondering how the sketch is going to end up on my ankle, Steve walks over to a machine and runs the sketch through it. It looks like some sort of copy machine and soon spits out another image of my pear, lined in purple. Next, Steve sets up his work area. It looks sterile, everything is covered in plastic and the needles (yikes) are in individual packages, very modern. He motions for me to sit down on the chair at his station. He has wrapped a stool with plastic for my ankle. I put my foot up and turn it so the side I want tattooed is facing up. Steve dons his gloves. I look at the table and at all the tools of the trade. There are little red cups, like tiny thimbles, lined up on a paper sheet. The cups are sitting in petroleum jelly to keep them in place. Each cup is filled with various colors of ink: black, red, yellow, green, and brown.

Steve attaches the disposable needle bar on to the tattoo machine and presses a foot peddle to start it whirring. My body jerks at the sound. Shit, it looks like a flippin' sewing machine with that needle going up and down.

"Just testing the gun out," he tells me. I nod as I work to recover from the shock of seeing the *gun* work. Steve grabs a spray bottle and squirts a cool liquid on my ankle. Next, he takes the purple copied sketch and lays it carefully on the wet skin. After pressing down and smoothing it out, he carefully lifts the soggy paper. Underneath I can see it has left a purple outline of a pear on my ankle.

"Cool."

"Why don't you get up and look in the mirror to see if that's where you want it?"

I walk up to the full-length mirror and turn sideways, taking in the view. It looks good and it's not even a tattoo yet. I turn this way and that, stand up on my toes as if I'm wearing high heels, trying to imagine how it will look in various outfits and situations. Satisfied, I return to my chair.

"Okay, let's do this," he announces. The hum and whirring of the gun starts again and my heart starts to race.

"Is it going to hurt?"

"Yes. It hurts. If it didn't everyone would have one, right?"

I don't know if that makes me feel better. Couldn't he have lied?

He must have seen the panic in my eyes since he adds, "Think of it as a rite of passage, a sacred event. This symbol, chosen by you, is like a totem to mark an important part of your life." Wow. He really is a philosopher.

"You're right. Let's do it!" I take a deep breath, waiting for the pain to begin.

Chapter 12

In less than an hour it's all done.

"It wasn't as bad as I imagined, Jared. I mean, don't get me wrong, some areas were like someone slicing me open with a razor blade, but the majority of the time it was an irritating repetitive scratching. When it got bad, I would think of Steve's speech on 'rite of passage' and that carried me through. Well, that and gritting my teeth, pulling up my hair in a ponytail as I started sweating, and gripping the chair with all my strength. The end result—a beautifully colored, realistic piece of art. I love it and want to keep checking it out, but Steve wrapped it up in some absorbent gauze and told me I had to wait until this evening to take off the bandage. Bummer."

On the bike ride home I worry about my ankle. It's not like the tattoo is going to fall off; I feel like I want to coddle that area. My ankle feels like I got a sunburn, actually I'm surprised it doesn't hurt more. I'm humming a little tune as I ride back. It's the tune that Thomas sings to Kathleen in my dreams. I wonder if it's a real song. Maybe someday I'll try to look it up. Happiness wells up in me, like I overcame a hurdle in my life. I already feel like a changed person. Me and my pear.

When I arrive home, I look down and notice my foot is streaked with blood-tinged fluids. My tattoo is leaking, must've been the pedaling. With care, I take off the bandage and wash off the raw area. It feels like I've been through a meat tenderizer. Looks good, doesn't look like any of the color ran. I text Wade, again.

Wade, guess what? Got a tattoo. Your mom is cool now! Love you.

For dinner, I heat up some leftover mac and cheese and prop my ankle up on pillows on the coffee table. Not that it needs to be elevated, thought I might as well give myself a little extra attention.

Sleeping was difficult since I was so afraid I would mess up the design if it rubbed on the sheets. In the morning, I was relieved to find the pear still there. Okay, that is enough of this worrying. Many people get tattoos and the tattoos don't disappear from sleeping wrong.

I'm bouncing along with anticipation to see Doug—can't wait to show off my new ink. It is overcast, as usual, and he is already doing tai chi. I sit down near him and watch how he effortlessly moves from one position to another. It's beautiful to watch—sort of a mixture of dance and martial arts. I wish I could move like that. Doug finishes his last pose and sits down next to me.

"I got a tattoo yesterday," I start the conversation. Doug merely nods his head. "It's to signify a change in me—from old Tess to new Tess," I explain.

"Who are you behind the name?" Doug asks me.

I'm confused. Is he talking about me being Jasmine before? No. I get it. He is talking about something deeper.

"I don't know . . ." I answer quickly since I can't think of anything profound to say. Doug doesn't respond. I'm not sure if he's irritated with me for being so shallow or if he's doing his meditation thing.

"Do you think we're here to play games, get tattoos, and sit on the beach?" he points out.

"Uh, no. I'm working on things." I cross my arms.

"Is that what you're doing? Or avoiding?"

"Avoiding? Avoiding what?"

"Your gift. Your intuition." Doug pokes his finger into my shoulder.

"Stop," I tell him. He's starting to piss me off. What happened to my safe beach buddy?

"Stop what? Forcing you into addressing your truth? Tell me."

"Tell you what?" My voice rising.

"Why do you fight your intuition?"

"Intuition? I don't follow intuition." I feel for Jared's necklace under my shirt.

"Why?"

"I hate damned intuition. Is that what you want to hear? Goddammit! What good is it? What good did it do, huh? Answer me that. Did it save Jared? Could it save Jared? No!"

I stand up to leave. I don't need to put up with this crap from Doug. "What business is this of yours anyway?" I shout at him. After walking a few steps I pause. *What am I doing?* I take a deep breath and return to my place on the sand, slumping down in my spot.

"Go on," he starts again.

"I don't want to talk about it. Okay?"

"No, it's not okay."

"How dare you tell me what's okay or not."

"It's *you* that sat back down. Now tell me about your intuition," he pries.

"Intuition is fucking useless. There, I said it. Did it help on Jared's twenty-first birthday when he and his friends all drove to Las Vegas to celebrate? No!" My stomach feels like it's holding an angry ball of fire waiting to erupt. I rummage through my bag for tissue since the tears are now flowing. "Yeah, intuition was so helpful. Mom, Dad, and I were riding in the car to go to dinner in the valley and oblivious Mom was wondering if Jared struck it big on the roulette table and all of a sudden . . ."

"Yes?"

"All of a sudden, I got the clearest vision of Jared in a roll-over crash in the desert." My chest feels like it's burning. The ball of fire in my stomach is spreading. I can't breathe. I gulp air between sobs. "I was in the back seat of Dad's car and gasped and I couldn't get any air. Mom turned around to ask if I was okay . . ."

I stop and suck air deep into my lungs as the fire feeling moves to my head and legs. My heart is pounding. My body is remembering that horrible experience from many years ago.

Jesse, the lifeguard, who looks to be chatting up a young blond in a bikini, turns his head towards me. His face shows a look of puzzlement. Guess it's due to the scene I'm causing. I don't give a shit right now. Jesse turns his attention back to the more enticing blond.

I continue. "So much for damn intuition. I didn't say anything to my mom and dad. I mean, what was I going to say? I just saw Jared die? C'mon. I've never been able to do anything about these visions. If it was to happen, I couldn't control it. I felt helpless. I hated these visions. They were torture to me!"

I pull up the sweatshirt hood to hide my tear-streaked face and lie down in the sand in a fetal position. My body jerks with silent sobs as the fire feeling consumes me.

Doug sits silently as I continue to lie there and cry for a long while. Slowly the fire feeling leeches out into the cool grains of sand beneath me. My lungs suck in fresh air. Eventually my breathing and heart rate return to their usual rhythms. I push myself back up to a sitting position and blow my nose.

"And?" Doug asks.

My voice a little softer now, I continue and let out a sigh of resignation. "We went out for dinner, but I was quiet, withdrawn, and worried sick. My appetite, which was usually ravenous, was nonexistent. I was on pins and needles waiting for the dreaded phone call, which, unfortunately, did come. After we arrived back home, the phone rang and my heart sank. I heard my mother wailing, my dad yelling and punching walls. I didn't have to ask what was going on. I knew and closed myself off in my room, turning my stereo on full volume to drown out everything else. My life as I knew it was over."

I place my head in my hands. Although the fire feeling is gone, I feel scorched inside, raw. My head aches and my throat is dry.

"Please continue."

My energy is depleted; I continue in a whisper. "With Jared gone, our family disintegrated. Mom had an affair with her boss. But she never found out that I knew." I sigh. "I had seen the letters they wrote back and forth. Dad must've found out because they soon divorced. Mom, I think out of guilt, moved away. She took me with her, which was a disaster since it was to be my senior year in high school and I had to go to a new school where no one knew me. Yeah, that's when I decided to re-create myself. I started introducing myself as Tess. And that's when I vowed not to pay attention to visions anymore. They were a hindrance in my life. I decided I would only use logic and be practical in all decisions from that point on. Why do you even care?"

I'm completely drained from unloading my story. I'm not sure if I'm still pissed off or relieved. Doug is quiet—never answering my question. I wait since I'm all talked out. We sit quietly like that for what seems a long time. Doug places his hand on my knee and peace floods my body. My breath steadies and the pounding in my head diminishes to a mild throbbing.

Doug stands and turns to me. "Still, you must believe in something supernatural; you continue to talk to Jared."

"No. That's different. I don't really think I'm talking to him. It's a habit. He's not going to answer back." Searching through my memory—I didn't tell him about talking to Jared, did I? I just don't know now.

"You sure? Maybe your path is not about re-creating, but about undoing," he cryptically says and walks away. As I watch him leave my head starts to pound again.

And once again, I'm alone.

Chapter 13

Saturday is here. I won't be seeing Doug. I'm sure he could use the break, as can I. Last night I crashed from exhaustion after my encounter with him. I have mixed feelings about his behavior. It seems like he purposely provoked me. Why? Logically I realize it wasn't good to stuff my feelings about Jared for so long but I sure didn't like the way Doug handled it. Maybe that's the only way he could get it out of me. No one has ever been able to get me to open up about Jared before. Still, I'm not sure why he gives a damn anyway.

I can't keep ruminating about Doug. Much to my surprise, I actually spend the morning journaling about Jared—something I've never been able to do before. I take that as a move in the right direction.

Naomi is due over soon. We're off to the women's festival today. I'm not sure if I'm excited about the festival or excited about having some girl time with my best friend. I admit I'm excited to show off my new tattoo. Naomi will be shocked when I show her. I can't wait to see the look on her face. I'm wearing my usual tank top and khaki pants outfit, but hey, I'm wearing flip-flops now. Rolled up the pant legs so my tat shows, too.

My cell phone rings. Digging it out of my bag, I'm silently praying it's not my mother or Richard. Maybe it's Naomi telling me she is on her way. Nope, it's Mother. Deep breath and then I answer as cheerfully as possible.

"Hi Mother."

"Jaz. How are you, dear?" Mother never calls me Tess and insists on calling me "Jaz" no matter how many times I tell her I can't stand it.

"It's Tess, Mother."

"I did not name you that. You will always be Jaz to me."

"I give up. What did you need?" I answer.

"I only wanted to check in on my daughter. Are you done with your little time away and ready to come home? I'm sure Richard would love that."

"Mother, it's not time away. I moved here. I'm not going back. I'm happy." Okay, so I lied about being happy, but really what else was I supposed to say? Mother is always siding with Richard. She doesn't understand that I was suffocating in that house. I'm sure everyone is siding with Richard. "How could she abandon her family?" I imagine the neighbors saying.

"But, come on dear, you have a fine life here, a beautiful house, family, good business. Why did you feel the need to throw it all away?"

"Really, a guilt trip? So supportive."

"We all care about you, that's all."

"Well then support my decision. Look, I gotta jump off the phone now. Talk to you later."

"If you want to talk . . ."

"Yeah, bye." I click off. I need a drink and it isn't even noon. She makes me crazy. Talk about being a hypocrite, didn't she bail on Dad after Jared died? And don't even get me started on her affair. Arrgh! I take a few deep breaths, the way Doug taught me. I need to calm down before Naomi arrives. In . . . out . . . in . . . out . . . much better.

The doorbell rings as I'm finishing up putting on mascara. Right on time. I rush to open the door. And, of course, Naomi looks amazing. She is in a floral dress of pinks and corals that accentuates her curves. How does she do it?

"Ready, dear?" she asks.

"As I'll ever be. Hey, notice anything different?" I turn my ankle out in a dramatic pose.

"Ohmygod, Tess! You got a tattoo?!" she screams.

"Yeah, cool huh?" I grin.

"It's gorgeous. A pear, how perfect."

"I know. Right? Okay, let's go have some fun." I'm looking forward to this event, surprisingly.

We head down to Irvine taking the scenic drive along Pacific Coast Highway. Naomi rolls down all the windows for the fresh, cool air. I barely notice the scent of salty ocean in the breeze. We're quiet and comfortable together, taking in the views of the ocean and palm trees.

The fairground parking lot is almost full. I'm surprised how traveling a few miles inland can increase the temperature so much. I guess I won't need my windbreaker today. At the entrance we are greeted by three overeager women decked out in colorful t-shirts with rhinestone butterflies emblazoned on their chests. In their hair, they're wearing glittering butterfly clips. I'm puzzled by all the butterfly images on the signs and posters displayed, but then Miss Yellow T-shirt hands me a program. *3rd Annual Women's Festival: Transform Yourself!* Ahh, got it.

"Maybe they wanted to call it the 'Metamorphosis Festival,' but they couldn't spell it?" I pose to Naomi. Naomi is used to me by now and merely rolls her eyes. Darn, she won't play.

Miss Orange T-shirt attaches an armband to my wrist decorated with, you guessed it, butterflies. I'm already sick of the butterfly motif before I even enter the grounds. This is going to be a long day. We meander through the merchandise area. To my right is row upon row of vendors selling everything a transformed woman could ever need. There are flowing dresses and skirts. Maybe this is where Naomi stocks up on her clothes? There is one table devoted entirely to crystals and gemstones. According to the signs, they heal all sorts of ails. I pick up a pink one; the sign says "love." I don't think it will help and put it down. Another bin advertises black stones being useful for "Magick"?

I pick up one of the lightweight black stones and ask Naomi, "What's with the strange spelling?"

"That's how Wiccans spell it. That's so everyone knows they're not talking about magic, like magicians in a show."

"Oh, sure, now I see." But I really don't. We move on to the next table of jewelry. Oooh, sparkly.

Nothing is really catching my eye; glancing around I spy the food area and instantly become hungry. "Let's get something to eat," I suggest.

Naomi and I head over to the food stands. Hmmm. What are my choices?

- Vegan Wraps—nope
- Indian Tikka—maybe
- Soy Kabobs—nope
- Chicken Caesar Salad—Yup! Finally something I understand.

I grab a salad and a glass of Zinfandel from the wine bar and park myself on a table in the shade. From here we can see the stage where the belly dancing show is due to start soon. As the cool wine whirls around in my mouth, I start feeling the effects and relax. After we eat, I review the program for the day.

"There are many interesting lectures going on today," Naomi points out.

"Really?"

"Yes. Look, at two p.m. there is a talk on the Law of Attraction in Building 5. And, there's the one I really want to hear on Tarot. It's at two-thirty in Building 3, across that way." She points over my shoulder.

"Yeah, I'm not sure . . ."

I sit in a large room. Am I in a theatre? No. It's more like an auditorium. I glance around, noting the illuminated Exit signs and the back of the heads of women sitting in front of me. The chairs are teal in color, plastic with black armrests. Naomi sits next to me. I'm six rows back from the stage. Up on the stage is an elderly woman with a commanding presence. She's wearing a red, expensive looking business suit. I'm mesmerized by her speech. She's talking about . . . soul mates. Oh . . . it makes so much sense now . . .

"Hello, Tess, are you in there?" Naomi is asking me.

"Huh, oh yes, just thinking."

"No, you weren't thinking, you had that glazed look in your eyes again. Where were you?"

"Okay, fine. I was having one of those 'vision' things." I make air quotes with my hands.

"Ooh, tell me, tell me." She sits upright.

"It's not a big deal. I was sitting in this lecture and was very interested in what the woman was saying."

"Lecture, woman?" She grabs the program from me and starts scanning for woman lecturers today. "What else can you remember? You're supposed to be at that lecture. The vision is trying to guide you." She sounds convincing.

"Uh . . . well, we were in a very large room. Like an auditorium. And she was talking about . . . uh, soul mates."

"Soul mates, soul mates . . ." Her finger is moving down the page of the program. "Yeah, here it is. Dr. Alberta Feinberg at one-thirty p.m. is holding a lecture in the main hall. Listen to what the title is?" Naomi pauses for dramatic effect.

"Tell me, already."

"Okay. It's called, *Finding Your True Love: Soul Mates Through Time*. Come, we can just make it."

Before I can object she is pulling my arm and standing up. I take a deep breath and follow. Another thing old Tess wouldn't do. Old Tess would not pay attention to any vision guiding her. Well, let's see if it works out better for New Tess. Into the auditorium she drags me.

The first five rows are already filled up with women hoping to glean some nugget that will lead them to their "true love" and sure enough there are two seats together in the sixth row, exactly as I saw in my mind's eye. We make our way to our seats and await the presenter.

A few minutes later Dr. Alberta Feinberg takes the stage, wearing the suit I saw too. This is freaking me out a little and I start to fidget in my seat. I feel like bolting. Naomi, sensing my anxiety, gives my hand a squeeze. The lecture begins and right away Dr. Feinberg launches into a tale of soul mates reuniting.

"A woman who had spent her entire life in Florida was resigned never to find love. She admitted although her life was content and she was grateful for the comfortable life she had grown accustomed to, she longed for love," Dr. Feinberg tells the audience. "This woman had begun to learn a meditative practice called Tonglen whereas she would breathe in all the pain of the world and breathe out love and compassion. She felt as this was her small part in healing the world. She rationalized that if love was not meant for her, she would give love to the world instead. After months of practice, she noticed that certain images would appear in her mind. Only flashes, yet they were consistent and repetitive.

"The images in her mind's eye were of New York, the Statue of Liberty and, most often, the prominent lion statues in front of the New York Library. Even though she would attempt to redirect her mind to breathing compassion, the images persisted. Soon after, she began seeing New York references in her everyday life. Ads for New York Pizza, billboards of New York travel. This woman was bombarded with the images even in her sleep. Finally out of desperation and a large dose of curiosity she left Florida for a five day trip to New York. Mind you, this was quite an adventure for an introvert who never left the safety of the Florida beaches.

"She visited all the sights that tourists do: the Empire State Building, the Statue of Liberty, Ground Zero. She looked for signs and clues on this trip, hoping to understand the meaning of the strange images in Florida. She thought her instincts would lead her to the answers. No luck." Dr. Feinberg takes a sip of water from her cup before continuing.

"Finally, on the last day of her trip she set out for the library, the only landmark she had missed. As she stood in front of one of the large lion statues that guard the entrance to the library, she wondered, 'Now what?'" Dr. Feinberg takes a deep breath and scans the audience, making eye contact with someone behind me. She smiles.

I glance behind me to see who she's looking at. There are too many behind me to tell. I sit forward in my chair waiting for her to continue.

"As this woman is about to enter the library, a gentleman approaches. He explains that he is from California and is quite lost. Would she be able to help him with directions? She was about to explain that she was also a visitor when she looked into his eyes. Immediately and suddenly images of past lives with this man poured into her head. She knew him and he was her love over many lifetimes. He took a deep breath of recognition and then tears came to his eyes. 'It's you,' he revealed. Both recognized each other instantly and found their love once more in this life."

Naomi squeezes my hand.

"The woman was me many years ago. And . . . David," she calls to a person behind me, "David, please stand. Everyone, this is David, the lost traveler from California. We have been together fifteen glorious years."

The audience erupts in applause and joyous outbursts. My cheeks are wet and I notice Naomi is sniffling. "Tissue?" Naomi hands me one as she dabs her eyes with hers.

Dr. Feinberg sips more water as she waits for the audience to settle again. Now that she knows she has our attention, she explains the research being done in this field. Dr. Feinberg discusses how we find our soul mates again and again throughout our various lifetimes.

"Sometimes they show up as a lover, or a sibling, or even a parent. You will always find each other. If you haven't found your soul mate yet, don't despair—he or she is out there looking for you too." She concludes, causing a standing ovation for the many of us longing to find this special someone, myself included.

"Wow. That was some speech—so inspirational," says Naomi as we exit the auditorium.

"Yeah, especially for desperate Tess."

"Stop. You're not desperate. Just open and available."

"Oh. So that's what we're calling it? Huh?"

The rest of the afternoon Naomi and I attend the lectures she has been dying to hear. It is fine with me since my mind is still working on what Dr. Feinberg said. While Naomi is engaged in deep conversation about the "Hanged Man" in Tarot, I sneak off to see if I can snag one of Dr. Feinberg's business cards in case I have any further questions. You never know. The auditorium is empty except for flyers and business cards of the various presenters throughout the day. I grab Dr. Feinberg's card and glance over the other cards: past life regressionists, psychics, yoga, meditation, and nutritional counseling. On a whim, I take both the past life regressionist and psychic's cards.

"Never know when it might come in handy. Right?" I tug on my necklace.

On the way home, I'm unusually quiet. Naomi, however, is in one of her jabbering moods, like she is on too much caffeine. It works out great when you don't feel like talking—can't get a word in edgewise anyway. I'm looking forward to sitting alone, maybe on the beach, and thinking about what Dr. Feinberg alluded to. Maybe Doug will be there to listen. Nah, I need to do this one on my own.

Chapter 14

I decide, after all, to sit next to Doug this morning. I still feel a little awkward because of my outburst and his behavior the other day, but he doesn't mention it. He doesn't even ask where I was yesterday. He accepts what is. God, what is that like? Talking is not what I feel like doing today. I only want to sit, next to him, and mull over the words I heard yesterday. They keep playing over and over in my mind. "You will always find each other. If you have not found your soul mate yet, don't despair—he or she is out there looking for you too." It's an echo in my head.

I keep going back to my relationship with Richard and how it never felt like the romantic, soul-mate love I had envisioned. My mind replays the dreams of Kathleen and Thomas. I want what they had. Maybe my soul mate is out there right now, like Dr. Feinberg said. Here I'm sitting on an empty stretch of beach alone and somewhere my love is sitting . . . where? Where do I even start looking? How would I know him if I saw him? It's not like he'll be wearing a neon sign that flashes "Tess' Soul Mate!" There must be a way. For a minute I feel energized, like I have a purpose. Someone is searching for me, I want to participate. But then I sink. There are seven billion people on the planet. I'll never find him.

Wait. If we were together in a past life, according to Dr. Feinberg, and if we find each other over and over, we can't be too far from each other. Again I'm feeling energized. Doug looks over at me curiously as I keep vacillating from sitting up in excitement to slumping in depression.

"I'm working something out," I offer.

"I see," he adds, more out of politeness, I would guess.

"It's just . . ." I start. "Never mind." It's too hard to explain right now.

In my mind, I start to come up with a list on what my next step should be:
- Make a list of potential soul mates from people I've met
- Talk to a psychic, maybe they can see who it is
- ~~Take out an ad in the paper.~~ Nah, strike that. Too crazy. I can see it now. "Are you my soul mate? Call 555-5555."
- Go to a past life therapist and get clues to my past
- Ask Naomi for suggestions

I did take a couple of business cards from the festival. If I recall, there was one from a past life regressionist and another from a psychic. I have the urge to call one of them now, and pop up to leave.

"See you tomorrow, Doug," I announce.

"Looks like you made a decision."

"Sure did." And I'm off towards home.

An hour later, I'm still staring at the two cards. In my right hand is a business card from *Psychic Serena*. The card has a photo of a bleached-blond woman, smiling too big. The card has some Egyptian symbols and a decorated hand. It's kind of freaking me out. In my left hand is the other one. This card is a brown, non-descript card that simply displays a woman's name, *Barbara Johnson, C.Ht. Past Life Regression and Hypnosis*. It lists her office hours and on the back is a place to write in the appointment time. This one seems so . . . clinical. I'm torn. I would think a psychic could help point me in the right direction quicker. I can imagine her saying something like, "I see you walking into the restaurant on 4th and Main on Thursday. He'll be waiting for you, holding a bouquet of roses." Okay, maybe it wouldn't be that easy, but she might be able to tell me about the here and now, which is where I am, and not some dead past, where I'm not. The past life regressionist may help me find my soul mate too, but I wonder if it will feel like I'm under a microscope. I'm not sure I can even be hypnotized. I'm such a non-trusting, nervous, skeptical person anyway. Can I relax and trust someone enough to get in that vulnerable state?

I can't make a decision right now. I'm a bundle of nerves and indecision. A bike ride will help me clear my mind. I pack a snack bag with an apple and some almonds. Attaching my water bottle to Ms. Glimmer, we're ready to ride. Today, I'm off to explore Seal Beach. Wonder if I will actually see any seals? It's a nice ride, my legs are pumping and my heart rate elevated. Enjoyable exercise, who would have thought they could go together. For a moment my mind is off my soul mate, "Prince Charming" search. My breath, synchronizing with my legs pumping, becomes a rhythmic meditation for me. I wonder if moving while meditating is okay. I'm going to ask Doug sometime.

Seal Beach comes into view in no time. My mind was lost in the scenery; the time flew by. Seal Beach has been called "Mayberry by the Sea" and I can see why. Main Street is a cute, attractive drag of shops and restaurants. There are many Irish pubs on this strip. Is there a large Irish community living here? I lock my bike to a rack at the entrance of the long wooden pier, grab the backpack from the basket and cinch up the tie. Looks like a hobo sack, I think as I toss it over my shoulder.

The sound and unevenness of this worn and bumpy pier adds to its charm. To my left are preteens skim-boarding on the calm waters. To my right are the surfers. Since the beach is also surrounded by breakwater walls like my quiet stretch of Long Beach, it's a good area for novice surfers to work out the kinks in their styles. As I walk along I scan the waters, hoping to catch a glimpse of a seal. At the end of the pier is a 50s style diner and surrounding it on three sides are people fishing over the edge of the pier. The closer I get to the diner, the stronger the aroma of burgers cooking. I'm famished. Somehow the fruit and nuts I packed seem like a letdown after the smell of burgers and fries.

The diner is done up nicely with 50s memorabilia displayed throughout. A peppy girl in a candy-striped uniform and hair up in a high ponytail takes me to a booth overlooking the ocean. There is a real jukebox playing tunes of a bygone era. Not really my style, but fun for an afternoon. I order a peanut butter shake, a turkey burger, and fries. Well, at least the turkey burger was healthy, and I will burn off calories on the ride back, I rationalize.

After lunch, I'm stuffed and I leisurely walk back up the pier. On my right side I catch some movement in my peripheral vision. I strain to see in the dark waters. There it is again. It pops its head up and looks at me. A seal. I see one.

"A seal!" I call out. No one seems to care. Guess they see them all the time.

I unlock my bike and start the ride back home. In the shopping center off of Pacific Coast Highway, there is a sign for cat adoption. Hmmm. Maybe that's what I need—someone to give my love to, an animal that loves unconditionally. I don't need to search for a man. A cat would be perfect for me. On impulse I stop at the center to take a look.

There are so many to choose from. I'm considering an orange tabby and then I notice a black cat with the most penetrating yellow eyes. His eyes hypnotize me. When I think that he's the one, I spy another option. I can't decide. Then I see him. In the far corner is a white and tan cat. He has dark patches on his feet that look like socks and his tail, my gosh . . . that tail is the bushiest thing I've ever seen. It looks like a squirrel tail. I cautiously move toward him and he regally sits waiting for me. No fear, pure confidence. He lets me pick him up and then he does something that clinches it. He hugs me, both paws wrapped around my neck. He holds on and hugs me like we are meant to be together.

"I see you met our hugger," a woman volunteer tells me.

My new-found friend is not letting go. I guess it's a done deal.

"I'd like to adopt this one," I announce. "How late will you be here because I need to get my car to take him home."

"We'll be here 'til seven. I can hold him for you."

"Great."

The volunteer pries off my new pal and I take off as fast as I can. I'm eager to get my car so I can take my cat home. What should I call him? I consider names as I ride like the wind:

- Socks?
- Chico?
- Max?
- Bushy tailed?—Nope

When I first saw him he was sitting so regally, like a prince. And since I seem to be obsessed with finding my Prince Charming, maybe I should call him "Prince." Yes, I can see it now—crazy woman thinks cat is her soul mate. I do think "Prince" suits him, though. So, that's what it will be.

That evening, Prince is checking out his new home. I'm surprised at how well he seems to have adjusted to being here. Prince acts like he has been here all along and that we have always been together. Can we reincarnate into animals? I wonder.

"Are you my soul mate?" I ask him as he jumps on the kitchen counter and examines the broken tiles. Speaking of which, when is Jim planning on getting these fixed? I haven't heard from him in a while.

"No matter, I have a new love now, right Prince?"

After both of us are fed, I get situated on the couch with my laptop to work on some editing for the latest article. It's about incorporating exercise into your daily routine. I have my favorite writing spot now, sitting on the left side of the couch, propping my feet up on the coffee table and my tea cooling down on the end table. It's perfect. Prince is on the right side of the couch perched up on the arm rest. Without any reason that I can tell, he jumps down, walks under the coffee table and appears on my left side. He jumps up on the left arm rest then very slowly walks across my keyboard. Halfway across he pauses and stretches dramatically. He's trying to get my attention, the little brat. I can't help but laugh. Prince resumes his stroll across my computer and finally settles down on the right side of me, inches from where he started.

"What was with the circuitous route?" I ask him. He yawns as if I bore him. Cats.

Prince's eyes dilate suddenly. "What is it?" I ask. Someone knocks on the door. "Aw, so you're like my watch dog, er cat? Huh? Heard them coming before they knock, eh? You're useful already."

I head to the door. "Who is it?"

"Just Valerie."

"Come in," I tell her as I open the door. "Meet my roommate, Prince."

"Oh. He's gorgeous. Prince, huh? Figures, since ya been looking for your Prince Charming, right? Well honey, who ain't?" Valerie makes herself comfortable on the couch as Prince makes a bed on her lap.

"Can I get you something? Wine, tea?"

"Nah, needed a break from my four walls. Closing in on me you know."

"Sure. I understand." I sit down next to her and straighten the mess of scribbled pages spread on the coffee table.

"So you working on a big article for some fancy mag?" She points at my papers.

"No, only a short article on fitness."

"You hope to be a famous author someday?"

"Oh, I don't know. Would be nice. It's really a far off dream. Remember when I told you I changed my name to Tess?"

"Yeah, sure do. How can I forget that day?"

"Actually, I wish you would. Anyway, when I was seventeen I changed my name to Tess Estrada. I thought it would look great as a by-line when I became a writer. At least that was my dream back then. Remember how I said I hate nick names? Well, Tess Estrada ended up being Tesstrada—all one word. I didn't think that one out very well."

"Ha! That's a riot," Valerie snorts.

"Yeah, funny now, but not so much then."

"So how did you meet your ex? Richard, right?"

"Good memory. I met Richard when I was in college. Notice I don't call him Rick or Richie like his family and friends do. Richard was taking courses in physical rehab. One day he was showing off in the school gym and dropped a weight on his foot and broke his toe. Instantly, I ran up to help. I felt this strong impulse to take care of him. We got married a year later. I became Tess Whitaker, a great name I thought."

"Yeah, pretty good name. Almost as good as Valerie Snyder."

"Yes. Almost as good as yours." We both laugh.

"And you have a kid, right? I never had any. Didn't want to mess up this bod." She pushes out her breasts to make her point.

"Yeah, I can see that. Anyway, I have one son, Wade. I chose a name that was one syllable on purpose—nickname issue. Richard and I started a gym that became quite successful. We had the suburban house, the middle class cars, good neighborhood and schools for Wade. Perfect, except it wasn't. And that is pretty much the whole story of how I got here."

"Hmm. Your story seemed more exciting when it was a mystery." She elbows me.

"You're a trip, Valerie."

"Oh, honey, you don't know the half of it. Well, I'm off. Need that beauty sleep."

At nine p.m. I'm winding down from the day and head to the bedroom. Prince has already assumed his spot smack in the middle of the bed. He is a royal alright . . . a royal pain, that is. I carefully try to find some room for me and take a deep breath to relax. My neck is cricked from writing, but that's one of the things that come with the writing package. If I plan to write a book someday, I better get used to having a sore neck. As I start drifting off to sleep the sounds I've become accustomed to lull me to sleep . . . yappy dog . . . fireworks . . . wind chimes.

"Come make love to me again," Kathleen begs him. Thomas leans in close. Kathleen throws back her head. Her breath is catching, her heart is racing. Thomas gently tugs on her earlobe with his teeth. She pulls his head to her bosom. "Oh," she sighs.

I wake with a start. What time is it? My bedside clock informs me it's 5:23 a.m. I've been having that dream again. It feels so real. My body was feeling what Kathleen was feeling. It was getting *hot* and then I had to wake up. Okay, that does it. I'm going to see that past life regressionist. Maybe she can shed some light on these dreams. They don't feel like normal imaginative dreams. They feel more like a memory—a real honest-to-God memory. Now, I have to wait until a decent time to call her office.

Chapter 15

"Well, I did it, Jared. I made an appointment for tomorrow at three p.m. I'm really going to see a past life therapist! Yeah, it's shocking to me, too. She actually seemed quite kind on the phone. I appreciated the way she withheld judgment when I briefly mentioned my strange dreams. I've gotta tell Naomi. She'll be excited, I know it."

Naomi works as a massage therapist so I never know if she is between clients. I'll send a text.

Made appt. with past life therapist

A few minutes later my phone chimes with a text. It's Naomi.

OMG, I'm so glad. U will love it. Let me know everything

OK, will do, I text back.

Right away, I get another text from her.

Btw, having few friends over for healing circle Thursday at 6 p.m. Come?

OK.

What the heck is a healing circle? Guess I'll find out Thursday.

The rest of the day passes leisurely; I spend some quiet time with Doug, take my bike ride—more for keeping my mind clear than for exercise—and then come home to spend time with Prince. Prince acts like I'm annoying him when I try to pet him, but as soon as I get distracted by reading or putting away the dishes he's all over me.

"You play all the games people play when they are dating," I tell him. Once again he acts disinterested. I'm bored so I start cleaning out my backpack. Out dumps some old gum, coins, receipts from the various restaurants and coffeehouses I've visited recently, and a few business cards. I pile up the business cards:

- *Inkblaster's Tattoo* parlor—good memories, I'll keep that
- *Long Beach Cat Adoption Center*—I'll keep that one too
- *Psychic Serena*—just in case
- *Belmont Bikes*—former home of Ms. Glimmer
- *Sandy Beach Kayak Rental?*—I don't remember picking that one up

I turn over the card and spot Jesse's name and number. Oh, I completely forgot. He's going to think I'm a total flake. It's only coffee. Surely, I can spare some time to go out for coffee with a hunky, muscle-bound lifeguard, right? I pick up the phone to call him before I forget again.

"Jesse? This is Tess."

"Hi." I can hear the hesitation in his voice. Probably thinks I blew him off.

"I was wondering if you still wanted to grab a coffee?"

"Yeah, sounds great. You free Wednesday afternoon?"

"Um, I think so. Do you want to meet at *Skye Coffee* at four?" I suggest.

"Sure. See you there."

And as simple as that, I have a date. My first date since . . . well . . . since Richard and I dated a million years ago. It's just coffee. I can do this. Great, now I have another thing to be stressed out about:

- Past life therapy session—Tuesday
- Coffee with Jesse—Wednesday
- Healing Circle with Naomi—Thursday
- Life, in general—Arrgh!

Tuesday morning greets me much as any other day except I'm too uptight to enjoy my time on the balcony or at the beach. I'm uneasy and restless as I force myself to stick to my routine. Meditation is getting easier. Doug has been teaching me to sit and not have an agenda. I find my mind will jump around from one topic to another for a while but then finally start to settle down. It's not like I've found any deep secret about the universe or that I'm at peace like Doug, but I definitely have made progress since my first days of struggle. Today, however, I feel like I'm back at square one. My leg is jittery and my thoughts are what Doug calls "monkey mind." When he first told me that, I cracked up. I could see, in my mind's eye, a million monkeys jumping all over the place causing total destruction and chaos.

Doug notices my nervousness and reassuringly places his hand on my knee to stop its bouncing. It's comforting. Instantly, I have this calm wash over me just like before when he made me talk about Jared. It's as if his hands are infused with some kind of anti-anxiety medication. *Xanax hands.* They should bottle that. Wow, that's amazing. I feel a hundred times better. After a few moments, he removes his hand and resumes his controlled posture. The feeling of calm persists in me and I can settle into my meditation. I'm appreciative of this odd friendship or relationship we have. I actually don't know what to call it. It's never been defined. It simply exists. This is something new for me.

I leave the beach to go home. I want to get ready for the appointment. Since I hate being late, I end up being extra early for most things. Today will be no exception.

"What do you wear to a past life session, Jared? Period clothes?"

I chuckle to myself as the image of time travel pops into my mind. I really have no idea what to expect from today. Looking over my partially unpacked wardrobe, I choose loose fitting jeans and a fitted cotton t-shirt in a soft green. I don't want my clothes to bind if I'm trying to relax. Slipping on flip-flops and grabbing a water bottle, I head to my car.

Since I'm so early, taking the scenic route down Pacific Coast Highway sounds like the best idea. Jumping on a freeway in bumper to bumper traffic is not conducive to relaxation. I roll down the windows to feel the fresh air. With the ocean to my right, I drive towards Newport Beach where Barbara Johnson's office is located. When I stop at the red light at Seapoint Street in Huntington Beach, I notice I'm on the top of a little hill and have a superb view of the water. This is the first stoplight I don't mind waiting for. All of a sudden, I spot movement in the ocean.

"Dolphins! I can see dolphins swimming from here!"

I'm overjoyed and, of course, there is no one to tell except Jared, but he never answers back. *Honk.* I look in my rearview mirror. The light turned green and I was still admiring the view. Guess the driver behind me is not as delighted.

"Sorry," I mutter to the air.

It's tricky and confusing in Newport Beach. The town has tiny, curving streets that somehow dump me back where I was a few moments ago. I feel like I'm going round and round. After three wrong turns, I finally find the office. It's off of a main street in a location that appears to have residential homes and businesses. In fact, Barbara Johnson's office looks like it may have been a home at one time. She's on the second floor, per the directory. I climb the carpeted stairway. The railing is too beautiful for an office. It is made from a rich wood with delicately carved decorations.

Barbara's office is at the end of the hall. As I enter, some little bells, attached to the top of the door, tinkle. There is a small, pleasant waiting room where her professional certificates are displayed on the walls. The room is furnished in maroons and greens, tastefully done. Off the waiting room is another door. It's closed. I'm not sure if I should knock or wait. Not wanting to be rude, I decide to sit and wait for a few minutes.

Good time to practice my meditation, I decide. I follow my breath as a focus. After five or six breaths, a woman in what looks to be her mid-sixties comes out from behind the closed door. She is smartly dressed, in tan slacks and a burnt orange blouse. The necklace she is wearing is an interesting silver pendant. It looks like a complicated swirl, maybe a Celtic knot?

"Tess?" she asks and reaches out her hand for me to shake it.

"Yes."

"I'm Barbara. Why don't you come in and have a seat," she invites.

I follow her into the office. It's warm and comfortable. It makes me feel like I'm in someone's home, not in any way clinical. There is a large bay window with a window seat covered in patterned cushions. The walls are decorated with framed mosaic art of birds and plants that looks to be handcrafted. I want to go around and examine each piece more closely but know that I'm here for another purpose. Barbara notices my interest in the art and elaborates.

"I picked those up at a local art fair. I fell in love with them right away. In fact, I have three more of them in my home." She laughs. Her laughter is pleasing to the ear. In fact, so is her voice.

Against the walls are antique book shelves filled with books. There is a large throw rug over worn hardwood floors and two chairs. One is more of an arm chair. The other, which I presume is for me, is a plush reclining chair with a blue and yellow throw lying across it.

"Have a seat." She motions me to the reclining chair. I pick up the blanket and look for a place to put it. It's warm in here; I don't think I need a blanket now.

"Just hold on to that. You may want it when you're under hypnosis. People tend to get cool when in a trance. There is also a comfort to having a blanket, I've found," Barbara explains.

"Okay," I answer as I settle into the chair.

"Do you have any questions before I explain the process?"

"I don't really know what to ask right now."

"Fine, if something comes up, let me know. I understand from your phone call that you have been having dreams for a while now. And you're curious as to whether they could be past life connected. Correct?"

"Uh huh."

"Since this is your first time being hypnotized, I'm going to clear up some misconceptions many have. I'm a board certified hypnotherapist and have been in practice for over twenty years. I use hypnosis with my clients for various issues: weight loss, pain control, past life regression. No one has ever been 'stuck' in a past life. If something is unpleasant, either open your eyes or view the scene as if you are watching a movie. All hypnosis is self-hypnosis. I can't make you do anything you don't want to do. I know you've seen the stage hypnotists having the volunteer perform all kinds of outrageous acts. They volunteer because they like the attention. They're enjoying themselves, but they wouldn't do any act that they didn't want to do. Any questions so far?"

"Not yet, except I worry that I can't be hypnotized. Relaxing has never been my strong point."

"Well, we will take it slow. All you need to do is follow my voice. Just go for the experience. You can judge and analyze later. Okay, so how this works is, if you are willing, I'm going to play some soft music in the background and I'm merely going to act as your guide. You're always in control."

"Okay."

"Good, now, if you choose to, close your eyes, and with each breath you take you will find yourself more and more relaxed. That's right." Barbara begins guiding me into hypnosis. Her voice is soothing and I feel comfortable closing my eyes. I take the blanket and cover myself up with it. She's right; I do feel more secure with the throw covering me.

She continues by talking me through the relaxation process.

". . . and your neck and shoulders completely relax . . . many hold a lot of tension in this area . . . it feels so good to relax. You are feeling deeply peaceful and relaxed . . ."

I am indeed feeling relaxed, drifting, and calm. This is easier than I thought it would be. Barbara coaches me to relax all my muscles, and as she is talking I feel as if the tension in each part of my body melts away. After she completes the inventory on all my muscles, she guides me down an imaginary stairway.

"I would like you to visualize or imagine that you are at the top of a beautiful stairway. In a moment you will begin to walk down the stairs. With each step down you will go deeper and deeper into hypnosis, and at the bottom of the stairs you will be in a very deep state of peace and relaxation. Stepping down . . . down . . . deeper and deeper . . . down . . . down. At the bottom of your staircase you find yourself in a beautiful garden full of manicured trees and bushes, flowers of all colors, and a comfortable bench for you to rest your body. As your body rests in this peaceful garden your mind is free to travel. You notice that at the far end of the garden there is a bridge. On the other side of this bridge is another lifetime, a previous lifetime that you can visit. Do you want to visit a lifetime before this one? Lift your finger if you would like to go on."

I lift my right index finger slightly, not wanting to arouse from my sleepy state.

Barbara continues, "Good. In a moment you are going to begin crossing over the bridge. There is a fog obscuring your vision, but as you cross the fog will clear. Starting over the bridge . . . halfway there

". . . the fog is clearing. Be there. As you emerge from the fog you find you are in a lifetime before this one. It's the lifetime that is meant for you to see at this point in your life. Take a moment and look around. Are you inside or outside? You can talk and still remain in a deep state of hypnosis."

"Um . . . inside. It's dim. I'm in clothing that feels restrictive," I mumble.

"Can you look down and see what you're wearing?"

"I am wearing a long skirt. It trails along the floor . . . I have a blouse with a high-boned collar. Oh, it's my corset that is so restrictive." The images are coming so fast. It's startling and for a moment I want to analyze the experience, then I remember Barbara's words and take another deep breath to be in the moment.

I continue, "My hair is blond. It's long and wavy. I'm wearing it swept up and tied in a knot. I feel beautiful. There is someone singing."

"Kathleen, you look lovely tonight," Thomas whispers in my ear, causing me to blush. He pulls me close. My breath catches.

"Thomas, manners please, my parents are in the next room," I scold.

"We'll be as quiet as mice." He leans in and tries to kiss my cheek. I pull back and laugh.

"Oh Thomas, you are trouble." We dance in my parent's parlor. My Thomas looks dapper in his dark colored sack coat with a matching waistcoat and trousers. Thomas takes off his bowler hat and tosses it on the table. He sings close to my ear. "You are not singing the proper words," I tell him.

Again I'm startled, how did I even know what a sack coat was? I'm using words I never said as Tess.

"That's right, continue. You are doing fine. Take an easy breath and continue when you are ready," Barbara encourages me.

"Oh, I'm so much in love. How did so much good fortune come to me? I am the luckiest woman in the world."

"Can you get an idea of a date?"

"Yes, it's 1900. We are in New York. Thomas has asked for my hand in marriage. My parents are, of course, thrilled. I mean, why wouldn't they be? He is handsome. I know we will have handsome children. He has a good job, a policeman. Thomas looks so dashing in his uniform.

He will take care of me. He told me we will always be together. I know that he speaks the truth. We are to live in this glorious city. Yes, I am so fortunate."

"Do you want to move forward to the next significant period in this lifetime?"

"Alright." I take a deep breath; the scene opens up before me. "We are planning our wedding. My parents are helping out and loving every minute. They love Thomas more and more each day. Thomas and my father get along splendidly. Some of my lady friends from our sewing group are helping me crochet doilies for our home. We usually sew blouses and skirts; this is a welcome change. It is a pleasure to drink tea, crochet, and laugh with these women. Margaret, however, is raising some eyebrows of late."

"Go on. Who is Margaret?"

"Margaret is one of the women in the sewing circle. She is causing a stir. She has been speaking about a group of women she meets with. They are having a séance. Margaret believes in Spiritualism. I come from a proper God-fearing upbringing and I find her talk scandalous."

"And her talk is concerning to you?"

"*Kathleen, you should join us. The ladies are meeting a week from next,*" *Margaret tells me.*

I put down the doily I am working on and look her straight in the eye. "Margaret, I ask you not to speak of such things in my home. This is the work of the devil." The other women stop what they are working on and stare at me.

"*It is not demonic, I assure you. We have been studying these arts and have found them illuminating. You have a gift, Kathleen.*"

"*Stop this nonsense this instant or I shall ask you to leave these premises.*"

"*If that is your wish. I hope you reconsider another time,*" *Margaret adds and continues crocheting. The other women quickly resume their work as I sip some tea to calm my nerves.*

"Well, I can see that upsets you. Why don't you visit a time when you and Thomas are enjoying each other's company? At the count of three you will be there: one, two, three."

I relax back into the dreamy world.

Thomas is sitting close to me on the settee. He caresses my arm ever so gently and looks into my eyes. I could gaze at his handsome face for eternity . . .

"Tess. It's time to temporarily leave this lifetime behind and return to the garden where your body has been resting and healing. Each time you do this you will go deeper and effortlessly into a deep state of hypnosis. As I count from one to five you will find yourself back in the present. Your mind will be clear, your body refreshed, feeling wonderful. And you will remember everything. One, two, feeling wonderful, three, halfway there, four and five, wide awake, refreshed, and renewed."

I open my eyes and stretch. I feel like I've had a good nap.

"Give yourself a minute. You may want to stand up and move around a little. You seemed like you wanted to stay in that moment. You were lying there humming and smiling for a long while. After some time I decided to bring you out of hypnosis. So, how do you feel?"

"I feel great. So that was me? I was Kathleen?"

"It would appear so."

"All those years having that same dream, and now to find out that I was remembering another time. I'm blown away. It was so strange to be in her . . . my . . . Kathleen's body. It was like I could feel all she felt and hear her thoughts and, at the same time, think my thoughts. That's the weirdest feeling. As she was thinking, I was also thinking 'I don't think and talk that way.' I don't know why I didn't want to move ahead in time. Guess I was so happy where I was. I want the kind of love she had. I think I've always wanted that."

"Well, it appears that he is your soul mate and we do reconnect over and over in many lifetimes with our soul mates."

"So he may be out there then?" I ask.

"It's possible. I've seen it happen time and time again with clients. Over the next few days and in your dreams more information may surface for you. Also you may start to have some doubts as to whether you imagined this all or if it's true. This is common. If you would like we can set up another appointment to revisit that life and see how Kathleen and Thomas' life turned out, or we can work on another issue."

"I definitely want to know more about Kathleen and Thomas. If he's out there, I need as much information as I can get. I would like to set up another appointment."

"Let's give you a few weeks to process and assimilate this new information. Many realizations may occur and time is your friend to integrate this. I have an opening three weeks from today."

"Okay, sounds good," I tell her as I enter the date into my phone.

I leave the office in a daze, not from being hypnotized, but from the actual experience. I could feel and see everything as if I was in the year 1900. It felt so real. History has never been my strong suit and I'm not really sure if what I remembered is true from a historical standpoint. I want to read up on that time period in America. If I can verify some details then I would be convinced that I didn't imagine the whole thing.

As I'm driving home I keep having the strange feeling that Kathleen is still residing in me. I can still feel her. Her emotions, her love for Thomas, her frailty, it's all rolling around in my heart and head. I'm still entrenched in my mind when I enter the apartment and am rudely snapped out by persistent, mournful meowing.

"Oh, Prince, hold on, I'll feed you." I guess he wants to remind me that he is my first priority. The remainder of the evening is spent journaling about the experience. I want to make sure I don't forget any of the small details—like the comb, the way my hair was worn, or the clothes Thomas wore. It feels like those images are so embedded in me now that I wouldn't forget, but I don't want to take the chance.

Sleep comes easily and, like any other night, the dream comes. Tonight, however, there are a few changes. Instead of me observing them dancing, I am the one dancing. I jerk awake. The smell of cigar smoke wafts through my room. Someone's hand presses on my low back. How can that be? I can feel Thomas' hands on me. Kathleen and I merge in my dream and it is startling, yet heavenly. I want to go back to sleep.

Chapter 16

My first goal, after my morning meditation with Doug, of course, is to head to *Pacific City Central Library*. I've got to find out some information about life in the 1900s. I really feel that I need to validate some of the things I saw, er, remember, during the past life experience. I make a list of things to look up. The first thing is the clothing. I remember distinctly what Kathleen was wearing, and Thomas, too.

There is a surge of energy through me, like I'm on a mission, of sorts. I bring my laptop to enter any information I find and head out. With a twinge of impatience I'm swerving in and out of traffic.

"Why are there so many cars out today?" I yell to the sky. "Go home!" Nope. Everyone is taking their sweet time. Don't they know I have to find out if Kathleen and Thomas were real? Doesn't anyone care? Arghh.

Eventually I make it in one piece to the library and make my way over to the computer to search out what I need. Hmmm. I'm actually not sure what to put in the search engine: 1900s, New York, women's fashion, popular songs? I really don't know. Deciding on "early 1900s" I get tons of hits for WWI. That comes later in time. Not much before that is listed and there's not much on women. Well this is a dud, a wasted trip. Wait, why didn't I look this up on my own laptop?

I make my way down the circular stairway to the café in the basement. Here there are plenty of tables near convenient outlets for students to work. My jacket on the chair announces that this table is claimed. Here I can enjoy a view overlooking the large fountain and beautiful tailored grounds of the park that the library borders. A latte and onion bagel, smothered with cream cheese, from the café to keep me fortified and my laptop set up, I'm all ready to get the facts.

Women's fashion, 1900s, America is the first entry I plug into Google. And lo and behold, I am rewarded with Wikipedia articles, images, and a college history paper. I glance at the images first and . . . oh, my! I freeze as I'm about to push more bagel into my mouth. My mouth is agape as I stare at the image of a woman that looks much like I recalled. Her hair is swept up to the side of her head. She is wearing a long skirt and white blouse with a high collar. That's what I remember! I'm not sure if I'm more freaked from this validation or relieved that I'm not crazy.

Well, it could be that I'd seen this in a book or movie at one point and it implanted somewhere in my brain, I rationalize. There are two sides of me that argue constantly: the logical, practical Tess and the more "feeling, intuitive" Tess. Usually, practical Tess wins out, but lately I've been giving some leeway to touchy-feely Tess. I skim over the Wikipedia articles and find that women did wear corsets like the one I was so uncomfortable in during the regression. Come to think of it, how odd that I could actually feel the sensation of the binding corset, the smokiness of the room which I could smell and breathe into my lungs, and the lovely touch of Thomas. I'm absolutely amazed by this. Naomi needs to hear this surreal tale. How would I even begin? Barbara is right. I do need time to integrate the experience.

Okay, back at it. Let's try *Men's fashion, 1900s*—hitting "Enter" yields less results. I guess women's fashion is more exciting. There's an article posted on clothing in America, 1900s. Opening this article I scan the page looking for information on what men wore during this time period and once again gasp. There it is in black and white: sack coat, trousers, and bowler hat. Everything I had recounted to Barbara is right in front of me on my trusty laptop. Take that, Practical Tess! Even my practical side can't argue with this. I know I never heard the words "sack coat" in this life. Of that I'm sure.

Now what? I would love to find the song that plays over and over in my head. Thomas has sung it to me/Kathleen many nights in my dreams. I hum it unconsciously when I'm cleaning house or biking, but he changed the words. I wouldn't know where to start. I can't merely enter "Kathleen's song" and find it. I can't enter the words he said. Oh, why couldn't he have sung the correct words so I would have a starting point? Since I'm here anyway and in research mode, I pull up the popular tunes from the early 1900s on YouTube. Putting in my ear buds so I can listen without disturbing the students studying frantically for some final, no doubt, I start listening to one tune after another.

A deep breath, eyes closed, I attempt to put myself back in that dancing scene. I hit play on the first tune:
- Turkey in the Straw—nope
- The Laughing Song—not this one either
- Maple Leaf Rag—seems like Ragtime was popular then, still no

This is frustrating. Song after song, they all seem to roll together where I can't distinguish any tune and, to top it off, I can't seem to remember the tune that I thought was so embedded in my noggin. I'm just tired. Maybe I should get away from it for a while and then try again. Stretching out my back and rubbing my eyes, I glance at my watch. Three-thirty seven p.m. Oh shit! I'm supposed to meet Jesse at four for coffee. I'm going to be late. I hate that. He's going to think I'm such a flake. What am I going to say, "Sorry Jesse, but I had to find out if I really lived in the year 1900." No, that'll never fly. I pack my stuff up so quickly, just putting my computer in sleep mode and throwing out my cold latte. How many hours have I been camped out at this table? I'm insane.

I drive as fast as possible in speed-demon mode without killing anyone and arrive at *Skye Coffee* at four-twelve p.m. Not too bad, if I do say so myself. I don't even know why I'm meeting him. Today I'm not in the mood to chit-chat with anyone. My mind is back in another time and place and it is content there. Funny, but I think I'm wasting my time. Jesse's time, too, I guess. It's just that I feel that only Thomas will do for me. I can't settle for anything less. I want to stay focused on my search for Thomas. Jesse is just an obstacle in my path. That's horrible to say, but it's the way I feel. Yet, here I am. Taking a peek in the vanity mirror in my car, I pick out the bagel's poppy seeds from my teeth and apply some lip gloss. I undo my ponytail and let my hair spill around my shoulders. Okay, now I'm passable for a casual coffee date.

"It's show time," I announce to my mirror as I apply my best "greeting people" smile.

Jesse is dressed in jeans and a surfing t-shirt from the *U.S. Open of Surfing*, a couple of years ago. It's a popular annual event held in Huntington Beach. What else would I expect a Southern California lifeguard/surfer to wear? At least I don't feel so bad about my dress-down attire now.

"Hi." I give a small wave.

"Hey. What do you want to drink?" Jesse asks as he walks to the counter.

"Umm. An iced coffee sounds good. Thanks. I'll find us a table."

I sit uncomfortably waiting at the window table for Jesse to return with our drinks. This is only coffee, I tell myself, nothing more. You can do this. Life with Richard may have been boring at times, but at least there was no stress of trying to come up with conversation or trying to look cute. We were two people living in the same house doing our things, predictable but safe. Now, this . . .

"Here you go." Jesse interrupts my thoughts as he hands me my large iced coffee.

"Thanks. So, Jesse, tell me about you." It's a little trick I learned long ago when I didn't want to focus on me. People are really only interested in themselves so they never mind when you encourage them to tell their story. It's been my diversion technique for many years. Doug, however, is the only one who does not fall for it. What is it about him? Jesse has already launched into his tale and I, of course, have spaced out. Typical.

". . . and the waves were epic. I was on dawn patrol . . . Tess? Were you listening?"

"Oh, yes, of course. You were on patrol . . . go on," I fumble again. I'm really going to have to start paying attention to people.

"Yes, dawn patrol. That means going surfing really early in the morning. I surf before my lifeguard duties. Surfing is my life. You?"

Dawn patrol? Who knew? "No, never surfed in my life. Raised in the valley and didn't go to the beach much."

"Okay. That's cool. What about music? Do you like AFI? Danzig?"

"Um, never heard of those, sorry." I feel bad. Jesse is really trying to find some common ground, but what could we have in common. He looks to be ten years younger than I, hobbies and likes appear to differ. What now?

Jesse tries again, "What about movies? You like horror, sci-fi? Did you see the last Spiderman movie?"

I almost feel bad for him, trying so hard. It feels like I'm having a conversation with my fifteen-year-old son.

"Sorry again, Jesse. I'm more of a romantic comedy type of girl. You know, the chick flicks."

Jesse, it appears, is out of questions and sits silently poking his straw into his frozen berry drink. After a few moments of uncomfortable silence, I decide to save Jesse from this disastrous date. I let him off the hook.

"Jesse, you seem like a nice guy. You're cute and gifted, but truthfully I'm too screwed up right now to waste your time. I'm going through a divorce and I'm really not all-together. I really appreciate the kindness that you have shown me. I hope that we can continue this friendship though."

"I understand. You do seem a little spaced out. I knew something was going on with you after your freak-out on the sand that day, all yelling and screaming."

"You mean the day you were chatting up the cute blond?"

"Oh, yeah, she's an old friend."

"Oh okay. Sorry, that came off wrong. Well anyway, it's his fault for pissing me off." I try to downplay it.

"Who was pissing you off? Your ex?"

"No. Doug."

"Who?"

"Oh never mind. It's water under the bridge anyway."

"Well, if you change your mind—that is, after you get it together, we can try this again."

"Yeah, sure will. Thank you." I get up to take my leave.

"See you at the beach."

Back in the car, I let out a big sigh of relief. Really, Tess, what were you thinking? You might as well date Wade's buddies. Yikes!

"Next time, I'll use some common sense. Sometimes I wonder if I lost all my senses when I moved to Belmont Shore, Jared. First, letting Naomi talk me into attending that festival, then following the vision that led to the lecture on soul mates and, last but not least, having a past life regression session. I have officially flipped out. I need to get a reality check. Oh, wait, didn't I agree to go to Naomi's healing circle tomorrow? Will this insanity ever end?"

Chapter 17

Thursday arrives and I'm still crazy as ever. I had my same dream and, once again, my mind is consumed with what I discovered by scouring the internet. Last night I convinced myself to stop this nonsense and start focusing on the real world, but when I tried to come up with something to focus on, I drew a blank. Here I am, thirty-eight years old with no husband, a son who avoids me, and no job—focusing on all that is depressing. Better to live in denial and think about life in another time, right? Someday the money I'm living off from selling my half of the business is going to run out. I'm going to need a job besides the occasional article assignment . . . eventually. What kind of job eludes me, I could go back to personal training, ugh. Or maybe I could work in rehabilitation in a hospital setting? Nah, I can't see myself there either. It's hopeless.

Avoidance seems to be my major coping mechanism. Run away and pretend it doesn't exist, that's my motto. When Jared died, I changed my name and personality. It was easier than facing Jasmine's life. And now with Richard and Wade, I'm still running. My habit of avoiding phone calls and letting mail pile up makes it easy to escape to the beach and bike riding—and now escaping to the idealistic dream life of Kathleen and Thomas. It seems to me they had the perfect life. They found true love. Why can't I have that? Don't I deserve it too? Or maybe I'm being punished for skipping out on Richard and Wade? Don't get down on yourself again like when you were stuck on the curb for God- knows how long.

That's it, I'm going to call Richard and see if he's getting on okay. It's time to stop avoiding him altogether. I mean, how bad can it be? He's not contesting the divorce. The paperwork has been filed and we're waiting for the time period to be up. I understand the business is thriving and

Wade has been doing well in school. See, so much better without me to hold them down. Well, here goes.

"Hello?" Richard answers.

"Hi, it's me. Just checking in. How's it going?"

"As well as to be expected, I guess. Except that I don't have a wife anymore and Wade pretty much doesn't have a mother. You?"

"Richard, I don't want to fight. We both agreed this was for the best."

"No, I never agreed. You were all too eager to get away from here."

"We talked about this, Richard. We both weren't happy. It wasn't fair to both of us."

"And what about Wade? Was he figured into the equation?"

"Of course. You know I would love to have him visit here, but we have to wait until he is ready. Does he want to talk to me?"

"No, he says he wants nothing to do with you and I don't blame him."

"Richard, I'm sorry . . ." I trail off, and then tear off some toilet paper to wipe my tears and blow my nose.

"Yeah, well. We're fine. Look, I gotta go. Got a business to run and a son to look after."

"Okay. Talk to you later. Tell Wade, I love him."

"Sure thing."

I plop myself on the toilet seat with my head in my hands. Seems avoiding it all was a less painful option. I feel like crap. At least I'm not on the curb. Nope, now I'm on a toilet where no one can see me fall apart. Yeah, much better. Progress. It's late morning now, but maybe I can make it to the beach before Doug takes off. A Doug fix, that will surely help sort me out. Up you go.

I splash some cold water on my face and jet out the door and down the steps. I'm almost running to the beach now, as if somehow seeing Doug will put it all in perspective. He has been my rock, the person who grounds me. I feel like if I don't see him I'll go crazy. He has to be there. He has to be there. I'm chanting to myself as I run breathlessly to our spot. I'm running full speed now and get to our area of the beach. *Not here.*

I'm too late. He'll be here tomorrow, I'm sure, like he is most mornings, but I needed him today. I'm angry, hurt, guilt-ridden, a mess. My body collapses in his spot. I cry and wipe my nose on the back of my sleeve. My breath is ragged from the sobbing. No wonder I avoid confrontation. Look at the alternative. Richard is obviously hurting. Taking it out on me with his sarcasm doesn't help the situation. It only makes me want to back away further. Can't he see that?

I sit here for a long while breathing, watching the water, and imagining that Doug's calming presence is sitting next to me. I think it's working because I do feel calmer. Actually, I realize I feel pretty good. I called Richard! I'm a brave woman. It's okay if he's hurting. He will heal with time, as I am. Huh, I can do this. I calmed myself down and came to some good insights all by myself. I did it without Doug. Yippee.

I spend the rest of the day at home, listening to more 1900s tunes. Still, I can't place Thomas' tune, but I'm enjoying being immersed in that time period, escaping this year for a while. Hey, I deserve it after what I went through this morning. Prince seems to enjoy the old tunes too. He curls up next to me napping the afternoon away. How come cats always look so comfortable in their skin? I wish I could be that way, to be at home in myself. At five p.m. I stop my nostalgic trip to get ready to head to Naomi's place.

Naomi lives in Torrance so it's not that long of a drive to get to her place, although the 405 Freeway is never predictable and bottles up quickly. With me living in Belmont Shore now I'm actually closer to Naomi than when I lived in the Valley, another positive point of moving. Her apartment is typical for this area, nothing spectacular. The grounds are manicured and there are a couple of fountains, one at the entrance to the gated complex and one in the center court area where the pool and gym are located. The interiors, however, of the apartments are the same seen everywhere. Seen one, seen them all. However, Naomi, with her flair for color and pizazz, has her apartment fixed up in "Naomi Style." Once you step through the doors, it feels like you have been transported to a foreign land, like Nepal or India: exotic, colorful, and wildly alluring.

Tonight is no different. I arrive at six-twenty p.m., not my fault, it was that damn traffic, but Naomi is not upset. She seems genuinely delighted to see me, maybe because she feels free to share a part of her that I haven't been receptive to, until lately. Naomi is wearing the most vibrant peacock blue jumpsuit. I feel sheepish because, like always, I'm wearing, you got it, khaki pants and a tank top. It has become my uniform. Naomi is all about color and me, not so much. Hey, I made a stab at it with my Tibetan prayer flags, right?

"You're here! So good to see you, sweetie." Naomi hugs me and plants a kiss on my cheek.

"You too." The sights and smells of her apartment bombard my senses:

- Incense
- Strange, spacey music
- Colors galore
- Four women, whom I've never met, all vibrantly dressed

I feel like the grey crayon in a box of Crayolas. It's obvious I don't belong here and from the look on the women's faces, I bet they're thinking the same. I desperately scan the kitchen for some wine to take the edge off.

Naomi grabs my arm and introduces me to the group. "Everyone, this is my dearest friend, Tess."

"Hi," I say.

Naomi continues, "Tess, this is Lillian. Lillian is a talented Reiki practitioner . . ."

I shake Lillian's hand. Her hands are soft but strong, her smile warm. Naomi continues around the room.

". . . and this is Sandy. Sandy is a psychic . . ."

Sandy takes my hand in both of hers and looks deep into my eyes. Her gaze is unnerving, penetrating. Even with clothes on, I feel exposed and vulnerable. Instinctively, I drop my head, allowing my hair to fall in front of my eyes and break the connection. I pull my hand away. It tingles from Sandy's touch.

". . . and Monique is a massage therapist like me, but also works with Tarot . . ."

I nod my head at Monique as the coffee table is between us. I'm still a little freaked out by Sandy's stare.

"Lastly, we have Bobbi. Bobbi has been practicing Wicca for over twenty years and loves to do crystal healings."

"Oh, okay, crystal . . . nice to meet you all," I mumble. This is all too weird for me, yet here I am.

"So what is it that you do, Tess?" Bobbi asks.

"Oh, no, not Tess," Naomi giggles. "She's just here to observe. She's only recently been introduced to this world," Naomi explains to the group.

"Right," I agree.

"No, I sense there's more to you, Tess. You have power. You've been denying it for many years," Sandy chimes in.

Okay, that does it. Where is that damn wine? I head right to the kitchen, grab a glass and fill it to the brim with cool zinfandel. Naomi, sensing my discomfort, follows me.

"Hey, you okay?"

"Yeah. I mean no. Oh, I don't know."

"It's okay. Let me explain to you what a healing circle is about. Then if you're still uneasy, you can go home and no one will think you're weird or anything. No worries."

"Okay, thanks." I take a swig of the wine.

"Good. So this is what we do. If one of us has a personal issue and wants help for it, they will sit in the middle and the rest of us will sit around her. She can tell us her problem or think about it. We then will do what we feel is the best way to heal her. Usually that can be praying, wishing her good thoughts, using our hands to send energy, or using a crystal to send healing. That's all. Nothing weird. No voodoo dolls or sacrifices. See, nothing to worry about. We eat, drink wine, talk, and laugh. It's a good group. I think you'll like it here."

"Yeah, but."

"I know Sandy gave you the willies. She can be pretty intense, but Sandy's a great psychic. She's a little vocal about what she sees. You may want to talk to her, maybe she can help give you some clarity."

"Uh."

"Only when you feel comfortable," she inserts. "Come sit and eat. You need some food with that wine."

"Thank you, Naomi. You're a good friend, even if you get me involved in these crazy gatherings."

I relax a little and fix myself a plate of tabouleh, hummus, stuffed grape leaves, and pita bread. Finding a comfortable spot to sit on the overstuffed couch, I dig into the food. With the wine and the New Age music playing in the background, I feel myself start to unwind a bit. The conversation and wine are flowing and I'm content listening to the others discussing their passion.

"I did a healing on a man the other day," Lillian shares. "It was amazing. He was so uptight and distrusting, so I approached him carefully and told him I wouldn't touch him. I held my hands about two inches from his body and imagined him encased in healing white light. I sent love and healing to him and all of a sudden he started crying. He said that he could feel the love and warmth spread through his body. He told me that he had horrible, crippling pain in his back for many years, but when I sent healing into him, the pain melted away. Afterwards he stood straight and gave me the most heartwarming smile. That made my day."

Wow. Pretty amazing is right, I'm thinking. And she said she never even touched him. Is that possible? The stories went on and on, each one a variation of the same theme, someone desperate for help and these women able to provide it. Is it the desire for help that makes people susceptible to the help these women say they give? Is it a placebo? I don't want to offend anyone so I stay quiet. Bobbi recalls a tale of a client with Rheumatoid Arthritis.

"When Amber came to see me she couldn't straighten her right arm. The arthritis in her elbow was fierce. I had her lie down on my crystal bed. My massage table is set up with hundreds of crystals and healing stones underneath. Amber set her intention to heal and the gemstones did the rest. I invoked the archangels and deities and used my wand to clear any blocks in her energy bodies. After the session Amber moved her arm with ease and was completely pain-free. Still, even months later, she tells me her elbow is completely healed."

I'm blown away by their reports and a little skeptical. I mean, it really sounds too good to be true. It would be great if it was that easy, and if these women do have these powers. But, come on.

After we finish our plates, Naomi announces that it's time to begin the healing circle. Monique asks to be healed and sits in the chair in the center of our circle. Bobbi leads the ceremony. She stands facing north, and lifts her right hand in the air and points her left to the ground. Then she turns to face east.

"She's invoking the four directions, to make a sacred circle," Naomi whispers to me. I nod my head. Bobbi starts her prayer.

"Oh, Power of the East, Element of Air, new beginnings, I invoke thee. Come protect our circle." Bobbi turns to the south and continues. "Power of the South, Element of Fire, cleansing and purging, I invoke thee. Come protect our circle." She turns to face west. "Power of the West, Element of Water, soothing, restoring, and washing of our ills, I invoke thee. Come protect our circle." Finally facing to the north, she continues, "Power of the North, Element of Earth, grounding Mother, I invoke thee. Come protect our circle. As above, so below. Our circle is unbroken and sacred. So mote it be."

"So mote it be," the group chimes in.

Bobbi continues, "Monique, you've asked to be healed tonight. If you wish, you can share what area you are having issues with or you can think of it and set your intention silently."

"I'm not sure Gary and I are going to make it. Our marriage is falling apart. I think he is cheating on me. There have been many signs over the last year." Monique is tearing up and I feel myself getting emotional for her sake.

"Everyone please set your intention on what is the greatest good for all parties. Healing and love to Monique and Gary—that they find love, peace, and happiness whether together or apart. Monique, please send love and healing to Gary, too. For the next five minutes let's set our intention on the healing of Monique and Gary."

Bobbi starts waving a crystal wand over Monique in counter-clockwise circles. Lillian starts chanting "Om Mani Padme Hum" over and over. It sticks in my head, *Oooommmannii . . . paadmeeeehummmm . . .* The repetitiveness and simplicity of this phrase is soothing. Next thing I know, the words flow from me effortlessly. Naomi is holding her hands out towards Monique as if she is sending energy to her. Sandy is doing the same. Monique has her eyes closed and looks peaceful.

I'm not sure what to do. To me everyone has a part to play. I don't know what my part is. I stick with the chanting. Om Mani Padme Hum, Om Mani Padme Hum. Words blurring together, becoming a seamless blend of sounds. Sounds that vibrate off my lips and reverberate in my chest, dropping down to my sacrum and moving up my spine. The sound pulse finds its way back up to a spot between my eyebrows and dissipates to where, I'm not sure. My body ripples with each syllable.

Finally, I close my eyes to pay attention to the chant and sensations that arise from it. Then, I notice it. Subtle at first, but it starts to grow. There is a palpable energy here. I can see it in my mind's eye, an energy not only originating from the chanting. It's red in the center with a white glow encasing Monique. It pulsates and undulates. There is energy streaming from Naomi's fingers straight into Monique. It's coming out in reds and yellows, so beautiful. Keeping my eyes closed I scan the room. I can see energy coming from Sandy too. Hers is yellow and a warm, glowing orange.

Something inside pushes me to give it a shot. Not knowing the proper procedure I try imagining healing energy going from me to Monique. *What color would healing be?* I wonder. *Green* pops into my head. As fast as I think it, I feel a ball of energy pooling in my solar plexus. As it grows with each outbreath of Om, it transmits through my body.

Green bands of energy shoot down my arms, through my hands and out my fingers. It streams effortlessly in the air and into Monique. A swirl of all of our combined colors of energy surround Monique's frame. Monique and I gasp simultaneously. Did I do something wrong?

I open my eyes, halting the energy flow. I wonder if I messed up their circle or maybe used a wrong color. As I look around, the group is staring at me, smiling wide. Whew.

"That was powerful!" Monique announces.

Naomi is beaming like I'm her little pet project. "See, I told you she would fit in nicely here."

"Well done, Tess. With some training you could really hone those natural abilities," Bobbi tells me. I'm feeling a little embarrassed with all the attention. Yet, it's nice to be appreciated for something. Even if it's woo-woo stuff.

Bobbi then closes the sacred circle by thanking the four directions. This time though she does the circle backward or counter-clockwise.

"So mote it be," she states at last to the group and we all repeat, "So mote it be."

Afterwards, we all spend time laughing, talking, and drinking more wine. It's weird, but in a good way. I'm not freaking out as I would've in the past. In fact, it felt quite natural. When I was sending energy, I didn't have to do any special ritual. I simply thought about sending and it occurred. Is it my intention that really is the true power here? Wade would have loved this. He has always been into anything supernatural or outside of convention. He loved to expound on his ideas of time travel, witches, and vampires. He once told me there were real vampires today, but they sucked off of people's energy, not their blood. I can believe that; just a few minutes with my mother and I'm completely drained. A smile comes to my lips. Wade would have thought that was funny, too. I'll send him another text. Not that he will reply but, you know, I keep trying. At least he knows I haven't forgotten about him.

Wade, you'll never believe, your mom just sent energy to heal someone. You would've loved this. They did some kind of magic circle. Love you, mom.

The night appears to be winding down and Bobbi gathers up her gear. I get up to help Naomi clean up the kitchen. It's been a good evening after all. Bobbi and Monique head out together after thanking Naomi for her hospitality. Monique gives me a tight squeeze.

"Thank you so much for your wonderful healing," she whispers in my ear. I'm touched and kiss her lightly on her cheek. Lillian leaves next, giving Naomi and me a quick hug. I notice that Sandy is hanging back, as if she is waiting for the others to leave. Does she want to talk to me privately? I feel a tad uneasy, but Naomi, sensing my tension, gives my hand a little squeeze. Personally, I'm also waiting for everyone to leave so I can share my past life experience with Naomi, alone.

Sandy looks like she made up her mind and with confidence walks up to me, looks me straight in the eye, and takes my hands in hers. Naomi and I freeze all conversation and wait expectantly for Sandy to speak.

"Tess, I hesitated sharing with you, so I went inside and asked Spirit. I've been informed that I should share with you some information. I see things . . . I see that you had a sibling pass and still grieve. Know that he is happy and at peace . . ."

I yank my hands away in shock. The tears start to flow immediately. I dab my eyes with a napkin. How did she know? Did Naomi tell her about Jared?

On cue, Sandy answers my unspoken question, "I didn't know about your brother until Spirit showed me." I glance at Naomi, who is nodding in agreement.

"Go on," I tell Sandy. Once again she gently takes my hands.

"You have gifts, but you've chosen to ignore them. You felt that they were a hindrance in your life. It's time to embrace your gifts, Tess. This is part of the reason you're here." She pauses as if she is listening to some voice only she can hear. I wait patiently, because so far she has been spot on.

"One last thing, I see the letter J."

"You mean my brother?"

"No. The one you are searching for, the one from your dreams."

I'm bowled over, mouth agape, and speechless! I can't even muster up a "thank you" or "good bye." In fact, I've got to sit down . . . now! And so, I do, right on the floor of the kitchen. Thank goodness for the lovely cabinets to rest up against. Naomi takes over the pleasantries and sees Sandy out, thanking her profusely.

"I'm sorry. I didn't mean to shake her up," Sandy apologizes.

"No, no, don't worry. Tess has been going through a rough patch. What you said, I feel, will be very healing for her. Thank you so much."

After Sandy leaves, I stand up carefully and splash some water on my face from the kitchen sink. How could she have known about my dreams and my longing for the elusive Thomas, or as she called him, J?

"Sit down on the couch," Naomi orders and grabs my arm to help me to the living room. Her touch is reassuring and I allow her to guide me to a comfortable spot.

Naomi fixes us some tea and brings over a plate of baklava to nibble on. With one of the napkins from the table I dry the remnants of water off my face. Strands of wet hair leave splotches on my shirt. After she brings my tea, she settles in next to me and waits patiently for my side of the story.

First, I fortify myself with two decadent pieces of honey-dripping baklava and in an un-ladylike fashion take to licking every bit of honey off my fingers. I can't ever imagine Kathleen doing this, I think to myself. Okay, I'm ready now to share with Naomi.

"So," I begin. Naomi is well aware that is my word before launching into a long tale. I continue, "Remember, I told you I was seeing that past life regressionist?" Naomi nods her head. "Well, I went under easily and found myself in the year 1900 and in Kathleen's body . . . the woman from my dreams." I pause to make sure Naomi is taking it all in okay.

"How exciting! What was it like? Could you feel her? Did you really feel like you were back in time? Did you get scared? What was Thomas like? Is he as dreamy as he is in your dreams?"

"Whoa, slow down. Yes, I could feel her and hear her thoughts. That was the strangest part for me. I could completely think my thoughts as Tess, and Kathleen's thoughts at the same time. And I could feel myself holding and dancing with Thomas, with him singing to me and . . . well . . . I still don't know how that's possible, but it felt as real as you and I sitting here right now."

"Amazing! You're so lucky."

"I guess . . . well, anyway, it was a lovely experience. It was romantic and everything I hoped it would be. Kathleen and Thomas were perfect together. They had the ideal love. She was supremely happy. I want that. And if he is really out there, he may be searching for me as I am for him . . ."

"Sandy nailed it then. She saw that he is out there and she gave you a major clue—J. Just as you are Tess now, he is J and no longer Thomas. I'm so happy for you."

"Naomi, the letter J doesn't give me much to go on. I don't know if he's local or even where to start looking."

"Come on, Tess. Let's think. Most likely he would have reincarnated close to where you are since you are soul mates. It would make sense that he would be close by. And we have to think about his name. Have you met anyone whose name starts with J?"

I stop a moment and rack my brain for anyone I know whose name starts with the letter J. Holy crap. There are many J's in my life:

- Jasmine Estrada—my birth name–nope
- Jared Estrada—my deceased brother–can rule him out based on what Sandy said. Whew!
- June—my landlady–eww, don't think so
- Jesse—my lifeguard friend and bad first date
- Jim—the tile guy that still needs to fix my tiles

"Well?" Naomi is still waiting for an answer. I know she saw the wheels turning in my mind.

"Okay, I can think of two J's currently in my life."

"Who, who?"

"There is this lifeguard I went out with, actually; it was yesterday. We had coffee and absolutely nothing in common. Cute, but young. His name is Jesse. And then there's this guy who is supposed to fix the tiles in my kitchen. I was checking out his ass when he came over to see what needed repair. His name happens to be Jim."

"This is good news. You have two potential prospects here. You need to go back out with Jesse and see if he's the one and then do the same with Jim." She speaks as if it is so easy.

"And how, do you suppose, I'm to tell if any of them is the one?"

"I don't know. Maybe look in his eyes. You know, 'window to the soul' and all that. Or better yet, kiss him, like they do in the movies."

"Oh God, you're worse than I am with this fantasy idea of romance." Suddenly, we both start laughing hysterically. The whole idea is insane and yet, I can tell we are both invigorated by it, like we have undertaken a quest of some sort.

Chapter 18

I end up crashing on the couch since we talked, laughed, and ate more baklava way into the early morning hours. I can't remember the last time I had that much fun. It was nice to completely relax with someone that I'm so comfortable with. What would I do without Naomi in my life? She is a God-send to me. When I open my eyes, for a moment, I'm confused as to where I am.

"Hi sweetie. You're up." Naomi, looking as radiant as ever, hands me a cup of hot tea. How does she do it? I look like crap when I first wake up, but Naomi looks bright-eyed and beautiful.

"Ugh. I'm so sorry I kept you up last night. I know you have to get to work. Did you get any sleep?"

"I'm fine. It was fun hanging out with you. It's been a long time. After you got married and I met Raj, our lives were taken up with other things. I glad we're making more time for each other."

Raj is Naomi's on again, off again boyfriend. He's okay, I guess. I mean, he is all manly, hair in the right places, and cultured, but sometimes he kind of gets on my nerves. There's really no good reason not to like him . . .

"Tess, you spacing out again?"

"No, I'm back one hundred percent. What time do you have to get out of here?"

"I don't have my first client until eleven so we have the morning together. I figured we could talk strategy on how you're going to find J. Come, sit down and let's make a list. You like lists," Naomi teases.

"Naomi, I can do this. You don't need to help."

"I'll start singing."

"Okay, okay you convinced me. Let me use the bathroom first." I grab my bag and head to the bathroom. I'm so glad I keep a travel toothbrush with me. Yuck, I look horrible. With my brush I try to comb out my tangled knots and make myself presentable. Finally, giving up, I pull my hair up in a knot, brush my teeth, pee, and splash water on my face. Much better.

"Come, sit." Naomi insists.

"Coming." As I sit down at the dining room table next to her, she has already set out muffins, fruit, and a pot of coffee. Pinching off a chunk of lemon muffin, I peer at the list she started.

"So, first, what I propose you do is ask Jesse back out on a date. This time choose something more romantic. I figure if you want to flesh out if Thomas is indeed inside of Jesse, a romantic spot would be the place. Last time it was just coffee, so of course it wouldn't work."

My god, does she stop to take a breath? "Uh huh" is all I can add to the conversation before she is off and running again.

"Okay, so you take Jesse to a romantic place for dinner, I'm thinking Italian, with soft music in the background, maybe sit by a fireplace, look deep into his eyes and then you'll see if Thomas is there. And if he is not the one then go to Phase Two: Jim, the tile guy. And with Jim you'll do the same thing. The most it will cost you is two dinners and maybe a little discomfort if neither is the one, but imagine if Thomas is one of them and how happy you'll both be that you found each other again."

"Got it, Naomi. Jeez. Look, I'll call Jesse again. Give me a few days though, will ya? I haven't gotten over that uncomfortable coffee date yet." My cell phone rings as if on cue. I hit speaker.

"Hello?"

"Ms. Whitaker?"

"Yes?"

"This is Jim Daly. I wanted to let you know that the tiles arrived and I was wondering when you're free for me to come over and replace your kitchen tiles? Are you free this afternoon?"

"Yes, she is," Naomi quickly answers for me.

I glare at her, but she shrugs and gives me her best innocent smile.

"Uh okay, Ms. Whitaker? Are you still there?"

"Yes, I am, that was just . . ." Now what? ". . . My assistant," I lie and add, "She was checking my schedule. Does three p.m. work for you?"

"That's fine. See you at three."

After he clicks off, I turn my head towards Naomi and await an explanation.

"See. I helped. This way you can find out if Jim is Thomas, and you don't have to wait or go out for dinner if it's not him. It's perfect."

"Great. Yeah, perfect."

"Look, I gotta get ready for work. Fill me in on everything tonight." Naomi gets up, kisses my cheek and strolls off to her bedroom, leaving me alone with leftover breakfast and Naomi's list entitled "How to Find Mr. J." It's kind of cute, but feels weird to be searching for Thomas this way. When I was mulling it over in my mind it seemed perfectly rational, but now that Naomi and I are starting an active search it seems . . . I don't know . . . like I'm some crazy past-life stalker. I mean, how weird is that? You can't get rid of someone even if you die. No, they come find you in your next life. I'm sure Thomas would have wanted to be with Kathleen/me again. So I'm not really stalking, right?

Okay, what else can I add to the "How to Find Mr. J" list, besides Jim and Jesse?

- Jim Daly—three p.m. appointment
- Jesse (don't know last name) lifeguard—make new date
- See Barbara (past life regressionist)—get more clues—see if I can move up appointment
- Ask Sandy the psychic if she sees anything else
- Start going out and see if I can meet any J's

The list stares back at me awaiting its next line; I'm out of options and my coffee is cold. Guess it's time to go home.

"Hey, I'm gonna get out of here," I call out.

"Hold on, let me see you out," she yells back.

I put the cups in the sink and wrap the remainder of the muffins in plastic wrap, then grab my bag as Naomi comes out in a robe with a towel wrapped on her head. She looks like a spa commercial, all fresh, clean, and glowing with health.

"Raj is having a get-together barbecue this weekend. He promises it will be special. You'll be there?"

"Oh, sure, of course."

"Good. You remember how to get to his place?"

"Rancho Palos Verdes, right? Text me the address and I'll GPS it."

"Okay, six on Saturday. Love you."

"Love you, too. Thanks for everything. You're the best."

"I know. Good luck today."

"Okay. You know that this is too weird."

"Yes, but weird in a good way. I'm so excited for you."

"You're crazy." We both start to laugh. Actually it sounds more like cackling, which cracks us up even more.

I mull over the last few days in my mind. It's been a whirlwind of emotions and experiences that I still haven't had time to properly digest. And yet, before I give myself time to process I'm off to meet Jim and see if he can be the one I'm looking for, my soul mate. Butterflies churn my stomach. Maybe I should eat something to settle my nerves. I wish I could've seen Doug today. I could really use his *Xanax* touch. Tomorrow, for sure. I'll get to the beach nice and early, I promise myself.

First thing, a shower. The water always helps to clear my head. Warm water sprays over me and I let my mind go blank for a few moments. No thinking of soul mates, or Kathleen and Thomas. No contemplating the seduction of Jim or Jesse. No worries about Richard and Wade. All gone, peace and contentment.

water . . . open ocean . . . bonjour . . . king bed . . . tan arms, his hands caressing my breasts . . .

What was that? Another vision? Premonition? Does this mean I'm getting close to finding Thomas? The image was beautiful, and sexy. Did it have to be that short? I finally get an image that's enjoyable and it's too brief. I couldn't even see his face. I was definitely in the middle of making love and enjoying it. A lot! Does Thomas/J take me to Paris? Ooh la la. I smile to myself as I dry off. I could get into that.

I dress quickly in denim shorts and a white blouse, my attempt at looking sexy. Comb out my wet hair and gaze into the mirror. So, you're really going to do this? I ask myself. How does one go about seducing someone? It's been years since I played that game. I apply a little light makeup on my eyes and cheeks and then, for added measure, put on some lip gloss. Jim will be here in less than an hour. I can't sit here waiting.

A walk will do me good. I grab an apple for the walk, after passing on the idea of a pear. I don't need an orgasmic out-of-the-body moment right now. I take the stairs lightly with a bounce in my step; there's much energy to burn. It's too bad I don't have time for a run. I head down my street, past my neighbor with the blue mustang—looks like he got it running as he's now waxing it.

"Hi, nice day," he calls out to me.

"Yes, it is," I respond and carry on. I'm heading to visit a dear friend of mine. As I approach he gets up from his spot and waits by the gate.

"Hey, Midnight! How are you doing, love?"

He's a quiet one, giving me the a-okay tail wag.

"So, it's a big day today. I'm going to find out if this guy is my love from a past life." I spill the beans to my friend. He's a good listener as long as I'm scratching him behind his ears and under his chin. "So how will I know it's him, you ask? Good question. I'm not sure. I guess I will look him deep in his eyes."

I stare at Midnight's eyes. They are deep pools. As I stare into them I feel as if I can see his soul. I see purity, honesty, and loyalty. I see deep, honest love in his eyes. I start to choke up.

"Oh my," I tell him. "You do get it." I kiss him on his muzzle and thank him for his gift of clarity and friendship. Maybe Naomi is right and this eye thing will work. It worked with Midnight. What I saw when I looked into Midnight's eyes was as if I was given a peek into his soul and it was illuminating. I'll look into Jim's eyes and see his soul. Time to head back and do this.

On the walk back home I feel empowered and have a renewed sense of confidence. I'm a strong woman with gifts, according to Bobbi. I repeat over and over, I'm strong and powerful, I'm strong and powerful. As I approach my apartment I see Jim pulling up in his white pickup truck. Suddenly, I want to turn and go the way I came. What happened to strong and powerful? I chide. Dammit, he saw me, no running now.

"Hello, Ms. Whitaker."

"It's Tess. Hi Jim. Come on up."

Jim grabs his supplies and heads up the stairs behind me. I hope my attempt at a wiggle spurs his interest. Boy, this going to be disastrous if he's not the one, or he's not into me . . . don't go there. Focus.

I open the door and stand in the doorway so he's forced to pass close to my body as he enters. He raises his eyebrows at me curiously. Okay, maybe I should be a little more subtle. I'll try conversation.

"So, Jim, those tiles were hard to find?" Okay, I know it's lame. It's the only thing I can think of.

"They're not exactly the same tiles. Your original tiles are not made anymore. I was able to locate, however, a tile that's very close in color and style. Here, take a look." He holds up the new tile next to the counter. "See, the yellow and crackling glaze is very similar."

I lean in as close as I dare without seeming like I am throwing myself at him. "Oh, yes, they are quite similar." My God, who gives a shit about tiles and glaze? I've got to think of something else.

"What type of work do you do?" Jim asks me.

Before thinking, I answer, "Oh, I don't work."

"I'm confused. Didn't you tell me the first time I met you that you came from a business meeting and today you indicated that your assistant was checking your schedule? Not that it's any of my concern. I only need to take care of your tiles."

Damn. When you lie you've really got to keep track of things. He's right. I must seem like a real winner.

"I'm sorry, Jim. I lied to you earlier because I forgot about the appointment. My mind has been other places and, today, that was my friend goofing around. I hope you can accept my apology." I figure the truth is better at this point.

"Not a big deal. Don't worry about it."

"Good. Let's start fresh. I'm Tess, divorced and learning about living at the beach. Currently, I'm not working and should be okay for a little while. I sold off my half of a personal training business I owned and I have an occasional article writing assignment."

"Nice to meet you. Are you planning on going back into personal training?"

"I'm not sure. I really don't know if it resonates with me anymore. And you?"

"Well, not much to tell. Been in the tile arena for twenty-three years, really can't see myself doing anything else."

How nice to know what you want to do, I think. Jim stops and focuses on his work. He really is good at what he does. He uses his tools with precision and exudes a confidence. I can see why he likes it. It fits him well. Jim looks up at me.

"Sorry, didn't mean to stare. I was noticing how proficient you are. It's like an art."

"Yeah, I guess you can say that."

I take a good look at his eyes. They are a soft blue, small with crinkles around the edge. Too many years in the sun by the look of his weathered face. Can I see if Thomas is in there? I move myself around so that I can get a deep look into them. There's no way to do this casually. Jim looks at me questioningly. Hell. He probably thinks I'm a nut.

"I just . . ." What am I going to say?

Jim stops working and looks at me. Now what? I feel those butterflies, or hormones I felt the last time he was here when I was checking out his ass. Well, I haven't had sex in a very long time. Is it so wrong to jump the tile guy? I lean over the counter and gaze deeper into his eyes. He also leans in. I can feel the heat from his body, his breath close to mine. I close my eyes and make my move. I kiss him on his mouth. Jim doesn't resist. My mouth is hungry for another human and forces its tongue into his mouth. Jim is receptive and also probes my mouth with his tongue. I'm worked up and kiss him harder. Finally we break free and he comes around the counter.

"Tess, you are one interesting woman." He grabs me by the shoulders and presses me against the counter, attacking my mouth with his. My hands make their way down to his jeans and start undoing his belt. Jim's tan arms reach for me. He fondles my breasts. Could this be from my vision—tan arms? No, there is no water and no French. Stop thinking of this now, enjoy the moment.

Jim breaks free from me, "Let's go to your bedroom and continue."

He pulls me towards the back of the apartment. Okay, so I didn't see anything in his eyes and didn't feel anything in his kiss, but, hey, he's kind of hot and I'm horny. Can you blame a girl?

I let him guide me to the bedroom. I stand at the end of the bed. Jim gently pushes me down on the mattress. I'm really going to do this. I haven't had sex with anyone except Richard in a million years, it feels like. I start to unbutton my blouse as Jim unzips his jeans. Jeepers. How can all of that fit in his pants? Richard was all of five inches so anything bigger is thrilling.

"Oh my."

"Yes, I hear that a lot," he says with a laugh. I start to laugh too.

This is going to be great. I hope I remember what to do. Just like riding a bike, I laugh inwardly. I push down my shorts and shimmy out of my panties and wait with anticipation. Jim straddles my right leg and leans down to kiss me as I crane my neck up to him. His penis rests on my leg. I imagine what it will feel like inside me. He trails tiny kisses down my neck and makes his way down to my . . .

Knock knock. Who's that? Not now! Maybe they'll go away. I try to ignore it.

"Where were we?" I say.

Knock KNOCK. Damn it.

"Tess, it's June. Is Jim there? I want to look at the work he's doing."

June, the landlady? Now? This can't be happening.

"Be there in a moment." I jump up as Jim is scrambling to tuck his now half erect penis back into his jeans, that beautiful penis that was so close . . . I knew I didn't like June.

"I'll get the door. Go to the bathroom and put yourself together. I'll cover for us," Jim tells me.

"Thank you," I whisper and give him a peck on the cheek.

I grab a pair of sweatpants and take off to the bathroom, locking the door. I'm breathless and feel like a child hiding from the teacher. With my hands on the sink counter and leaning forward, I stare at my reflection. My hair is mussed and my lips are swollen from his kisses. What was I doing? The mood has broken. He's not the one, but at that moment my body didn't care. I'm not sure if I'm relieved that June interrupted us or not. I didn't even think of condoms. Hormones are dangerous. June and Jim's voices are muted in the background. I splash some water on my face and brush my teeth, then flush the toilet to keep up with the cover.

"Oh, there you are. Jim was showing me the fine work he's doing here. You look dreadful dear, are you ill? You're flushed." June is in fine form, standing quite close to Jim.

The poor guy looks trapped; the look on his face reveals his discomfort. His afternoon didn't turn out the way he planned.

"I'm not sick. I feel fine. I didn't know you would be by."

"Yes. I thought I would see Jim about some additional work. Jim, if you're done here, shall we check the work I need in the apartment downstairs?"

"Sure, I'm done." Jim gathers his belongings and gives me an apologetic look.

"Feel better, Tess. Oh and I'll need a pet deposit of two hundred dollars, just add that to next month's rent." June points with her chin to Prince, as she and Jim make their exit.

"I'm not . . ." Oh never mind.

God, I hate her.

Chapter 19

Doug's in his usual place. It feels wonderful to see him, a relief actually. It's like I haven't missed a day from our routine. After yesterday's disaster with Jim, I'm happy to sit here in quiet.

"Sometimes I feel so confused," I blurt out after several minutes of silence.

"About everything?"

"About where I'm going, what I'm supposed to do. My life has been turned completely upside down and I don't know what the next step is."

"My guess is that you've spent a great amount of energy avoiding the world. The universe directs us if we only take a moment to listen."

"Is that what you do?"

"Yes . . . always."

Hmm, maybe that's why he seems at peace with himself and, well, everything.

"And what is the universe telling you right now?"

"It says that Tess needs a pointer to her path."

"Is that what you are?"

"For now. Open yourself to the infinite. Pay attention to the clues. All the answers are in front of you."

With that, Doug rises and starts to walk away, leaving me to ponder his cryptic statements again. I sit for another ten minutes or so, attempting to open up myself to the universe, as he directed, since he must have been pretty serious to utter that many words in one sitting. I better pay attention.

"Okay, I'm here. What do you want to show me?" I call out to the sky. I wait. Nothing.

Hmmph. I'm going to get some coffee. Brushing off the sand from my hands and butt I head towards 2nd Street to *Skye Coffee*, home of the smashing time with Jesse. The coffee can't be beat, though.

As I wait for my cinnamon latte with skim milk, to save on calories of course, I glance at the table of flyers announcing various local events. One catches my eye, a writers conference. A writers conference, that sounds right up my alley. It's in the Valley though. Ugh, not back to the Valley, but I'd really like to go. I would love to write a book someday. Maybe this is what Doug is talking about. Maybe I'm supposed to be at this conference.

I retrieve my latte and find a spot by the window. Sun filters in, warming my arms and casting light on the flyer. The conference is held over a weekend and features a variety of inspirational and educational workshops. While I sip my drink I peruse the flyer and scan the blurbs looking for classes that resonate with me. A few catch my eye:

- Character Development—Joan Berger
- Setting the Scene—Adam Ormand
- Marketing and Publishing Your Novel—Sid Fleming
- Query Clinic—Daniel Garcia

Right away the workshops on "character development" and "scene setting" jump out. These areas are something I would love to learn more about. I think I'm going to sign up. I pull out my phone to check the dates and, of course, I'm free. How much is really going on in my life anyway, besides figuring out who Thomas is, finalizing a divorce, and not having a relationship with my own son. Yup. Nothing going on.

Yet, I feel this conference is going to be great, except for going back to that damn valley. Even if I were busy, I think I would find the time to go. Heck, I'm going to do it. I fill out the online form on the phone, enter my credit card number, and press send. Done. See, universe, I can listen.

The rest of the week is uneventful. I spend the majority of my time writing and cycling. I know I haven't made another date with Jesse. I can't handle it; finding things to talk about is something I'm not willing to tackle right now. Jim hasn't called me. Well, I haven't called him either. Do I want to pursue it again? What would be the use? I don't feel that he is J. There was no recognition in his eyes or his kiss, for that matter. And I'm well aware that it was my hormones that were talking that afternoon, so again what is the point of pursuing anything? Except to find out if the sex would be as good as I was already envisioning. No. I'm going to leave well enough alone. If I do find J soon then Jim will only complicate matters. It's better this way.

"Naomi listened with a sympathetic ear while I aired my sexual frustration over the phone. I'm sure she'll dote over me at Raj's barbeque tonight. What do you wear to a barbecue anyway, Jared?"

I choose jeans and a silk blouse in beige and black, a pair of low black sandals and I'm set.

"Why did they put Rancho Palos Verdes so dog-gone far from anywhere else in Southern California? Okay, so it's pretty and has nice views of the Pacific. It's only a short distance from me as the crow flies, however, it takes an exorbitant amount of time to wind up the hills. I'm not sure whether my irritation is the drive or seeing Raj. I know it's crazy, but I'm almost jealous when I see them together. Weird, huh? I keep that to myself, another facet of my crazy life."

Raj has an older house. It's fixed up comfortably. It's the view that makes this house divine. From his back yard he has the most spectacular views of the blue ocean. There is a cove below and to the right. I stare down there and drift away in my mind. I imagine making love on that secluded stretch of beach. As for who I'll be making love to, I don't have a clue. He's more of a faceless form, some muscular man who wants nothing more than to please me. "Tell me what you want, Tess," he'll whisper huskily in my ear as I lie beneath him in the warm sand. I will melt, and then . . .

"You want a glass of wine?" Raj interrupts my delicious fantasy.

"Uh." It takes me a moment to reconnect with the present. "Sure, white if you got it. Thanks."

Naomi comes bounding up to greet me and gives me a hug.

"So glad you came. The views are terrific, huh?"

"Yes, they're amazing. Thanks for inviting me. So what's the special occasion?"

"I'm not sure. Raj said he wants to have his close friends over and has an announcement to make. Maybe he got a promotion. We'll find out soon enough."

"Here's your wine. Chardonnay, is that okay?" Raj hands me my wine.

"Great, thank you. I love your house. You're very lucky."

"Yes, I feel lucky. We will be eating soon. I hope you brought your appetite. We have ribs, chicken, corn—the works."

"Sounds perfect," I tell him.

Raj gives Naomi a kiss on her cheek and my stomach tightens. What's wrong with me? He's a good guy, treats her well for the most part, and has a good job and beautiful home. All is well. No worries, I tell myself.

Dinner is plentiful. The smell of barbequed chicken and ribs slightly charred spurs my appetite. I'm ravenous and tear into my overflowing plate in the most un-ladylike fashion. I covet the perfect spot outside to eat and enjoy views of the ocean and the man to my left. He's one of Raj's friends, I would guess. He's tall with tousled hair. I want to run my hands through his hair. While eavesdropping on his and a portly man's conversation across the table, I pick up that he's successful in business. He has looked over at me a couple of times and if I didn't know better, I would say he's interested in me. Hmm. No wedding ring. Good sign. Maybe he's the one.

He just smiled at me. I smile back, hoping I don't have barbecue sauce on my face. Be cool, Tess.

"You're friends with Naomi, right?" Mr. Tousled asks me.

"Yes, since high school. How long have you known Raj?"

"Not too long, maybe three or four years. We've done some business together and play basketball on the weekends."

"Oh." Okay, I can't think of anything to say so I go back to my meal.

"You live around here?" He's talking again.

"Not too far. Belmont Shore. You?"

"I'm in Hermosa Beach, not too far either."

Okay, I've got to find out what his name is before this goes any further. He already sounds promising:

- No ring
- Cute
- Lives close
- Successful

It all sounds good to me.

"I'm sorry. I didn't get your name. I'm Tess."

"Stephen. Stephen Butler of Butler Real Estate. Nice to meet you."

Darn. Not a J. Well, no use wasting my time.

"Nice meeting you, Stephen. I'll talk to you later—I need to catch up with Naomi. Enjoy your evening." I get up with my plate and wine and head for the kitchen. Stephen looks a little put off. I'm on a mission and can't be diverted by the first cute, successful guy I meet.

Naomi's in the kitchen, cleaning up and directing traffic.

"Hey, there you are, Naomi, need help?"

"Are you trying to avoid someone? I saw you out there talking to Stephen and then you suddenly appear here."

I can't get away with anything around her. "He's not a J," I tell her in a low voice.

"I know, Tess, but did you have to cut him off so abruptly? He's been through a rough divorce too, and is a little shell-shocked. He's fragile, and now he looks a little hurt."

"Look, I'm sorry. I thought it would be worse to waste his time if he wasn't the one. I should've asked for his name earlier in the conversation. Next time, okay?"

"Okay, all's forgiven." Naomi gives me a hug. I start helping her in the kitchen. It's enjoyable working side by side with her and for a moment I forget everything else and completely focus on the task of washing dishes.

"So, when's this big secret announcement?" I ask as I'm washing the last dish.

"I'm not really sure," Naomi admits and then turns her direction towards the door. The doorbell is chiming. "Can you get it, Tess?"

"Sure," I say as I carry a damp dish towel to dry my hands. Opening the door with slippery fingers, I'm gobsmacked at who's staring back at me: *Richard and Wade.* What the heck!

"Hi Tess." Richard greets me coolly and plants a hasty kiss on my cheek as he hands me a bottle of wine for the party.

"Uh. Hi. Nice to see you both." I quickly recover. How in the world did I not know they would be here? I mean, it makes sense that Raj would invite them. We've been friends for many years, no reason to exclude Richard since I left him. Still, it's quite shocking. And there is my dear boy looking as disinterested as usual.

"Hi Wade, honey." I try to act unassuming, not sure how it's coming across, desperate maybe?

"Hey," Wade offers, not taking his eyes off his all-important smart phone.

"Come in. Get something to eat. You must be hungry. Oh my God there is so much food here. You could eat for days. And wait until you see the view. You're going to die. Raj has some kind of announcement to make. I don't have any idea what it is. You? How was the drive? Bad traffic? My, it's good to see you. Well, don't stand there; let's get you some food and drink. Wine, Richard?" Oh my goodness, I've completely lost it. This is too much for me. I need a drink, bad. I lead them both to the kitchen.

"Hi Naomi, good to see you." Richard gives her a hug. She looks surprised. So she didn't know either that they would be here. I knew she wouldn't have let me be bowled over that way. I feel a little better. Whew, I'm so glad he didn't see me chatting up that Stephen Butler.

"Wade." I direct him away from the group, handing him a plate and pointing out the foods I know he likes. I'm tempted to pile up his plate for him like I did when he was young. "So, how's school?" I try.

"Fine."

"Doing anything fun?"

"Not really."

"Skateboarding?"

"Sometimes."

Jeez, this is like pulling teeth. Are all teenage boys this way? We plant ourselves at a table outside.

"Well, you look great. Getting taller." I notice that the little acne he had is clearing up.

"Yeah." He answers as he tears off some rib meat with his teeth, leaving sauce on his cheek. I want to wipe it off.

"Your new hair style is cool. Cut off all the waviness, huh?"

"Uh huh."

"Well it looks great, very mature. Get my texts?"

"Yeah."

"Okay, good. Want something to drink?"

"Sure."

"Okay, be right back. I think there's some cheesecake in the kitchen too; I'll snag you a piece." I get up and make a beeline to the kitchen, my refuge. As I pour a cup of soda for Wade, my hands are shaking.

"You okay?" Naomi grabs the cup from my hands and pours for me.

"I can't do this," I whisper to her.

"You're doing fine. I had no idea they would be here. I hope you believe me."

I nod as I face the wall. I don't want my face to betray my attempts to keep it together.

"Where's Richard?" Again speaking in low tones.

"He asked me to point him to the bathroom. He'll probably be out in a sec. I'll head him off at the pass, if you want."

"No, I've got to talk to him sooner or later. Give me a moment. Hey, can I get a piece of cheesecake for Wade?"

"Of course." She cuts a large slice and puts it on a plate for me.

I put on my best "I have it all together" face and steadily carry the soda and cheesecake out for Wade. Richard is sitting next to him. I see he found the wine.

"Here you go." I place the cake and soda down for Wade.

"Thanks mom."

I melt for an instant and feel my eyes start to prickle. Nope, get a grip. Not now!

"How are you doing, Richard? You look great." Asking to take the pressure off me.

"Good. We're adjusting well, Wade and me. Right, amigo?"

"Yup." Wade answers as verbose as ever.

"Business good? You and Terrence holding down the fort?"

"Yeah, thriving well. The clients miss you and your no-nonsense attitude. Mrs. Dupree says hi."

"Oh, that's nice. Good to hear." Who the heck is Mrs. Dupree? Has it been that long? That chapter of my life seems like a lifetime ago. "So, you want me to fix you a plate, Richard?" I offer, hoping he'll say yes so I can temporarily extricate myself from this scene.

"Sure." He looks up at me. Just like old times. Long after Wade wanted me to prepare plates for him, Richard still seemed to rely on it.

"Not a problem. Be back in a jiff," I tell him too cheerfully.

"Still okay?" Naomi asks me when I get back in the kitchen.

"Yeah, sure." I focus on choosing out food for Richard. Raj disturbs my hell and I'm grateful.

"Attention! Can I get everyone to gather outside for a few minutes?" Raj calls out to all of the guests. Naomi shrugs her shoulders.

"Come. Don't want to keep him waiting," I tell her as I carry out Richard's overflowing plate of chicken, ribs, beans, and corn.

I take Naomi's arm and we walk out to the patio. I hand Richard his plate with a smile. He looks grateful. Maybe this will be okay after all.

A mid-forties woman in a low-cut blouse is standing by a table and hands us a glass of champagne. Ooh. This must be special; we get champagne and big-busted women. There must be forty of us all waiting with bated breath for the big announcement. Naomi and I find a spot towards the back of the crowd. Richard and Wade are on a bench by us, watching the scene as they scarf their food.

Raj jumps up dramatically onto a low wall, waiting for the group to settle. I notice he's fidgeting with his watch. That's not like him. He's usually cool and collected.

"First of all, I want to thank everyone for taking time from their busy weekend to spend time at my home. I hope you have had enough to eat, there's plenty more. Well, enough stalling . . . er . . . This is harder than I thought." I glance at Naomi and we both look puzzled.

Raj continues, "As you are all aware, I've been blessed. My business is successful, I have wonderful, supportive friends and family, but I've never known true happiness until I met sweet Naomi."

Naomi looks down and smiles shyly. She's completely smitten.

He calls out to her, "Naomi can you come up here for a moment?" A man gives her a nudge towards Raj.

"Go. Go," I coax her. Naomi makes her way through the crowd and stands on the ground, looking up at Raj expectantly.

"Come up here." He reaches down for her hand and assists her up to give us all a good view. "You have given me joy; you breathed life into me. You taught me to color outside the lines and find the art in all things. You complete me, Naomi. The only thing that would make my life better is if I could spend my days giving you the same happiness you give me . . ." Raj stops and swallows hard. He reaches into his right pants pocket and pulls out a ring box.

"Oh," gasps Naomi. He lowers himself down on one knee in front of all these witnesses.

"Naomi, my love, I would be honored if you would agree to spend your life with me. I love you with all my heart. Will you marry me?"

Raj opens the black velvet ring box to display an engagement ring. Damn, I can't see it, being so far back in the crowd. My stomach is in knots. I'm just happy for her, right? That's it. Naomi's response indicates to me that she loves the ring. Tears roll down her cheeks.

"Yes Raj. Of course I'll marry you. I love you too." She looks my direction. "Tess, get up here," she yells out.

Uh. Okay. I make my way through the group to stand next to the happy couple on the wall.

"Tess, you are my dearest friend; tell me you'll be my maid of honor."

I'm dumbstruck. First, Richard and Wade being sprung on me, then the proposal that I haven't processed yet, and now I'm to be a maid of honor. I don't even remember what they're supposed to do. I've seemed to have lost the power of speech. The ring Raj presented to her is amazing. I've never seen anything quite like it. It's gold and displays a hand on the top and one on the bottom gently cupping a large cabochon emerald. The emerald green shows well against her skin and red hair. He did good. I hate to admit it, I'm jealous of her good fortune. I never had an engagement ring. When Richard proposed to me we were too poor to afford anything and then after the business got off the ground, promises of a "proper" engagement ring were long forgotten.

I nod "yes" to being her maid of honor. Naomi takes me in a tight squeeze and kisses my cheek. My face gets damp from her tears of happiness. I start to cry, from what I'm not sure—happiness, confusion, jealousy, and guilt over the family I left, being overwhelmed . . . the list goes on.

"Congratulations, sweetie, I'm so happy for you," I whisper in her ear. "Congratulations, Raj," I add for good measure. In the crowd there is much whooping, clapping, and "cheers" being called out. All are toasting and sipping their champagne. I down mine. Where can I get another glass?

Chapter 20

"Oh Jared, I have the worst headache. When did I ever drink so much? I only did it because it felt like it was the only way to get through last night. It was wonderful and terrible at the same time to see Wade. He looks like an adult. God, I miss him. My thoughts are conflicted. He didn't seem as angry toward me as usual. Maybe time away is what he needed. I'm confused and his lack of communication skills doesn't help the matter. My heart is heavy today as well as my head. I need quiet. Even Prince is too loud for me. Why the hell did I think wind chimes were a good idea? Help."

After a couple of Tylenol and a few more hours of sleep I feel well enough to eat some toast. The party girl scene isn't for me. I really didn't drink as much as the others and yet, I get hit hard the next day. Naomi had to drive me home and Raj followed so I wouldn't be stranded without a car today. They're too good, and good for each other too. I see that now. I want nothing but happiness for her.

Not wanting to drive today, I'm going to bicycle to the farmers market held every Sunday at Alamito's Bay, only a few blocks from me. I shower quickly and throw on some shorts, tank top, and flip-flops, and grab my backpack for my purchases. I head down the steps ready for another cycling adventure. Sun blaring and no wind, it is a perfect day for a ride. The familiar sound of a screen door slamming from Valerie's apartment causes me to turn.

"Hi Valer . . .," I start to call out, but stop short when I notice she's not alone.

Jim, my tile guy, is tucking his shirt back into his jeans. He leans in and kisses Valerie on her cheek. What's going on? Oh my, Valerie and Jim—they must have hit it off after he fixed her tiles.

That dog. Well, I really can't blame him; I did leave him hot and bothered.

"See you later, honey," she tells Jim. "Hey lady. Going for a ride?"

"Uh, yeah," I answer. After Jim climbs into his truck, I ask, "So you and Jim, huh?"

"Uh huh. He came to fix my tiles and one thing led to another."

"I can imagine."

"Man, he's got a great ass and . . ." Valerie waves her hand as if she is dismissing the subject.

"And what?" I tease.

"Well. Let's just say he's got a very large glue gun." She laughs.

"Oh?" I look away.

"What was that? Your eyes. What's up with that look? You didn't? No . . . Oh my, you did. You sampled him." She points at me.

"No, no, it's not what you think."

"Then what?" she presses.

How am I going to explain this? I can't tell her about my soul mate search, can I?

"Look, Valerie. I'm really happy that you and Jim found each other. You look cute together."

"And?"

"Ok. Yes, I did have a close call with Jim, but I promise you we did not have sex."

"Why? Not good enough for you?"

"What? I'm confused. First you're upset that you thought we had sex and now you're upset that we didn't?"

"Oh shit. I don't know what I'm saying. I'm a freakin' mess. I got it bad for this guy. I think he might be the one."

"That's wonderful. You're very lucky."

"Hey, don't worry. I'm sure you'll find yours someday."

"Yeah, I'm not too sure."

"There's someone for you, just not my Jim."

"Got it. I'll cross him off my list." I make an imaginary X in the air, causing Valerie to snort with laughter.

"You know . . . we're both crazy."
"Oh yeah, I know it."

Fresh air is the best cure for a hangover. Soon my head is feeling clearer. I'm in the moment, watching the gulls, the palm fronds sway and, of course, the traffic whizzing by—which I ignore. For this brief space in time, life is good.

The farmers market is congested, as it is most Sundays. I weave between the long lines of cars and find a close spot to tie up Ms. Glimmer. They hold the market in the parking lot of the boat docks. The boat docks are not locked. I love to wander up and down, imagining what it would be like to own one of them. Which boat would I choose? What would I name her? I play a fantasy game in my mind.

Today, though, I'm focused on the market. Where to start first—with the fruits and vegetables? Or maybe with the clothing, home, and yard decorations? I reach into my backpack for my water bottle since I'm suddenly parched and come up empty-handed. What? Looks like I forgot to pack a water bottle in my haste to get going. Sweet, juicy, thirst-quenching fruit is all I can think of. Almost pushing my way through the crowds, I've got to get some liquid in me.

"Excuse me . . . pardon . . . so sorry . . . got to get through . . ." I continuously call out to those in my way, getting some nasty looks in return. They just don't understand. If they were as thirsty as I am they wouldn't be as kind as I'm attempting to be.

Finally, rows upon rows of ripe fruits and vegetables. All the colors displayed for the shoppers' delight. The brightest greens of the peppers, orange-reds of plump tomatoes, yet, my prize is a little further down. Crates of the deepest purple plums I've ever seen, bursting with juicy goodness. They're so full it appears that if I looked at them too hard they would weep their juices on each other and spill onto the ground. I choose two large plums, pay the vendor, and immediately devour them, sucking straight through the skin and skipping the biting stage. I was right about them. They are every bit as delicious and satisfying as I imagined they would be. Plum juice runs down my chin and onto my shirt, staining it. My appearance isn't my primary concern at the moment. So now I have to walk around with a stained tank.

To my left are cherries, grapes and, oh my, pears, large green and yellow pears, all juicy and waiting to be chosen by a passerby. I can't pass it up. I have to have one. I need it. With careful consideration, I pick out the best of the group, pay for it, and take my prize over to the boat docks away from the throng. Sitting on the grass bordering the walkway, I examine my beauty. Taking in the color variations, shape, and then, taking a good whiff. My mind already starting to mist over, I feel the other world coming into view. I'm feeling the effects before I even take a bite.

I close my eyes and take a bite, letting the fruity meat and juice tantalize my tongue. The scent moves through my nostrils. I'm transported once more to that dreamy, illusory world I've visited before, courtesy of the pear. I lay back on the grass as my present-day vision and hearing are temporarily halted. This pear experience is different, more intense and sensory. Only one bite and I'm off on a trip similar to a drug trip. Has the experience been affected by the alcohol I drank last night? I can't think right now. The effects of the pear magic are consuming me.

Laying in the soft grass . . . we lovers embrace . . . feeding pears to each other . . . teasing to delayed ecstasy . . . rough hands exploring my body, my hands explore his . . . making love in the countryside . . . sun low in the sky . . . no rushing this day . . . this day for us and us alone . . . "One more time," I tell him.

"Hey, miss! You okay?" Someone is calling from far away. *Leave me alone,* I think.

He smiles knowingly as he gently caresses and cups my breasts . . . I give myself to him again . . . oh, my love . . .

"Miss, are you sick? Do you need me to call for help?" He's yelling this time.

"What? Who are you?" I'm jerked back into this time and feel momentarily confused.

"You passed out or something. I've been calling and shaking you for a few minutes with no response," answers a fifty-ish man in a Hawaiian shirt and shorts.

"You're kidding, right?" I'm puzzled. I took that bite a moment ago. I look around and notice the pear has rolled down the slope of the grassy incline I'm lying on and is covered in dirt and leaves. Huh? How long was I out?

"No, that's why I was concerned. You looked totally out of it."

"I was taking a short nap. Sorry. I had a long bike ride and had forgotten my water bottle so I stopped for some food and rest before continuing on. Thank you for your concern, but I'm fine now," I lie. Well, I couldn't really say I was having an out-of-body experience, could I? He would be calling for a 5150 mental health evaluation immediately. Please go away, I silently beg.

"Ok, no problem. Get hydrated before you ride. It's hot today."

"Yeah, thanks, I'll do that." I stand and retrieve my soiled pear and backpack and chuck the pear in the nearest trash bin. Hiding behind my sunglasses and keeping my head dipped low, I attempt to avoid any more confrontations. On the ride home, I have only one thought—get home safely, away from people and in a place where I can process what happened.

With Ms. Glimmer securely stowed in the garage, I make my way up the stairs and into my apartment, bolting the door. Prince is swirling around my legs, brushing his body up against me. He won't let me walk straight. The instant I take a step he runs towards the kitchen. Ah, he's sneaky. He's luring me into the kitchen for kibble.

"Okay. Hold on a moment. What's your hurry?" I tell him as I pour some kibble into his bowl. Now that he's happy, I can wash up.

"Oh my." I'm startled by my image in the bathroom mirror. No wonder that man thought there was something wrong with me. My shirt is badly stained with plum juice, but worse than that is my face. Ugh. Purple stains on my chin and neck. Grass bits in my tangled hair and smeared eye makeup from last night that I never washed off. I look horrific. What has gotten into me? I need to process after a long shower.

After I shower and dress, I stand in my living room. I feel the need to pace. There's this unspent energy in me. I can't sit still. I try my balcony and the living room couch, even a spot on the floor under the Tibetan prayer flags, but it's no use. I can't relax or think. I need to talk to someone.

Out the door and down the street—I hope he's there. I start walking faster. As I approach closer, I can barely make out a form. My heart beats a little faster. Yes, he's there. Thank goodness. I breathe a sigh of relief, looks like he's been waiting for me.

"Hi, Midnight," I call out as he wags his tail in response. "Wow, I'm so glad to see you. I hope you don't mind if I tell you what happened. I really need to talk it out." He pushes his wet nose through the gate as confirmation that he's all ears. I lower myself to a cross-legged position on the sidewalk outside his gate.

"I just had the weirdest experience, Midnight. I'm not sure if my drinking too much last night or being dehydrated this morning contributed to the experience, but even so, it was weird, to say the least. Usually when I eat pears the world falls away and I'm in an altered state, in a good way. It's all joy and a dreamlike happiness. This time it was different. Yes, I had all the happiness and bliss, but it was so much more. It was like I went to another lifetime. I was lying on the grass, eating pears with a lover. I couldn't see him or me. It was more of a sensation. And if that wasn't weird enough, it all occurred after only one bite and there was some kind of time lapse. I was out for a longer time than I thought. I'm kinda freaking out. Any thoughts?"

Midnight responds by turning his head so I can better scratch under his collar.

"Yeah, no thoughts about it, huh? Well, thanks for listening anyway." I guess I should ask my hypnotherapist about it sometime. I do have an appointment this week with her. Are my visions getting stronger since I haven't been fighting them? I wonder. "My life has really changed a lot since moving down here. I think it's better, right? At least I'm not bored . . ." I start to chuckle. I look up as I notice an elderly woman coming out of the house that Midnight lives in.

"Hi there," she calls out to me.

"Hi, so sorry, please excuse me . . ." I stammer and stand up quickly. How embarrassing.

"I've seen you a few times visiting Buddy. I thought I would say hi. He's a good listener, isn't he?" She comes over to shake my hand and places a gentle, gnarled hand on Midnight's, er, Buddy's head. He leans into her.

"Yes, he is. Thank you for allowing me to visit him. He's been my therapist of sorts. I've been calling him Midnight. Hope you don't mind, I didn't know his name."

"No. Midnight is fine. I'm sure he doesn't mind. I'm Esther Duncan, been here since 1964, seen many changes over the years. I've had many 'Buddys' over the years too. I find it easier to stay with the same name and breed, with my memory."

"Hi Esther. I'm Tess. Tess Whitaker. I moved to this neighborhood recently and your Buddy was sort of my first friend. I hope you don't mind me coming by to visit him like this."

"Anytime. I'm sure he loves the company. I wouldn't mind the company either, just sit here sewing most days. It was nice meeting you, Tess. Come on, Buddy, let's get some dinner."

Buddy follows Esther obediently up the walk, never looking back at me. Buddy, huh? Going to take some getting used to. At least Esther knows I'm not some kind of stalker now. Is it going to be strange confessing my deepest secrets to Buddy, knowing that Esther may be watching? I think I liked it better when I felt more anonymous.

Chapter 21

At long last, it's time for my second hypnotherapy session with Barbara. I feel excited and nervous, not like the last time, though, when I thought I was insane to do this. This time it's more of an excited anticipation. What am I going to find out about Kathleen and Thomas? Will I glean more details to help me find *him*?

There's no problem finding a parking space and traffic was light. All seems to be going well. Barbara is sipping tea when I arrive and looks quite relaxed. I'm taking it as a sign that it will be a good session.

"Good afternoon, Tess. How have you been since I last saw you?"

"Fine, thanks. Spent some time googling that time period and was surprised to see what I remembered right there on my computer screen."

"Yes, it's validating to be able to confirm some facts. I know that when I had my first experience I felt compelled to verify what I had seen under hypnosis. If I could confirm details then I could believe in the healing power of this type of therapy, I thought. Now, I've come to realize that it really doesn't matter if it can be verified or not. What's important is how it affects us, what we learn and how we grow from the experience. Of course there's nothing wrong with researching the past to help you along the path, many of us do that."

"Yeah, I guess that makes sense."

"Do you have any questions before we get started?"

"I can't think of any."

"Okay. I'll use an abbreviated form of the hypnosis process since you already know what it feels like and what to expect. You should be able to get to a very deep state of hypnosis quickly. If you're ready—let's get started. Get comfortable, making sure that your clothing is not binding."

I lie down on her reclining chair and lay the blanket over me. I close my eyes as her words guide me into relaxation. I find myself going into hypnosis easily, more so than the first time. I now have some idea of what to expect and feel more comfortable with Barbara. I can see the staircase in my mind clearly and walk down into the now familiar garden. Next she guides me over the bridge and once again I find myself in New York with Thomas.

Barbara is quiet, giving me a moment to adjust to the new surroundings in my mind. Then she asks, "Do you have a sense of a date?"

"It's 1904 . . .," I start. I can see my home and handsome Thomas. "Thomas and I are married. I'm keeping a fine home. We're in marital bliss and have been blessed with a son, Thomas Jr. He is handsome like his father."

"Was there anything significant that happened in your life before 1904, besides your marriage?"

"Well, there was a police riot in 1900. Thomas, thank goodness, was not involved. We've been blessed with good fortune and a bountiful, peaceful existence."

"Okay, with your permission, on the count of three, I would like you to go to the next significant event in that lifetime. One, two, three. Tell me what is happening," Barbara instructs.

In my mind's eye, I jump in time and find myself seven years ahead, in 1911. For a moment, I'm confused and the image is blurry. As it clears, I choke up.

"Oh, it's tragic." My mother cries as she opens the door. I had come to pay a visit to my dear parents.

"What is happening?" I ask as I enter her parlor.

"There is news of a fire at the shirtwaist factory."

"Say it is not so. Did anyone we know perish?" I take my mother's hands.

"Bessie. You remember dear Bessie."

"Of course, we played together as children. I had seen the picketing by many women over the work conditions there."

"Yes, I did too. I mind my own business and don't meddle in other's issues," my mother says.

"My heart breaks for Bessie's parents though. I'm sure they are overcome with grief," I add.

"Let us prepare a meal to bring over to Bessie's parent's house. We will pay our respects."

I wipe a tear from my eye, remembering the tragedy of that day.

"How about your life with Thomas and Thomas Jr.?" Barbara prompts.

Once again, I relax into that dreamy state I've come to love so much.

"It's simply divine. In fact, we've been blessed with another son. Robert, we call him."

"Come let's dance, shall we?" Thomas lifts young Robert up in his arms.

I hold on to Thomas Jr.'s hand. "Yes, I do so love to dance. And now I have three handsome dance partners," I tell my family.

"Who would need a phonograph when one can sing for his family?" Thomas brags and starts to sing. Robert squeals as his papa twirls him around our sitting room. We all laugh and dance as Thomas sings for us.

"Thomas, you are quite the entertainer," I say.

"And your lady friends? Are you still sewing?"

"Margaret and the other women from my sewing circle have been dabbling with Spiritualism. They look to be enjoying themselves. Although I was fearful, they convinced me to join them in a séance. They were connecting with spirits of the departed. It was frightening. I could feel something coursing through me. I worry that something evil entered me. The other women were frightened too. They said they never felt that vibration until I joined. They stared at me as if I were possessed. I pray I did not make a dreadful mistake."

"Okay. Take a deep breath of peace and relaxation and move a little ahead in time to the next significant event."

Again I jump ahead. As the scene clears I find myself shaking. It takes me a moment to find my voice.

"It's . . ." I stop and take a deep breath to relax. In a low voice, I describe the scene in halting phrases, pausing every now and then as the emotion is consuming me. "It's 1918 . . ."

These are trying times. My Thomas has been drafted into the war . . . I'm devastated . . . It has been a fortnight since he left. My love is out there fighting and I fear I may lose him . . . I won't be able to live without him. I try to be strong for Thomas Jr. and Robert.

"When is papa coming back?" Robert asks.

"Soon dear, very soon. We must be brave." I stroke Robert's hair. Thomas Jr. looks out the window as if he is waiting for his papa too. Thomas promised that he would come back to me, though. He said we are meant to be together. It was written in the stars that we will always find each other. I'm holding on to that promise. It is the only thing I have to hold on to . . .

I drift off in Kathleen's world.

"Go on. Take a deep breath. With each breath you take you will be more relaxed and at peace. You are doing well," Barbara says.

"Most men have gone to war . . . There are many deaths. Women have been forced to work men's jobs. And so many are dying here in New York; the Spanish Influenza is taking our children and the elderly daily. Both my parents have perished. My boys, thankfully, are healthy and strong. Thomas Jr. is now fourteen years of age and Robert is twelve."

"Anything else you can share about this time? You can detach from the scene, reporting what is around you like a journalist would."

"We all cut our hair and no one wears bright colors. Everyone joins in mourning . . . The mood is somber. Our clothing is more functional now. I'm wearing a cotton shirtwaist with a skirt that goes to my mid-calf. We do have proper bras now, no more binding corsets," I report to Barbara.

"Good, anything else?"

"I don't want to be here anymore. I'm too consumed with worry."

And with that statement I pop myself out of hypnosis.

Barbara gives me some time to fully come back to the present.

"How do you feel?"

"Um . . . I'm not sure. I grieve the loss of Kathleen's parents and I still feel Kathleen's concern for Thomas. Even though I'm back here, why do I still feel that sense of worry?"

"That's to be expected. Give yourself some time. It will recede. This *was* you and so remembering it will trigger those feelings you had years ago. If you were to recall a troubling time from earlier in this life, you would able to pull up and feel those emotions once again."

My mind goes directly to losing Jared and immediately the depression surfaces.

"Okay, I get it." I shake off that emotion and try to focus on being back in the room with Barbara, letting my eyes take in the comforting colors and textures around me.

"Do you have any questions for me?"

"Well, I don't feel like I got any more clues as to who Thomas is today. Is it because I popped out of hypnosis so suddenly?"

"You will only remember what you currently can handle. I would suggest that you let this experience sit with you for a while and then come back. I believe you'll know when the right time is. Give yourself permission to let this new information seep into you. Watch your dreams and journal your thoughts. Give me a call when you're ready for the next session."

"Okay, that sounds reasonable. I'll do that. Thank you."

Upon leaving the office, I decide to walk the adjoining neighborhood instead of going straight to my car. The sun feels fierce on my shoulders, pressing down much like the weight of this last session. Rationally, I understand that this was many years and past lifetimes ago, but I can't seem to let go of the nagging worry I'm carrying for Thomas, who I have not met in this life. At least I don't think I've met him. It feels like I have feelings for a fictional character, as if I was watching a Superman movie and suddenly felt intense concern for his wellbeing. How do I deal with these strange feelings? How can I get some perspective? If only I felt closer to discovering who Thomas is, but I only feel more confused.

With a deep inhalation, I try to clear my head. Doug would advise me to come back to the present moment by noticing what is around—kids on bicycles, people driving home after a long day's work, and dogs barking to welcome their owners return. Yes, this is real life. Doug is right. The dread feels a little lighter when I focus on now. For the moment, I'll leave New York and the early 1900s behind. In time, when I feel a little stronger, I'll go back and unravel this mystery. For now, I'm going to focus on the present. The writers conference is coming up and this will help me stay grounded. I'm already feeling more at ease. In fact, thinking of the conference is actually exciting to me. Learning about the craft, being with other writers, soaking up their energy, their inspiration, and their dedication to their lonely endeavor is quite appealing. I want to understand them and join their world.

Chapter 22

The thought of three days in the valley fills me with trepidation and excitement. A mixture of emotions well up, hating the valley yet loving the idea of getting away and schmoozing with other writers. Not that I'm really a writer, except for the occasional articles.

"One day, I hope I'll be able to call myself a real honest-to-God book writing author. Until then, I'll blend in and absorb as much as I can. Got my handy notebook to record copious notes, bags are packed, Prince is being watched by Valerie. It's all good," I say aloud as I play with my necklace.

The 405 Freeway is crowded as usual, so I'm glad I left early. Tonight, Friday, is mostly introductions, I would guess, and then tomorrow I'm signed up for workshops throughout the day. There will be a banquet tomorrow evening and, on Sunday, workshops until lunch. Then the long drive home and back to my life of limbo.

Stuck in traffic, my thoughts wander to that God-forsaken valley I left for the beach. My whole family, or what's left of it, is there. Am I going to visit any of them? Hell no! This is my time, my writers conference. Surely I don't want any guilt trips invading it. Richard and Wade probably don't want to see me either. Maybe, since I'm sitting here on the freeway, I can give Mother a quick call and appease my guilt.

"Hello." My mother answers on the second ring.

"Hi Mother, just checking in with you. How are you doing?"

"Fine, dear, and you?"

So far, so good, I think.

"I'm great, thanks."

"Doing anything this weekend? I haven't seen you in a long time."

Is this woman psychic?

"Uh . . . well, yes, I'm currently out of town . . . in San Diego."

Okay. I lied. I can't really say I'll be only a few blocks from her, now can I?

"Oh, drive safe. Talk to Richard? He misses you."

"Mother, stop already. We've been over this. I'm not going back to him. I'm happier this way."

"I never said to go back, just pointing out that he misses you. You made such a cute couple."

"Mother! Look, I gotta go. Need to pay attention to my driving. Love you." I click off before she can respond. Why is the back of my neck so sweaty? How does she have that effect on me, time and time again? I really need a past life session to figure out where she comes into play. Ugh.

The hotel isn't fancy. No matter, I'm ready and open to discover a new world. I can't remember being this eager in a very long time. The elevator deposits me on the fourth floor and my room has a lovely view of a parking lot. Oh well. I sprawl on the king bed and let the cool bedding soothe me. One hour before the "Welcome Workshop," I have a little time to rest and wash up before hitting the conference room downstairs.

Shit. What time is it? How long have I been asleep? Three a.m.? I slept through the welcome and dinner. This is turning out to be a productive conference. I'm wide awake with hours to go before breakfast. Breathe, Tess. Okay, let's make the best of this. The conference layout and workshop brochure is at the foot of the bed; I'll take the time to plan out my next two days. It will be fine. There is a coffee-maker in the room. I'll meditate first, then have coffee, plan what workshops I want to attend, hit the gym, and be ready for breakfast at six-thirty a.m., a little early, but doable.

Meditation is definitely getting easier. A wave of gratitude wells up in me for Doug's patient teaching. I must tell him the next time I see him. He really was a Godsend for me. Calming my mind, taking in the peaceful energy around me and breathing out any anxiety and worry, I fall into an easy pattern. I set an intention of openness and discovery for this weekend.

Before I realize it, an hour has passed. I feel calm, peaceful, and open. Stretching, I turn on the bedside light and make coffee and head to the bathroom while the coffee brews. In minutes the coffee is done . . . ack . . . hotel coffee . . . well can't be too picky right now. With pillows propped behind my back in the bed and coffee beside me, the conference program and pen in hand, I methodically weigh my options to maximize learning this weekend. Ahhh . . . making lists. Now, I'm in my element.

- 7:00 a.m.—Breakfast
- 9:00 a.m.—*Getting over Writer's Block*- Catherine Meyers
- 11:30 a.m.—*Setting the Scene*- Adam Ormand
- Lunch
- 2:00 p.m.—*Character Development*- Joan Berger
- Off for afternoon—networking
- 5:30 p.m.—Banquet
- Sunday
- 7:00 a.m.—Breakfast
- 9:00 a.m.—*Marketing and Publishing Your Novel*- Sid Fleming
- 11:30 a.m.—*Query Clinic*- Daniel Garcia
- Back Home

My schedule set, workout finished, showered and dressed in khakis (of course) and a black blouse, now I'm hungry. The breakfast room is already alive with, I assume, other workshop attendees. Ahh . . . breathe in the writer energy. I glance around and wonder what the others are currently writing. Are they already published? Anyone famous? My eyes dart about and fall on a man with salt and pepper hair, sitting up against the wall to my right. *Oh, there's that guy again.*

What? Why did I think that? I don't remember seeing him before and yet, there was a moment of recognition. In a trance-like state I make my way to the buffet line and grab a plate. Did I see him at check-in? No, I don't think so. Parking lot? No. Huh? I missed the orientation last night. Gym this morning? No, he wasn't there either. Who is he?

"Ma'am? You're holding up the line," a short, heavy man, who looks to be in his seventies, informs me. I realize I'm paused in mid scoop with the scrambled eggs.

"Oh, désolée," I reply and look up to see the man's puzzled look. I make my way through the line quickly. What the heck did I say to him? I meant to say I was sorry and yet I said . . . what was it? Oh yeah . . . désolée. Have I gone off the deep end?

Plunked down at a tiny table facing away from the mystery man, I call Naomi on her cell phone.

"Naomi," I whisper. "I hope I didn't wake you."

"No, Raj and I are sitting on his patio, sipping tea and watching a pod of dolphins. Why are you whispering? How's the conference?"

"Well . . . I missed last night's orientation, so I don't really know yet . . . don't ask. Anyway, I just had a weird experience."

"Another one?" she teases.

"No, this is different. When I came down for breakfast, there was this man and I recognized him. I swear I don't know him, though."

"Past life, maybe?"

"Hmm. I don't know. So, as I was trying to figure out why he seemed so familiar, I was holding up the buffet line and this guy basically told me to move along. Okay, so here is the weird part—I said some word I don't know."

"Wow. What did you say?"

"Uh . . . something like . . . dezo- something. Dezo lay? Maybe?"

"Oh, you must have remembered that from high school French."

"French? I didn't take French. I took Spanish for one year in the tenth grade."

"Well, you must've heard it from somewhere. You told him 'sorry' in French—désolée."

"Oh my God. I meant to say 'sorry' and that other word came out. What do you think it means? This is all too weird."

"I don't know. Stay open and see what happens. Don't get too freaked out. Okay?"

"Yeah, right. No problem," I point out.

"Tess. Seriously. Have a good time. Love you."

"Love you too. Thanks for listening."

I put away my phone and take a deep breath. Wonder if Mystery Man is still here? As discreetly as possible I turn my head. Nope. Good, now I can eat my breakfast in peace. I shovel a forkful of eggs into my mouth—cold and bland. Ugh, lost my appetite.

The first workshop on "Getting Over Writer's Block" was really helpful. Catherine Meyers, the instructor, looked to be in her early forties and was dressed in a bohemian style. She and Naomi would have hit it off. Thank goodness she was engaging and kept my mind from going back to the crazy morning. My notebook was filling up with great ideas and pointers for creating rituals for writing and avoiding the horrid writer's block. Really, what I need to do is actually start writing the book before I need to worry about getting a block. At least now I'll be well prepared for when it happens. Right? According to my schedule, "Setting the Scene" is next. I find room C42 quickly, sign in on the contact list and pick a seat close to the front to keep my mind from wandering.

The room fills up quickly and then *he* walks in. Shit. Mystery Man is taking this workshop too. Hopefully, he'll sit behind me so I can focus on the lecture, but he keeps walking right up to the podium. He's teaching this class? I quickly grab the program—"Setting the Scene"–Adam Ormand. *Adam Ormand?* No, the name doesn't ring a bell, either. I don't know him. No big deal. I'll just focus on what he has to teach. That's what I came for. Nothing more.

"Good morning, everyone. My name is Adam Ormand. Today I would like to share with you some of my tips for setting the scene in your writing." Adam smiles warmly and glances around the room.

My . . . he's kinda cute. Deep voice, a little grey in his hair, giving him that distinguished worldly look, crinkles by his eyes when he smiles. Oh . . . when he smiles. My stomach lurches.

"So, as I was saying, visiting the place you are describing helps convey a sense of realism . . ."

Oh . . . the smallest traces of stubble on his cheeks. So sexy. Wonder what it feels like to kiss him there . . . and . . . God . . . I have butterflies doing somersaults in my belly and a deep pulling down lower. I haven't paid one bit of attention to what he is saying. This is terrible. Here I am sitting right in front, merely feet from him. I need to get out of here; I'm hot, embarrassed, and very uncomfortable. What's wrong with me? This is ridiculous, lusting after this stranger. And he's not a J. I'm wasting my time.

"Thank you. If you have any questions I will be around for a few minutes to answer them," Adam concludes.

With that statement, I bolt out of the room and locate the nearest exit of the hotel—I need air. I gulp the air the minute I'm outside, as if I have been oxygen deprived. With a quickened pace, I head down the street, not having an intended destination, but an intense impulse to get distance between me and Adam. I walk and walk until the area is unfamiliar and holds no residue of the conference. It feels like I have been walking for hours. Eventually, some of the pent up energy has dissipated. Finding myself at *Shack-O-Shakes* I stop in to use the restroom and grab a black forest shake. Heck, I deserve it after that episode.

By the time I make it back to the hotel I have missed the afternoon session, have blisters on my feet, and barely have time to get ready for the banquet. This is turning out to be a winner of a conference. I can't even make it to the workshops.

After arriving late to the banquet, I search for an empty place at a long table. There's one at the end. I try to pull up a chair discretely and pick up the program for this evening. I glance at the planned dinner:

- Chicken—of course
- Roasted Potatoes
- Broccoli—ugh

Can it be any more boring? I roll my eyes in disgust. All these banquet dinners are the same. I must have made a face because I feel eyes on me. Looking up and to my right I see *him*. He has an amused smile on his face. Yikes! I should have scanned the faces first before I chose this seat. I did *not* want to sit across from him. He is way too distracting. What is it about him? I saw him speak earlier today and honestly don't remember a thing he said. I spent the entire hour and a half trying to calm myself down. It was downright infuriating. I felt like I had no control of my own body! My breath was shallow and fast. My heart was racing. My thoughts . . . well, I don't even want to recall that again. I felt like a hormone-raging teenager! This can't be happening. He is not J. I remind myself. *He is not J!* What am I supposed to do with that? I have to get a grip is what I have to do. I am only searching for J. The psychic says he is out there. I can't let him, my Thomas, down. Damn that Adam Ormand!

And now he is sitting across the table from me, smirking. "Not too fond of processed chicken?" he asks.

"No. No, it's fine. Had a little headache from all the lectures today." I stretch in an exaggerated manner. "That's all," I lie. "Oh, not that they caused a headache, just a lot to take in . . ." Sweat beads up on the back of my neck.

"Oh, I see. So my talk gave you a headache, huh? You did look a bit flushed."

Yikes! So trying to look normal earlier didn't work so well. "No, it was great. The rooms were a little warm though." I will him mentally to stop talking. I can't keep this up. I grab my folder and jot down some notes so he'll think I'm too busy to talk. Good idea, I think. Thankfully, my rubbery food arrives. Now I can focus on my meal and not him.

"So, did you enjoy my lecture on setting the scene?" Shit! He's talking again. "Because I feel the best way to describe a location is to walk it and experience it as your character does. For instance, I sail to my locations and spend time there to really let it seep into me," Adam explains.

I perk up. I can tell this is something that he is passionate about. His eyes lit up when he mentioned sailing. Actually, it was cute.

"You have a boat then?" Now I'm talking. Help.

"Yes, I live on it."

"All the time?" I'm intrigued. Live on a boat? Where does he put all his stuff? Does he get claustrophobic? How big is it? Can I go sailing? Where did that come from?

"Yes. All the time," he answers matter-of-factly.

God, that sounds . . . sexy.

"Have you lived on a boat for a long time?"

"A number of years. Buying my boat was one of my best decisions. Enough about me, tell me about your writing plans."

"Oh, they're dreams really. But I've had a few articles published."

"Well, there you go. Not a dream. It's a reality for you. Bravo!"

The server removes my empty plate and places a piece of key lime pie in front of me. Guess I was hungrier than I thought.

"The best key lime pie I ever had was in Homosassa, Florida. Spent time down there swimming with the manatees and writing. The trees and houses made a wonderful backdrop for many stories."

"Wow. I've always wanted to see the manatees up close. I don't have the Florida pie to compare to, but I rate this one a 9.5."

"I would give it a 9.0. However, if I factor in my charming dinner companion, I'd give it a 9.8."

"Ha! Not a 10?" I joke back. He makes talking seem effortless.

"Looks like we closed the place," Adam remarks. I look around and sure enough we're the last in the room.

"Oops," I laugh. "I've been enjoying myself too much tonight."

"See you in the morning?"

"Yes. Goodnight." I really don't want to leave, but what choice do I have?

Back in the room, I'm reeling. It's the best evening I've had in such a long time and yet, I'm sad since this can't go anywhere. If only his name wasn't Adam. Maybe, Jonathan or James, but it's Adam. No getting around that. I go over the night again and again as I lay in bed. My body is alive and tingling. My body wants him. I would jump at the chance to make mad, crazy love to him. My mind plays sexual scenarios—straddling him, him behind me, bathing each other, elevators. Yes, you name it and my mind is playing it, trying it on for size.

I can stand it no longer and have to take matters into my own hands. My hands explore my body as I imagine Adam's hands on me: his strong, slightly rough hands caressing my skin, exploring all the tender and sensitive areas, deftly making my body respond. Mmmm.

I doze off and on the rest of the night. I don't think I got more than three hours sleep, yet surprisingly with as little sleep and food I've received the last two days, I'm full of energy. The hotel gym is empty this morning. I lift weights and run for twenty minutes on the treadmill. Who am I? I get to the breakfast buffet a little after seven a.m., hoping that Adam is here. My breath is catching in anticipation. I feel a pang of disappointment when I don't see him. As I make my way through the breakfast line, I hear a familiar husky voice.

"Sleep well?" Adam is behind me in line.

"You startled me. Uh, yes, I suppose. You?"

"Not really. I couldn't get you out of my mind," he informs me. My heart and stomach are doing a happy dance.

"Oh?"

I make my way through the rest of the line in silence, not sure of what to say next, and head to a small table by the window. Adam, thankfully, decides to join me. How am I going to eat with my stomach all in knots?

"So, where were we?" Adam starts.

"Well, I was telling you about my bike, Ms. Glimmer . . ." As I start to relate my love of cycling, I absentmindedly grab the pepper shaker and hand it to Adam.

"Uh . . . okay. How did you know I wanted pepper on my eggs?"

"I didn't . . . oh . . ." What is going on with me? Somehow, I intuitively knew that he wanted pepper. Naomi is going to freak when I tell her. Adam takes the pepper and shakes some on his eggs. He runs a hand through his hair. He looks thoughtful, as if he is about to ask me another question, but changes his mind.

"Go on. So you named your bike Ms. Glimmer? Are you in the habit of naming things?"

"Yeah, I guess I am . . . the dog down the street, the lifeguard, my meditation teacher . . ."

"Wait, you meditate?"

"Well, learning to. Most of the time I'm struggling with my 'monkey mind' as Doug calls it."

"Doug?"

"Doug is my meditation teacher. He didn't start out that way. I mean, I didn't seek him out. Oh, it's hard to explain. You meditate?"

"No, but been meaning to learn. I guess writing is my form of meditation."

"Yeah, I can see that."

"So what do you write?"

"I've only been journaling my thoughts and I get infrequent article assignments about fitness, but I want to write a book. In fact, I've wanted to write for as long as I remember."

"Well, if the desire is present there is no stopping the words from coming out. I'm sure you'll write incredible work."

Wow. That's so nice to hear, and from a real writer.

"Thank you." I glance up at him and then look away. I feel a strong pull in his eyes and want to fall into them, but resist.

"You know, we'd better hurry if we want to make the next lecture." He checks the time on his watch. It's the first time I noticed it. The watch is stylish, but not pretentious. I love the way the gears are exposed. Good choice, I think.

"Okay . . . yeah . . . right . . . lecture. That's what we are here for, right?" I ask, almost hoping he sways me from the workshop.

"Yes, we are." He grabs my tray and heads to the trash bin. I'm a little disappointed that breakfast is over and, for that matter, the conference will soon be over and Adam will be gone. I shake it off and start after him to see what he's attending. Maybe we're going to the same workshops.

"Which lectures are you going to today?" I ask him.

"The ones you are," he answers easily. Secretly, I'm delighted.

Although we're attending the last two lectures of the conference together, I'm not sure what the point is. I, for one, am completely unable to concentrate. I take out my pad of paper, but can't locate my pen in my bag. Seeing my dismay regarding the loss of my pen, Adam hands me one of his from his bag. Instantly I feel a jolt when his fingers touch mine briefly.

"Thanks," I mouth to him. During the first lecture, "Marketing and Publishing Your Novel," I feel a strong connection to him and enjoy the tingling sensation on my left side, the side closest to his body. It was during the second lecture, "Query Clinic," when things got even stranger.

Maybe it's the close proximity to him or holding on to the pen he gave me, but I can feel his energy emanating from his body, encasing him and me in our own private bubble. Again, I feel short of breath and excited. It's one of the most bewildering and exhilarating experiences I've known. It feels as if the energy keeps building with each breath I take and the energy bubble increases in strength exponentially—breathing and increasing, breathing and strengthening, breathing and building. The power and intensity keeps up at a dizzying pace until I feel I can't contain it any longer. It feels as if the bubble wants to burst and spew its energy over the other workshop attendees. I'm lightheaded and near the point of hyperventilating. Is Adam feeling the same, or is this my private delusion?

No matter how much I try to slow my breathing, the bubble demands more. It is my master now and I breathe into it and increase its strength. Finally, the bubble is filled to capacity and instead of exploding as I imagined it would do, it implodes. I gasp audibly and draw a sharp intake of air. The energy slices through my body. This energy changes form and becomes a raven. The raven, as black as midnight, takes its sharp beak and pierces my heart. The raven soars through my heart, checking out all the chambers and then decides to explore my body by way of my arteries and veins. I can feel the raven diving and soaring through my blood, making its way to every cell of my body. The raven radiates a heat. My first thought is not, *what the heck is a raven doing in my body?* No, it's, *why is the raven hot—shouldn't it be cool like the night?* Mind you, this is all while I'm trying to be very inconspicuous in a classroom full of other people. I keep my eyes straight ahead, but my eyes are not focused on anyone or anything in particular. I'm completely immersed in this surreal experience. I find it both frightening and invigorating. Part of me feels that I'm given a great gift. One that old Tess would have dispelled immediately.

Each area of my body that the raven touches feels alive and awakened, as if it had been asleep my entire life. At this point, I'm not sure that I even care if others know something is going on with me and think I'm strange. I'm completely caught up in the experience and do not want to break free from it. The raven continues its journey, piercing each cell and brushing it with its long blue-black feathers as it flies by. It completes the around-the-body tour and suddenly the raven makes a sharp left turn and starts its ascent towards the top of my head. Straight through the middle of my body, along my spinal cord, it flies. As it reaches my throat, I feel as if I want to sing out, but keep silent. Then it continues between my eyes and as dramatically as it entered my body it shoots through the top of my head in a climax of energy, which pours down around me in all the colors of the rainbow. I feel each color as it bathes me and cools me from the raven's heat. And each color has its own sensation and temperature. Eventually, the sensations subside and leave me to sit quietly in peace, right in time for the lecture to wrap up.

All the lightheadedness and racing heart is gone, leaving me with a sense that all is right with the world. I could live in this feeling forever. Adam stays by my side as we walk out of the classroom. We're both quiet. Did Adam have a similar experience or was the raven's visit meant exclusively for me? I can't ask him, "Hey, did a raven just soar through your veins?" He doesn't offer up any clue that anything extraordinary happened to him either. We walk in silence.

The conference is over and the other attendees are saying their goodbyes and heading out to their cars or bus stops and train stations. What happens now? My mind whirls trying to work out what to do next. Since I can't come with anything to extend the moment, I break the silence.

"Well, I really enjoyed talking to you and hope to see you at another conference. Here's your pen. Thank you for letting me borrow it." I pull it out to hand back to him.

"No, you can keep it. That way you'll have no excuse not to write." He laughs uncomfortably.

Again we are quiet. I sense that neither of us wants to part but really don't see another option. I look up at his face, part of me trying to memorize the details. The soft crinkles around his green eyes, the straight nose, the strong chin, and most of all the mouth. His mouth, which I fantasized about kissing last night, is smiling kindly at me now. His eyes show a little sadness. Does he not want me to leave? *Tess, he's not the one. His name does not have a J in it. You need to be strong and walk away,* I tell myself.

There is a palpable battle occurring between my body and mind. My body wants to grab him and hold on for dear life, but my mind is telling me to get away, and quickly. The impulse to clutch at him moves down my arms. My hands tremble under the struggle as I force myself to keep my hands at my side.

"Okay then, well thanks again," I tell him.

Adam looks pensive as if he is also considering his next move.

"Okay then," he says. He reaches out to embrace me.

I hug him back and it feels oh-so-delightful. I could melt into this hug. His warmth transmits to me and for a moment I feel encased in a safe, snug cocoon. An all-out war rages between my body and mind. My insides tremble and shudder as the internal battle continues. *Not the one,* I remind myself again.

With my willpower, I pull away without as much as a goodbye. *Start walking. Go. Go. Go.* I urge my feet to move. Continuing the mantra of Go. Go. Go. I make it to the safe refuge of my car.

In my entire life, I have never fought impulses so persistent. My body was primed to run back to him the whole way. It was sheer willpower that helped me reach my vehicle. The drive out of the hotel parking lot solidifies that I won't see him again. My eyes tear up. I feel nauseous, a sign that my body is already grieving. It's going to take me a long time to get over this.

Chapter 23

By the time I reach home I'm dead exhausted and, so, quickly retrieve Prince from Valerie, thanking her profusely and promising to catch up soon. Then I crash in the bed with all my clothes on. Prince does his normal kneading on my chest with claws protruding into my flesh before, finally, settling in for the night. I find it strangely comforting, like the claws are a reminder that I am not entirely numb to the world.

I sleep the night through, although when I awake I feel like I have a slight hangover. Maybe it's the residual heaviness I feel that is making me ill. I've got to see Doug. That's what I need right now. I slip on my sweats and grab a travel mug of hot green tea. On the way to the beach, I pass Buddy's house, but he's not out and about at this early hour. When I approach the sand, I exhale deeply with relief when I see the back of Doug's head. He's sitting in his usual lotus position. I hadn't realized I was holding my breath.

I slide down quietly next to him, hoping once again to absorb his calming energy. We sit quietly for a long while and I synchronize my breathing with his. Each breath I take in seems to pull in calm and each breath I let out expels tension. I envision Doug's peace filling me up. Over time I notice that the heaviness has temporarily abated and peace has taken up house. Ah, I could stay in this space forever. In and out, I breathe contentment next to my mysterious friend and mentor.

"How was the conference?" Doug startles me with the break of our shared silence.

"Uh . . . good . . . I guess." I'm confused. I don't remember ever telling Doug about the conference. Maybe I had? I don't know now.

"So . . . you met someone."

"Sort of . . ." I trail off. Doug didn't ask me a question. It was more of a statement. I don't know how to respond.

"Sort of? You did or you didn't."

"Well. It's complicated . . ."

"Go on."

I take a deep breath. I can't explain this crazy tale about J and past lives and Adam not being "the one." What am I going to say?

"Well, technically I met someone, but it can't work out. I can't explain why, just trust me on this."

"Seems like you already made up your mind. Sometimes there is more to a story than you think. Don't limit yourself to what little information you currently have."

"Okay . . . well even so, I didn't get his number and there would be no way to get in contact with him. It's over . . . I'd rather not talk about it if you don't mind." I'm feeling that heaviness creep back in again.

"Tess. You've changed greatly since I met you. I've seen you grow, find more peace, and learn about you. You have learned techniques for grounding and centering and, most importantly, you have learned to trust yourself and your intuition. Don't be completely influenced by outside sources. Always go within and ask what is true for you. That is what you should follow, not what others have pointed out. To find what you seek you must look beyond mankind with his intelligence and wisdom. You must look to nature to see nature. Not just on this tiny speck called Earth, but the whole universe. Not just outside the city limits, but everywhere. Not just what you see around you, but what you see inside you. Everything you wish to know is inside yourself, learn to see it."

What has gotten into Doug? I rarely see him so verbal, or for that matter so direct.

"Uh huh," is all I can muster. Yup, so deep, Tess, I chide myself.

We sit in silence. Me trying to come up with something to say and Doug . . . well, who knows?

"It is time for me to move on, Tess."

"What!?" Okay, now I'm awake.

"A while back, I explained that I go where I feel called to go. Well, I also move on when I feel that my purpose has been fulfilled."

"You were called to be here because of me?"

"I believe so. And this morning I felt a deep sense that whatever it was I was here for was completed. It's time for me to move on."

"Where will you go?" I cry out an octave higher than I intended. A panic is rising within me.

"I never know. I go until I feel compelled to stop again. My instincts tell me to go north though, if that helps."

"Not really. This isn't a good time for me to be without you. Couldn't you stay a little longer, until I get over this gloominess I feel?" I know I sound desperate, but come on. I'm still reeling over Adam, and now this?

"You don't need me. You're powerful. You need to own it. Breathe it in."

I stare at him, dumbstruck. He's kidding, right? Nope. He looks darn serious. First I can't breathe and then something deep down takes over. I focus intently on just breathing. Natural breathing . . . we all do it, I tell myself. In . . . out . . . life is falling apart and I'm still breathing. It's something. For the next half hour or so, Doug and I sit and breathe. I try to imagine me being a powerful woman like he said I am. I visualize myself breathing in the energy around me from nature and fortifying myself with it. I do feel better, more sure of myself than when we started. Maybe I can do it.

Without ceremony, without a word, Doug stands up and walks away. I know I won't see him again and don't turn around to watch him go. I can't bring myself to. I don't cry, either. I just sit and breathe the way he taught me. Somehow, I know that's the best way to honor a dear friend that gave me so much.

I'm not sure how long I sat on the beach; my legs are cramped and hunger is gnawing at me. Standing up is slow and stretching painful. It's like I am purposely punishing myself, for what, I don't know. Slowly, I head home. My body and mind are still heavy, even after all that breathing energy. I feel alone again.

The stairs to my apartment look to be too much to tackle right now and so, as I did many months ago, I plop myself down on the curb. Hmm. Weeds need to be pulled again. Fear bubbles up inside me. Am I in the same spot I was on that terrible day on the curb when I had no energy to move? I'm secretly willing Valerie to come out and save me again. Paralysis takes over. I can't breathe. My chest is pressing down on me, strangling the air from my lungs. I can't go back to that day. Panic is setting in. I cross my arms to feel the whale-fluke tips press into my breasts, some reassurance that I'm alive.

Hush now. You're fine. Just breathe.

Was that me talking? Okay. It's confirmed; I'm officially insane. I'm hearing voices. Soothing, caring voices that seem like they are trying to help me, but voices just the same.

Hush dear. You're strong and I'm here with you. Breathe it in.

"Jared? Is that you?" Is he finally answering back? Oh God, could he really hear me all this time? How embarrassing. I really thought I was talking to myself. Who is with me? God? An angel? A spirit guide? What is it? At least I feel less of a panic; worrying about voices in the head does help one focus, I guess.

Call me whatever feels best. Labels do not matter, but you can call me your higher self. I am always here for you.

Okay. So am I literally talking to myself? Well, at least I know me well, no need for formal introductions.

Doug helped you to see what was always there. Don't dishonor him by not realizing your strengths and gifts. Follow your intuition. It won't let you down. Jared has his path, you have yours. Now get up off this curb and live your life!

Fine! Now I am in a shouting match with myself. It's strange, but the voice seems like it is me, a wiser me. And I hate to admit it but she, er me, is right. Doug did teach me a lot and yes it was nice having him around, but it really isn't necessary anymore. I've been hiding behind the safety of having him there. And I have been testing out my intuition, which proved correct many times. Before I would have ignored it, yet my life was falling apart. When I have been following it, life has improved.

As I mull over this tiny epiphany, I notice that, once again, I have weeded the curb. Guess some things never change. Hey, I'm improving the neighborhood, right? With one more deep cleansing breath, I stand up with ease. Lighter somehow, in my body and mind. Although it could just be that I missed breakfast. I may have lost Doug and a shot at Adam, but at least I didn't lose my humor.

Prince greets me at the door with his incessant meow. He's hungry too. I pour kibble in his dish, then grab a bowl of granola for myself and sit on the balcony. It's peaceful here listening to the wind chimes and watching the street below. I've got my whole life ahead of me. What shall I choose to do with it? I actually feel a tad inspired. I recite a new list:

- Well, I do want to write a book
- Hmm. I would like to have a creative outlet, something to do with my hands
- I'm eventually going to have to do something to support myself; my money from the business won't last forever
- I plan to continue my search for J. Maybe go out with Jesse again as Naomi suggested?
- One of these days, I need to make another appointment with my past life therapist to see what happens with Kathleen and Thomas
- Looking forward to helping Naomi plan her wedding

Chapter 24

It's been weeks since Doug left and, surprisingly, I've fallen into a nice comfortable routine. Still talk to Jared—it's a soothing habit. Been journaling a lot and thinking of writing either a non-fiction book on fitness and meditative bicycling or maybe a memoir. I find that it works well to jot down ideas in my journal that I keep in my backpack. If I'm riding around town and notice the way the sun glints off the sign of a Lebanese café, for instance, suddenly I'm mesmerized by its beauty. Next thing I know I stop, whip out my trusty journal and write in the moment. Writing has become part of my meditative practice, just like Adam talked about. I understand where he's coming from now.

I feel a lot stronger, too. That experience on the curb where I was talking to myself really helped me turn the corner. Doug's old spot on the beach, I've claimed for my own. It feels comfortable to sit daily where he sat for many months. The sand in this special place, seems to me, is imbued with his energy.

"I know it sounds crazy, in fact, don't tell anyone, Jared, but I took a little of it home with me and put it in a small, clear, glass vase. It sits on my counter with some other shells and pebbles I have collected during my many contemplative walks along that stretch of beach. The vase of 'Doug's sand' gives me a constant reminder of his teachings."

Color fascinates me like it never has before. I'm not sure if it's because I'm more attentive to details for writing or it's due to my new perspective. But I can't live in the drabness anymore. For years I have dressed in somber colors, like Kathleen did during the war. I feel a fog lifting and those colors don't suit me anymore. Last week I bought bright tanks and festive yoga pants. I feel alive in these new colors. I've also been thinking about my desire for a creative outlet.

In my new vibrant attire I ride the strand. I have my trusty backpack in the basket and once more stop to write on the spot. This time I'm inspired by a three-legged shepherd that does not seem at all troubled by the fact that one of his legs is missing. As I'm pulling out my journal from the backpack, I get to thinking—I can make a backpack too. Not that I have ever been much of a seamstress, but it occurs to me that I probably have a latent talent for sewing. Kathleen could sew so that means if I'm her then, I too, can sew.

With this new conviction, I head straight to Esther and Buddy's house to discuss the idea. Esther's delighted and offers to assist me with my notion to be creative. We head to the fabric store and choose a variety of fabrics, from soft suede to bright cotton and flannel patterns. Basically, I let my intuition guide me as we stroll through the shop, touching each fabric and eyeing all the colors that dazzle me. I have my arms full of my new treasures, including a small sewing machine that Esther recommends as we leave the store. She assures me that I will learn quickly. "Okay, sure thing," I tell her. But I have a huge smile on my face. Somehow, I know I will create something fantastic.

Back at Esther's home, we lay out all the various fabrics while Buddy watches us with interest. Esther spends the time teaching me the basics of sewing, from laying out the fabric, cutting, and working the sewing machine. After two hours I feel I have the basics down on how to make a cute and attractive bag for my bike basket.

"Thank you so much, Esther, for taking the time to teach me."

"Are you kidding? I should be thanking you; I had company for many hours and got to talk about a subject I love. What could be better?"

I give her a big hug, gather up my belongings and head for home to start my new project. As soon as I get home Prince takes to checking it all out. I'm not sure if he likes the fabrics or smells Buddy. He's probably thinking I'm a traitor. With blues playing in the background, I make a cup of tea and set to work. I grab my scissors and choose a piece of fabric with dragonflies on it just as Prince decides that is where he wants to lie down. Humph. I need a decoy cloth for him.

"Wow, this corduroy is fabulous. I'm definitely going to use this one first," I call out to the air and make a move to grab it when Prince gets up from the dragonfly fabric and heads for the corduroy.

Hah! It worked. Now with the preferred fabric, I cut out the pattern that Esther taught me. And then consider the other rolls of fabric, choosing a lining of flannel. In a meditative state, I assemble a bag and sew it together. By the time I look at the clock it's after midnight. The time flew by and I felt completely at home and peaceful the entire time. My project is complete. I'm left in awe of my handiwork. It's a colorful, drawstring bag lined in emerald green flannel with shoulder straps and a pocket for small change and keys. I take my bag out the front door and down the steps to my garage where Ms. Glimmer is resting. I have to see how my new creation works in the bike basket. Aha! It fits perfectly; the opening is large enough to spread around the lip of the basket if I choose to use it as a basket liner. And then I can tighten up the drawstring to close and sling the straps over my shoulders for a fun purse/backpack.

Yippee! I'm ecstatic and spontaneously start doing a little happy dance in my garage. I want to sing out. I am creative! Who knew? And I went completely by instinct. Well, with a little help from Esther. This is most definitely a good day. I kiss my new bag and hug it to my chest then close the garage. "Good night, Ms. Glimmer. We'll go out tomorrow," I whisper to my bike and head up the stairs to go to bed.

I awake early, as always, but with a new happiness in my heart. My mind is already planning new color schemes for other bags. I can give them as gifts. Naomi has asked me to help her pick out flowers for her wedding this afternoon, but I have the morning to meditate, ride a bit, and then start a new bag. Maybe this one will be for Naomi. On impulse, I text Wade.

Hi. Hope you are doing well? I'm doing good. Been riding my bike and sewing and writing. Miss you.

I don't expect an answer. At least he knows I'm still here and ready for him if, or when, he wants to talk. I got a two bedroom apartment hoping he would someday visit. It sits empty, but for the first time, I'm okay with that, surprisingly. Boy, have I changed.

When I ride up and down the strand, I note an energy buzzing in me. Maybe it's the colors I now wear or my new bag. I'm not sure, but I like this new me. Sewing yesterday felt right, like it was a natural process. I feel grateful for Kathleen giving me that, if she really did. It may have come from another life. I'm sure I've had other lives and have talents from those that I haven't tapped.

It's been a while since I looked into that time period. I feel like I hit a wall and could go no further. Thomas' song still plays in my mind in the early mornings and no matter how much internet research I do I can't find that tune. Why couldn't he have sung the right words? Maybe I need to see Barbara for another regression to get more information and finally get to the bottom of how their lives turned out. I feel that until I do, Thomas' song will continue to play in my head.

That's it. I'm done sulking. It's time I got off my ass. I'm going to make another appointment with Barbara. Find out more about Thomas and Kathleen and the children they had. And I am going to go out on date with Jesse. Keep focused on the search for Thomas/J and forget about that distracting Adam! Wait until Naomi gets a load of the new and improved Tess. Shit! I'm going to be late to meet her if I don't hurry.

*

"Naomi!" I yell out from across the street where I've parked. She's standing on the corner in front of the florist. Does she look peeved? I squint my eyes in the sun.

"You're twenty minutes late." Yup. She's peeved.

"So sorry, got sidetracked. I'm all yours now. Please, please forgive me." I give her my best sorry puppy look.

"Stop." She smiles at me. I can see all is forgiven. Man, I gotta patent that look.

"So, sweetie, what are you thinking of, colors, type of flowers?" Get the subject back on the bride, quickly.

Naomi grabs my arm and we walk inside the shop together. "Come, let's see what strikes us? Deal?"

"Sounds perfect." I love seeing her this happy.

"Can I be of assistance?" A well groomed sixty-ish woman with alabaster white hair and red, trendy, plastic framed glasses asks.

"Oh yes. My dearest friend here is getting married early next year and she would like to look at flower choices," I announce.

"Well. We have some exciting choices for a winter wedding. Come over here and we can go over some suggestions. I'm Gretchen, and what is your name, dear?" gesturing to Naomi.

"Hi, Gretchen. I'm Naomi and this is Tess. She's helping me plan a few things for the wedding."

"Fabulous. What colors were you thinking? Winter whites are always popular, like calla lilies, amaryllis, tulips. Or there are reds. For instance, roses, anemones, gloriosa lilies . . ."

"Hmmm. Can you give us a moment?" Naomi asks.

"Of course. Let me know if you have any questions or want to know if a specific flower will be available."

Naomi pulls me to the side and Gretchen graciously makes herself scarce.

"What's up?" I inquire.

"I don't know. There are so many choices and decisions to make. I'm feeling stuck just on the flowers. Tell me what kind of flowers to get. You've been married before, you know what to do." There is a hint of panic in her normally even-keeled voice.

"Hey. Hey. Naomi, breathe. It's all fine. I don't need to tell you anything. Look inside yourself. You already know what the perfect flowers are for your wedding." I shock myself with my words. This sounds like something Doug would say. Has he rubbed off on me?

Naomi closes her eyes and I hold her hands. We breathe together, synchronizing our breath, connecting and calming.

"You're right, Tess. I see the perfect flowers in my mind's eye: orchids. I see white orchids. It's beautiful. Thank you. That really helped." She hugs me tightly and kisses my cheek.

"Let's go find Gretchen," I encourage.

"Yes and then let's go to the café for coffee and catch up. Then you can tell me what you did with old skeptical Tess? And where in the world you got that adorable bag?"

"Oh that old thing," I laugh. "Actually I made it last night."

"Get out of here. That's amazing."

"Thanks, yeah, I'm happy with how it turned out."

"So, have you come to a decision?" asks Gretchen.

"Yes, I was wondering if white orchids would be available?" Naomi replies.

"Oh, yes, we can get that. We can pair it with a sage green lamb's ear. It would be exquisite. Good choice."

"Okay, let's write it up," Naomi gushes.

"Do you have a restroom?" I ask.

"Yes, it's down the hall and to the right," Gretchen directs me.

"Thank you." I head off towards the bathroom. Looking back I can see the two of them sitting down with a catalog and order form. As I return, they're still discussing corsages and boutonnieres.

"Hey, Tess, gotta pen?" Naomi calls to me.

"Yeah, check my bag," I yell back at her. I'm distracted by the vibrant orange of a gerbera daisy. Can that be real or is it dyed? I wonder.

I wander back to Naomi and Gretchen who are engrossed in conversation and freeze mid step. *No!*

"No! Not that pen! You can't use that pen. Not Adam's pen," I cry out louder than I expected to.

"What the heck, Tess? What's the big drama about?"

I grab the pen from her hand and simultaneously reach in my bag to grab another, benign, writing instrument. I hand her the substitute and clasp tightly to Adam's pen. Naomi looks at me with this look that says, "Yup she's really lost it," but takes the approved pen and continues with her form.

"We'll talk about *this* later." She waves her arm up and down at me as if to emphasize what "this" is. *Got it.* That's when it dawns on me that I'm acting irrational. I look down to find that I'm still grasping the pen tightly with both hands to my chest. Maybe I have lost it?

With my wits gathered, I place the pen safely in the side pocket of my bag and walk outside for some fresh air and away from prying eyes. Breathe in peace, breathe out stress. Breathe in . . .

"There you are," Naomi interrupts my meditation. "Let's get some coffee and then you can explain."

"Ok." Why do I feel like a child about to go to the principal's office?

The coffeehouse is packed with mostly teens and young college kids cramming for exams. Although they seem to do more chatting than studying while they sip their frozen drinks and munch on pastries. I don't blame them. I did the same when I was in college, hanging out at cheap diners and munching on French fries with bleu cheese dressing. Ah . . . good times.

Naomi claims a table by the bathroom and I grab us two lattes. Naomi discretely twirls her red hair. A dead give-away to me that she's anxious. Even though I can see she's nervous, to the rest of the world she looks calm and serene. She would be great at poker. I'm completely the opposite. I would give my hand away every time. I can't hide a single emotion. Naomi smoothes her hair and skirt and sits poised waiting for me to return. My, she's lovely. She'll be a beautiful bride.

"Here you go." Setting Naomi's drink down, I pull my chair in close to her so we can talk over the background chatter.

"Thank you. Now that we have the flowers ordered and I can cross that off my long to-do list, I want to know what got into you back at the shop? Who are you? Where did you put Tess?" Naomi tells me half teasingly, trying to hide confusion.

"I'm really sorry about that. I don't know what got into me."

"Come on. Don't lie to me. You've shared all the weird happenings with me, don't close up now."

"You're right," I admit, defeated. "It's not that I don't want to share, it's more that I don't know where to start. I've had a confusing time since the writers conference."

"Okay. Start there. Last I heard you were speaking French out of the blue."

"Just one word," I correct her.

"Yes, it was désolée. I remember. Go on. What happened next?"

"There was this guy at the conference. I called him Mystery Man. I felt as if I knew him."

"Yes, I thought maybe it was past life related."

"Yeah, right. Well every time I tried to avoid him, there he was. He was even teaching one of the workshops I went to. We ended up talking at dinner and the next day at breakfast. I really enjoyed his company. On the last day I couldn't find my pen and he gave me his."

"Ah. *The Pen*. I get it. So far, so good. What's his name?"

"There's the problem. He's not a J. His name is Adam Ormand," I sigh.

"Oh. I see. And now you are trying to focus on other projects. Like sewing?" She points to my new bag.

"Kind of. There's more to the story. When I got back from the conference I was depressed and needed to see Doug."

"Doug?"

"Yes. My transient, beach-sitting, tai chi-practicing, meditation-teaching, guru and friend."

"Wow. That's a mouthful," she giggles.

"Guess it is." And I start laughing too. How else can you explain the enigma that Doug is?

"And did he help you?"

"I met him at our spot on the beach and sat for a while and then, that day, he announced that it was time for him to move on."

"What!?"

"Yeah, that's what I thought. I practically begged him to stay, but he told me I didn't need him anymore. He said that I was a powerful woman who should trust her intuition."

"That I agree with and have been telling you for years."

"I know. You're right. After he left, I felt even more depressed and sat again on the curb in front of my apartment. I'd wondered if I hadn't progressed and was back at square one. Then I heard a voice."

"A voice? Wow, your stories really keep one interested. You should write them down."

"Hmmm. I've been thinking of writing a book. Maybe you're right. Back to the voice—first I thought I was crazy and then the voice told me it was my higher self. It told me that Doug was right; I should trust my intuition. Then it yelled at me to get off my ass and live life."

"Yelled out?"

"No, in my head. I yelled back."

"That must have been a scene."

"Thankfully it was not out loud. At least I don't think it was."

"Ha."

"Then I got up from the curb and something sort of shifted in me. For the first time in a long, long time, I decided to take control of my life. All of a sudden I saw possibility. I made a list."

"A list . . . some things never change."

"Okay, I like lists. On this list were things I wanted to do. I wanted more color in my life."

"Hence the new clothes?"

"Yeah, and I wanted to be more creative. Hence the bag. And I decided to focus my attention on finding J, learning the rest of the story of what happened to Kathleen and Thomas and, most of all, forget about Adam."

"Yeah. How's that working? You know, the forgetting about Adam thing?"

"Fine. So I had one little setback with 'The Pen Incident.'" Rolling my eyes, I make air quotes with my fingers.

Naomi reaches out and gives my hand a squeeze. "I'm just saying that maybe there's more to this pen incident than you realize. Maybe you shouldn't completely shut Adam out."

"What are you saying? First you tell me that I should be doggedly focused on finding J. If you remember, it was your psychic friend that gave me the initial J and you helped me make a list to find him and now you're backtracking?" I say a little louder than expected.

"Shhh. People are turning around."

"Sorry." I lower my head and hide behind my hair.

"Hey, no big deal. I don't know what I'm saying. I can tell that this guy really affected you and no matter how much you try to deny it, I don't think it will go away. I've never seen you like this about any guy, even Richard."

"I know. I know. Oh, Naomi, he's so sexy and funny and smart and we talked for hours without me even realizing how much time went by. He writes and teaches and lives on a boat. A boat! I couldn't sleep or eat much that whole conference. It was insane and amazing. And, I forgot to tell you, I had this connected energy bubble thing with him. I don't even know how to explain it."

"Wow, sounds great. So what are you going to do?"

"I don't know and it doesn't matter anyway; we didn't exchange numbers. Even if I wanted to contact him I couldn't . . ." Suddenly I'm feeling sad again.

"I get it. I don't mean to bring you down. So that's why the creativity is coming out then?"

"I'm not sure what sparked it. I feel like I tap into Kathleen when I'm sewing—probably my imagination."

"Maybe not. Let me see your bag."

I hand over my bag to Naomi. While she examines my handiwork I chew on my coffee stirrer, making it unusable.

"My God, Tess. This is really amazing. I can't believe you did this yourself. Without a pattern?"

"Yes, used my 'intuition.'" I air quote again, causing both of us to laugh.

"Seriously, it's remarkable. The stitching, the design, all of it. It's practical and attractive."

"Yes, it fits perfectly in my bike basket and then I pull the drawstring and it makes a cute bag to take around town."

"You're planning on making more, right?"

"Um. I thought I could make some and give them as gifts."

"No. You have to sell these. They'll go like hotcakes. I know some people that may be interested."

"Really?" Blushing at her praise, I wonder if it's plausible.

"Yes really. How long did it take you to make this?"

"One evening."

"You're kidding. That's amazing. Well, we have to think of a name for it. Have any ideas?"

"Uh, I haven't thought about it . . . *Bike Gear?*"

"No. It needs to be catchy and appeal to more than bicyclists."

"Okay. Do you have any ideas?"

"Well, let's think of something you like."

"Like cycling or writing, cats, beach, pears, boats?"

"That's it!"

"What's it? What did I say?"

"We'll call it *Pear Wear*. It's perfect."

"*Pear Wear?* Yeah, *Pear Wear*. I love it."

"Okay, it's a done deal. Get to work, make a few and get them to me a.s.a.p. I'll see what I can arrange on my end."

"I don't know how you end up talking me into these things, first searching for J and now creating *Pear Wear*. But, you're right. It's a good idea. I'll get to work on it tonight."

This time, before I set to work on the bags for Naomi, I pick up some comical pear patches at the fabric store and put together a makeshift studio in the unused spare bedroom of my apartment.

"Well, if Wade ever comes to visit I can pack this stuff away—it's only temporary," I tell Jared.

I kinda like my new "sewing studio." I put a cheap fountain in the corner and hang more Tibetan prayer flags around so I'll be surrounded by color. Put a desk in there and my sewing accoutrements in the drawers. On an old bookshelf, I neatly stack the fabric—in order of the colors of the rainbow.

A feeling of contentment wells up in me as I pause to take in my new workspace, but it's quickly squelched by my inner taskmaster telling me to sit down and sew, dammit. Okay, tea next to me, the CD playing my favorite blues singer belting out his raspy tunes in the background, phone turned off, Prince checking out the new layout, I'm set.

The evening seems to flow without too much effort, except for poking myself with the needle twice. Overall I'm getting the hang of it and have already figured out shortcuts—cutting more than one piece at a time, sewing more than one seam at a time. By the end of the evening I have three bags done. All that is left to do is to place my pear patch on the lower right corner. That can wait until tomorrow morning. I'm beat. I turn off my sewing machine and power up my phone again, tidy up the office, grab Prince, who had made a bed on a pile of suede fabric, and close the door to the studio.

Two voice messages? No one calls, but the minute I turn off my phone I miss two calls.

"Hi Tess. This is Jesse. Just wondering what you're up to and maybe if you wanted to grab a drink sometime. We haven't talked much since we had coffee. Hit me up when you can. Later."

Jesse, that's weird. I've been meaning to call him up for a date anyway. Maybe it's a sign. I hit "save" and play the next message:

"Uh, ahem . . . This is Adam Ormand. I hope it's not inconvenient or inappropriate for me to contact you like this. You see, uh, you left your contact information on my sign-in sheet and well . . . to tell the truth . . . uh, you've been on my mind. Let me tell you what, if you would like to go out for dinner and talk some more, give me a call. If not, and if my call was unwelcome, then please accept my apology. Your cell phone should have captured my number. Good night Tess . . . and oh . . . okay well . . ."

Chapter 25

Shit! How am I going to sleep now? I press save, then double check to make sure *his* message is still there and head to the bedroom, flopping on my bed. Shit . . . Shit . . . I never expected to hear from Adam again and now there's that familiar fluttering in my belly. Damn him. What was the long pause at the end of his message? Did he want to say something else or . . . maybe he was rethinking calling me?

"Oh, he's so polite and his voice is sweet and sexy. Seemed earnest . . . right, Jared?"

Let me listen to the message just one more time to check.

I play his message, listening to his voice again and again . . . and again. In fact, I'm not sure how many times that message played, but soon I'm quite familiar with his intonation and pacing. Eventually I must have drifted off to sleep with my phone lying on my chest.

You're singing the wrong words, Thomas . . . no don't leave . . . I can't live without you . . . need peace . . . wait, I hear you singing again . . .

Mmmm . . . the warm sun, lying in the soft grass and looking up at the green leaves of the pear tree. Overripe pears cover the ground . . . strong arms, hands caressing my breasts, moving down to my belly, down to my moist rose . . . oh . . . please . . .

I awake drenched in sweat and horny as hell. Why can't I ever have sex in my dream? No, I always wake before I get to the good part. I haven't had sex in what feels like forever and then I get teaser dreams. Was that Thomas in the pear orchard with me? Well no wonder I'm damn near orgasmic when I eat pears—must be past life related.

With my computer across my lap, I google "pear orchards, New York, 1915." Sure enough there were pears in the New York area. I sure don't remember that with Thomas, but who knows. I see that pears were prevalent in France and China too. Don't remember being in China. France . . . hmm. Désolée . . . I said a French word. Probably just a coincidence. And ,while I'm thinking about it, since when do I refer to my vagina as a "moist rose"? Jeez! That definitely was not me from this time period. Get with the times, girl.

*

When I wake up again, I'm blurry-eyed from lack of deep sleep. Between the voice messages and the past life dreams I feel exhausted and yet wired with excitement, or maybe it's due to anxiety. What am I going to do? Do I make the date like I planned with Jesse, or skip over him and move right to Adam? Even though my stomach flips at the mere mention of Adam I know I'm wasting my time. He's not a J. How many times must I remind myself? Maybe I should talk to Naomi about it. I wish Doug was here. He would at least let me ramble on about my issues. No. I'm a strong independent woman. I can figure this out by myself. A cup of tea, the beach, and a visit with Buddy will help me clear my head. That's what I need—a predictable routine. I feel better already.

*

I covet my spot of the beach, well, it used to be Doug's spot. It's mine now and I've noticed I'm quite territorial. I become uncomfortable, close to hostile, if I see anyone encroaching on our spot. It has become sort of sacred to me. I know that's not rational, but it does make me feel better and somehow still connected to Doug. I wonder who he's helping now; another lost girl like me? Maybe a drug addict that wants to clean up his act, or an elderly homeless woman that doesn't know where to turn. I'm sure whatever it is, he is giving them one-liners and opening them up to healing. They're fortunate to have him come across their paths. I miss him so, but happy that someone else can benefit.

And so I sit quietly, breathe in and out with the in and out of the waves, and find my serenity once more. While I listen quietly to my deep inner self I silently ask my question, "What should I do?" I know that's not very specific, but that's all that came to me. I wish I was more profound. Oh well. Away, I push the worries and replace them with peace until I'm no longer caring about the answer to my question and I'm content.

Just as I'm resting in a peaceful place . . . *call Jesse* speaks in my inner mind. Call Jesse? So I was right. I shouldn't go out with Adam. Jesse is the one? Can it really be? I open my eyes and desperately scan the beach for any sign of him. I want to see now if he is Thomas, but he's nowhere to be found. Okay. I will put Adam out of my head and focus on Jesse. Time to start my life.

I head over to Buddy's house and visit my good friend. He's waiting for me like he knew I was coming. It's uncanny. I start my routine of scratching him under his collar as he prefers. He has me well trained.

"Good morning Tess. Out visiting Buddy, or Midnight as you call him?" Esther asks as she opens her front door to greet me.

"Yes. He always brightens my day."

"He has that effect on most people—special boy. How are the bags coming along?"

"Good. Made three more last night. My friend, Naomi, says she may know people that are interested in buying them. Can you believe it?"

"Well, of course, after all you did learn from a master seamstress," she teases.

"Yes, I sure did. I really appreciate you taking the time to help me out that way."

"It was my pleasure and I enjoyed the company."

"I hope you have a good day. Talk to you soon. Goodbye Buddy." I give him a kiss on his head and start for home. Time to call Jesse. Why don't I feel more excited?

We decide to meet at a local Mexican restaurant known for their good food and better margaritas. I feel like I could use one now as I fidget with my blouse. I was at a loss as to what to wear tonight. I'm not feeling sexy, but I don't want to come off as prudish. I opted for linen slacks and a blouse of corals and muted greens—classy and understated. While I wait outside of the restaurant my mind wanders back to the writers conference and Adam's eyes when he smiles. My stomach flips. No! Focus on Jesse. Doug told me to trust my inner voice and my inner voice told me to call Jesse. Don't listen to your head or heart. It has steered you wrong many a time. I close my eyes and take a couple of calming breaths. When I open them Jesse is standing no more than two feet from my face, breaking me from my hard-sought calm.

"Whoa, you scared me."

"What were you doing? Sleeping standing up?" he jokes.

"Yeah, good one. No, I was practicing some of the meditation techniques Doug taught me." "Doug?"

"My friend that did the tai chi on the beach?"

"I don't know who you're talking about."

"We sat together almost every day." I shake my head in disbelief.

"What are you talking about?"

Now my calm is completely gone and I'm getting pretty darn annoyed.

"What are *you* talking about? We were good friends. I miss him," I exclaim.

"Okay. Okay. Don't mean to upset you." He shrugs his shoulders in resignation.

This date is not starting off on a good note. I rack my brain trying to find a way to get it back on solid footing.

"You want to go in and get some food?" Jesse asks.

"Sounds good." I grab his arm in a gesture of peace and smile sweetly. I'll deal with my feelings of anger later.

We're led to a small table in the center of the room where I feel as if I'm the center of attention. I much prefer tables against the wall or out of the way, but I'll make the best of it. Jesse is dressed pretty casual in keeping with his laid-back surfer persona. In jeans and a pull over long sleeve shirt he looks relaxed. Am I over-dressed? Don't get fixated on your outfit now, focus on connecting with Jesse, I remind myself.

Our waiter arrives to ask us what we would like, saving me from awkward conversation for the moment. I peer up from my menu and meet Jesse's eyes. I sure don't see anything there that looks familiar or especially deep. All I see is that he's hunky and so dang young.

"You wanna drink?" Jesse asks me.

"Yes, that would be nice—a margarita on the rocks, no salt, please."

"I'm having the chimichanga, you?"

"Uh . . . chicken enchiladas sound good."

Jesse gives the server our order and we are left, once again, with each other. Now what?

"So Jesse, is there anything else that interests you besides being a lifeguard and surfing?" Why did that sound like a mother disapproving of a child's career choice?

"Well, I like skateboarding too."

"Oh, skateboarding is cool. My son lives for skateboarding." Now I sound really old.

"How old is your son? Does he surf too?"

"Almost sixteen years old. And no he doesn't surf. He lives in the valley with his father."

"What about you? What interests you?"

"Well, I like writing, meditating, and fitness. I ran a gym for many years."

"Oh. So you're a personal trainer? I was thinking of doing that."

"You would probably be really good at it. You're in great shape and I'm sure you would have no trouble passing the test. I don't work right now. We, my ex-husband and I, owned the gym, but I sold out my portion in the divorce."

"That must've been hard."

"No, not really. The hardest part was leaving Wade, my son."

Our food arrives and we eat in silence. My margarita is gone and I'm feeling more relaxed. Jesse isn't so bad after all. I could do worse. He's young, cute. I would make others jealous if I walk down the street with him. Yeah, not a bad image. But what about when I get older and my body goes to hell in a hand basket or we run out of things to talk about. It's not like we really have that much in common. In fact, I feel kinda bad.

I'm basically only going out with him because his name starts with a J. Tess, what the hell are you doing? Deep down I know he's not Thomas. He couldn't be. I'm just not feeling it. I can't figure out why my inner voice told me to call him for a date though.

"Tess. Earth to Tess."

"Oh, sorry. Spaced out for a moment."

"Yeah, you do that a lot. Hey . . . why did you agree to go out with me? You don't seem too into it?" Jesse seems earnest.

Wow. I didn't expect that. How the heck am I going to respond? I really can't tell him the truth. "Oh hey, Jesse. I only went out with you because your name starts with a J and I'm looking for my love from a past life." Yeah, that'll never work.

"What do you mean? Of course I wanted to go out with you. You're a catch. I went out with you because you're sweet and cute. It's just that I realize we have quite an age gap and many different interests. I really don't want to keep you down. I hope you understand."

"Yeah, I can see that. Thank you for being honest. I like you, but I see we're very different. Hey, we share the love of the beach, right?"

"Right. Thank you for being so understanding with such a flaky girl. I know I must have frustrated you."

"A little. No worries. It's all good."

"Spoken like a true surfer. Let me pay for dinner since I caused all the turmoil."

"Thanks," Jesse says without protesting.

After I pay the bill, he walks a little ahead to get the door for me and once again I notice how perfect his ass is. Am I being a fool? Nah. It's for the best. It's really not fair to either of us.

"Hey, thanks for dinner, Tess. Good night kiss?"

"Sure."

He leans in to kiss me and his soft, full lips meet mine. His lips are warm and his breath has a hint of alcohol from the margarita. I keep my eyes open for a moment and look deep into his, in case there's a moment of recognition. Nope. I give in to the kiss. Without any expectations, I actually enjoy his short kiss. Soft, supple, not demanding like Jim—sweet. But not Thomas.

Chapter 26

"I want all the details," Naomi demands as we are served our glasses of Pinot Noir from Sonoma. We are tucked into a quiet corner of a wine bar in Seal Beach. Quiet, simple, and with Naomi—perfect.

"I don't know what to say. I'm a little confused. The date was fine, maybe a bit uncomfortable since we don't have much in common. Overall, it was fine."

"But . . . you said you were confused?"

"He's not Thomas."

"How can you be sure?"

"I just know. There wasn't a hint of recognition in his eyes or kiss."

"Kiss? You kissed him?" She leans forward as if she is about to receive juicy gossip. I feel like I'm back in high school.

"Yes. Sort of a goodnight/goodbye kiss. We talked about it. We're okay."

"You told him about your search?" Naomi's eyes widen.

"No, silly. I gave him some song and dance about our age differences and interests. Not really a lie and not the whole truth. To tell the truth, I was feeling bad for sort of leading him on. It felt good to have closure."

"Okay, well that's good, I guess. You said you were confused, what about?" Naomi asks, then finishes her glass of wine. With the pita chips and cheese they put out, I end up making a meal of it.

"Well . . . after I made you the three bags, I had two voicemails—one from Jesse and one from Adam."

"Yes. I remember. You were a basket case over what to do."

"I wouldn't exactly say basket case. Anyway, as Doug taught me, I went to meditate on the beach and my damn inner voice, that everyone is telling me to trust, tells me to call Jesse. It steered me wrong. I don't get it. Jesse is not the one."

"Wait a moment, Tess. Think it out. It actually makes perfect sense."

"How in the world can you say that?" I down my wine and clank my glass on the table forcefully.

"Don't get all huffy. Hear me out." Naomi places her hand on mine and motions to our server for another glass of wine for each of us.

"Okay. Sorry, it's been a rollercoaster of emotions for me this last year." I soften and gratefully cradle my freshly poured wine.

"I know." She looks at me gently, ensuring that I'm paying attention and then continues. "Had your inner voice told you to call Adam, you would have always wondered if Jesse was Thomas. Now that you know that he isn't the one, you can see Adam with a clear conscience."

"What good is that, Naomi? Adam isn't the one either."

"Can't you go out without the search? Does it always have to be about finding 'the one'?" She makes air quotes.

"Uh. Guess not."

"Stop frowning. Look, he obviously means something to you. You had a wonderful time at the writers conference. Your eyes light up when you talk about him, and let's not forget the pen incident." She laughs, causing me to giggle.

"Yeah, the 'pen incident.'" I copy her air quotes.

"It's not as if I'm asking you to marry him. It's only a date or two or three. Have fun, Tess. Haven't you struggled enough?"

"You're right. I'm going to call him." My stomach flips, for joy or fear. I'm not sure which, but think I'll go with joy.

"Good. Do it now."

"What?"

"I want to make sure you're not going to ruminate and rationalize and talk yourself out of it. Do it. I'll start singing, or worse, I'll take your phone and call myself. Remember your handyman?"

"Damn, you're bossy. Fine, I'll call. But I'm going outside first. Then catch me up on your wedding planning."

"Okay. Go! I have much to share."

After a deep breath and another gulp of wine, I'm primed for the call, I think. The night sea air hits me in the face as I exit the wine bar. The chill sharpens my mind. I don't want to call him with slurred speech. Around the side of the building I find myself shielded from the wind. I stare at my phone. Can I do this?

If I hadn't saved his number in my phone when he left that voicemail, I'd never have been able to push the entire ten digits with my hands shaking so. Breathe, breathe, I remind myself as I hear the ringing.

"Hello."

"Hi, Adam?"

"Yes?"

"This is Tess. Tess Whitaker. Uh, we met at the writers conference."

"Yes, yes. Tess. So good to hear your voice."

I breathe a sigh of relief. It's good to hear his, too. I feel flushed even though the night is cool.

"I hope you've been doing well," I tell him.

"I'm better now."

My heart skips a beat. How does he have that effect on me?

"Oh . . . um . . . I got your voicemail . . . and I was wondering if the offer still stands? Er, what I mean . . . are you still free to go out sometime?"

"Of course. I would love to go out. I know a great Italian restaurant in Belmont Shore. I hope you like Italian?"

"Yes. I love it. Sounds perfect."

"Are you free tomorrow?"

"Uh, yes, I am."

"Okay. Wonderful. Can I pick you up at six p.m.?"

"Sure. I'm in Belmont Shore. Do you have something to write with?"

"No. Remember, you took my pen."

"As I recall, you gave it to me." I'm grinning from ear to ear.

"Ah yes, you may be right. Okay, what is your address?"

I give him my address and brief directions. He mentions he's coming from Huntington Harbour. How strange, he's only minutes from me.

"Okay, then, see you tomorrow night."

"Looking forward to seeing you again, Tess."

I put the phone back in my pocket and notice my hands are still shaking. At least Naomi will be pleased. I have to admit I'm pleased too. No, that's not it. I am ebullient! I want to jump up and down. But being the civilized woman I am I saunter casually back into the wine bar and over to Naomi. I cannot, however, contain my grin.

"You did it!" Naomi jumps up and hugs me hard.

"Yes. I did, didn't I?"

"Good for you. When are you going out?"

"Tomorrow, for Italian in Belmont Shore."

"Great. You will fill me in on all, and I mean all, the details." She pinches my arm in play.

"We'll see," I tell her. "Okay, enough about me. I don't want to overthink this date; please tell me how your wedding planning is going?"

"Okay." Naomi closes her eyes and a look of enchantment comes over her. "I found the most lovely dress. I feel like an angel in it and Raj and I have been working on the invitations, writing our vows, and had a tasting with the caterer. It's been hectic, but a lot of fun."

I love watching her light up when she talks about the wedding. It's nice to see her this happy. I hope I find that kind of happiness someday.

"Oh, I almost forgot. Here are the three bags I promised you. I added a little pear patch for the *Pear Wear* motif. Hope you like them?" I hand the bags to her.

"Tess. They're perfect. Let me get back to you about these and maybe more you can sell. It's getting late and you need your beauty sleep for tomorrow's big date. Let's get out of here."

We hug each other tightly and say our goodbyes. It's been a good evening between catching up with my dearest friend and making a date with that sexy, mysterious Mr. Adam Ormand. Mmmm.

Chapter 27

Adam arrives at my door promptly at six. Normally I would've been still fiddling with my makeup, but tonight I'm ready when he arrives. For once, the day seemed effortless. I'm nervous, not anxious nervous, more of an anticipatory, excited type of nervous. It feels nice.

From the look in his eye when I open the door it appears that my burgundy silk-crepe dress with spaghetti straps is the right choice for this evening. If we would've gone out months ago it would have been an outfit of olive or black. I'm so glad I discovered color. Naomi would be proud. Adam is dressed in dark jeans, a long sleeve blue pinstripe shirt and a dark sports jacket. He looks like a picture portraying casual sophistication from a magazine ad. Should anyone look this good in real life?

"Hello, Tess. You look stunning." He hugs me warmly and I soak in his smell. There is a faint hint of alluring cologne on him. It's the sexy Adam scent that I savor, however.

"Hi there." I pull back to recover from his intoxicating aura or power or whatever it is. It's driving me crazy. I want to dive my head into his neck and drink him in.

"You hungry? There is this great Italian restaurant right up the street from here. I'm sure you've eaten there before since you live so close. It's been around for thirty years or so."

"Uh, no. I really haven't checked out many restaurants, mostly been journaling, sewing, and riding my bike."

"Ms. Glimmer, right?"

"You remember?"

"How could I forget something as important to you as Ms. Glimmer?"

Wow, what do you say to something like that? No one, except Naomi, has ever shown that much interest in what I enjoy. I'm speechless.

"Come. Let's eat." He grabs my bag and coat and leads me out the door. "Shall we walk?"

"Yes, that sounds nice." I glance down at the pear tattoo on my ankle. I sure hope tattoos don't turn him off. Nah, he seems non-judgmental. "So what is the name of this restaurant?"

"*Tramonte's*. You've been there before?"

"I'm not sure. I went to this great Italian restaurant around here when I was a child. I won't know if this is it until I walk in the door. I know I'll recognize the aroma."

Adam was right—the restaurant is up the street from me. Why didn't I check out this place sooner? *Waiting for Adam.* A voice whispers in my head. I shake it off and walk into the restaurant.

The delicious aroma of pizza fills my nostrils and takes me instantly back to that day many years ago. It's exactly like I remember. The lobby is warm and welcoming, with a fireplace. Along the windows they have checkers and backgammon tables set up for the patrons. We're shown to our booth. Each booth is private, as if we are in our own personal cubicle—so cozy and romantic. My mouth is already watering, probably both from the delicious aromas and the memory of that great pizza from years ago. On our table is the typical red candle jar that I've seen in many Italian restaurants.

There's no need to look at the menu. I want exactly what I ate that day so many years ago with Jared after our wonderful time (minus the teacup episode) at Disneyland. From where I'm sitting, I lean my head out towards the aisle and spy the large table that we, as a family, shared so many years ago. It seems like yesterday—*Jared sitting to my right and Mother to my left. Grandma and Grandpa are sitting across the table from me and there's Dad, engrossed in his menu, on the other end by Jared.*

I pull back into my protected booth as soon as the pizza arrives.

"My, that's a lot of pepperoni," Adam exclaims, but I'm only half listening. My mind is back in the past, not a past life, though. *Jared is giving me one of those horrid "Indian burns" whereas he's twisting, in opposite directions, the skin on my arm. "Stop. I'm telling," I squeal. "Jared, stop antagonizing your sister," my grandma chides. That makes him quit. Grandma sure had some power over us. We loved her so much—her generous and gentle nature. We always straightened up right away for fear of displeasing her. The rest of the evening was filled with laughter and pizza heaven.*

Yes, and now hot pizza is sitting in front of me once again. The spicy aroma is wafting up, keeping me in a place between two time periods—that of the bittersweet memories of Jared and Grandma and now with the newness of this unexpected date with Adam. Adam, a man that I fought so hard to keep out of my head and yet, here we are.

"Tess, are you planning on eating or to continue staring off into space? Where did you just go?" Adam breaks me of my reverie.

"I'm . . ." I start, but the words have left me, to be replaced by tears.

Adam reaches across the table and places his warm hand over mine.

"What's wrong? What can I do?" And suddenly it spills out—my memories of this restaurant, my feelings of loss, and Jared—those things I like to keep stuffed way down deep. The last time I spoke of this was with Doug. I thought I was done with this subject and here it resurfaces at the most inopportune time—on a first date! What a way to scare someone away. I'm mortified! I pull my hand from Adam's and attempt to cover my shameful face with my hands.

"No." Adam very gently takes my hand back. "Part of me is sorry that I took you to a place that holds such deep emotion and part of me feels that you need to heal this area. I'm glad I am here with you."

Where did this guy come from? He's not running at all from this situation.

"Please give me a moment." I get up and head to the bathroom to get control of this situation, passing *the* table that caused the upset. I take in my appearance in the restroom mirror. Shit, my eyes look like crap. All dressed up and now I look terrible. Okay, let's pull it together. I pull out my liner pencil from my purse, dry my eyes with tissue and redo my makeup. In my coin purse is Jared's necklace, one of the rare times I took it off because I didn't think it fit with my dress. I slip it back over my head. A few deep breaths and prayers later, I feel regrouped enough to join Adam. As I walk out of the bathroom and back toward our table I catch Adam standing by the lobby. Huh? Is he leaving?

"Come," he calls to me.

"We're not eating? I'm fine now, really."

"I know you are. But pizza on the beach is much more fun, don't you think?" He smiles and holds up the boxed pizza and soda.

"Yes. That would be fun." I smile back and feel warmth spread through me—a warmth and appreciation for his consideration and for not making a big deal of my mini-breakdown. I link my arm in his and we head down the street towards the beach.

"Let's sit in my spot," I tell him.

"Your spot? You have a spot on the beach?"

"Yes. I claimed it. I come here most mornings. This is where I learned meditation."

"From Doug, right?"

"My! I can't believe you remember that too. Doug moved on so it's my spot now. Do you remember everything I said?"

Adam shrugs his shoulders, then spreads out his coat on the sand for us to sit on. It's a warm night. A light breeze picks up once in a while, blowing my hair into my face. At least I'm not cold as we sit on the beach, eating our now cool pizza and sharing soda from a large disposable cup.

"You know, eating pizza on the beach, in the fresh air, is a perfect way to spend an evening."

"I know, right?" I laugh. He gets it. The beach is more fun, or at least more relaxing. I feel at home now, sitting in my spot with this bewildering man that seems to know the right thing to do in awkward situations. The night beach has an entirely different energy. I rely only on hearing and smell as the waves come in and crash on the beach. The sand disappears into blackness, creating a shroud of mystery, yet the sound of the waves console me, letting me know all is right. I move closer to Adam so that we are touching, laying my coat across our laps. I finish my third slice of pizza. I guess all that crying boosted my appetite.

With the food long gone, the conversation winding down, and the chill of the night air seeping into my bones, Adam stands extending his hand to mine to lift me off the cold beach. We brush the sand from our coats and he helps me into mine. We walk back to my apartment in quiet. *What next?* The closer I get to my place, the more butterflies show up in my belly. Once again confusion penetrates my heart and mind. I don't want him to leave and, yet, I wonder if I'm wasting our time. I worry about J out there looking for me—struggling, lonely. Wait. Is he even looking for me? What if he moved on? Maybe I'm being foolish when Adam, good and ready and so damn sexy, is standing right in front of me.

"Well, here we are." Adam points out the obvious as we stand at my door.

"Um . . . did you want to come in for a bit?" I ask him. Still not sure what's the right thing to do.

"No, but I would like to ask you to go out again—this time to not such an emotionally charged restaurant. What do you think?"

"Yes. I would like that."

"Tell you what. Why don't you come down to my boat in Huntington Harbour on Saturday around four p.m., Dock R, Slip 15. We'll sail over to Long Beach for dinner. Does that sound good to you?"

"It sounds perfect! And thank you for being so understanding tonight."

"Thank you for sharing with me." And with that he leans in to kiss me. I close my eyes and his lips meet mine. As our lips touch, a jolt sears through my body. The raven that visited me at the writers conference has returned, soaring through me in dramatic arcs, flying out of sheer joy. It's not a long kiss, but it's powerful—leaving me breathless, tingly, and wanting more.

"Wow," I say.

"Yes . . ." Even Adam looks like he needs a moment to recover. I'm glad it isn't only me. "Well. See you Saturday."

"Saturday," I whisper as I watch him walk down the steps, further away from my electrified body.

Chapter 28

I sleep surprisingly well and wake with lightness in my heart, as though telling Adam about Jared helped ease the weight I carried for so many years. Saturday can't come soon enough. Picking up the phone, I dial Naomi.

"Well, tell me all about it?" She answers the phone without as much as a hello.

"Not much to tell."

"Don't give me that. I want details," Naomi demands.

"Okay, okay. Well it was a perfect evening except for my emotional breakdown," I start.

"No, tell me you didn't!"

"Yeah, sure did. But it's okay. Adam was really great about it . . . I somehow decided to have a meltdown from memories of Jared . . . right in the middle of a crowded restaurant. Adam took it in stride and had our pizza boxed up and took me to the beach for an impromptu picnic."

"Wow. What a nice gesture. So what happened next?" Naomi hints.

"We just talked and then he walked me back to my place."

"And?"

"And nothing."

"Nothing?"

"Naomi! Stop, it was our first date. He was a gentleman."

"So no kiss, either?"

"Okay, well we did have a quick goodnight kiss."

"Yes?"

"Oh, Naomi, it was like electricity. In fact, it was a similar to a strange experience I had sitting next to him at the writers conference."

"Boy, you're the 'Queen of Strange Experiences.'"

"Seems like it. Anyway, it was this raven . . . never mind. It's too weird to explain . . ."

"Raven, huh? So are you seeing him again?"

"Saturday. He's taking me out on his boat." My heart skips as I say it out loud.

"Oh, yay! Well, I have the perfect way for you to focus throughout the week while you wait for Saturday. I have fifteen orders for your *Pear Wear* bags. Everyone loves them. You should think of setting up a booth at the farmers market."

"You really think so?" Hmm, I wonder if I could do that. Do I have it in me?

"Of course. Your bags are terrific."

"Okay, I'll get to work on the fifteen bags for you and look into the farmers market. Hey, thank you for that."

"What?"

"You know, your powers of distraction and encouragement."

"Hey, what are best friends for. Love you."

"Love you too." I hang up and run my fingers through my hair. Grabbing Prince, I twirl him around while he makes a mournful meow at me. "Fifteen bags! Can you believe it? We have our work cut out for us." Prince struggles out of my grip and gives me the "annoyed cat" look.

The rest of the week goes quickly. I've made twenty-two bags and booked myself to the Sunday farmers market the following weekend. By then I plan to have another twenty done. I've made them in all colors and themes to please a wide variety of customers and, of course, adorned them with my *Pear Wear* pear patch. I'm right pleased with myself. All that is left to do is figure out a good selling price and set up shop. Maybe I will bring one with me tonight on my date with Adam.

"I wonder what I should wear on a boat? It'll probably be chilly, but I still want to look cute. What do you think?" I ask Jared.

On the drive to the harbour, I'm ambivalent about my choice of attire—black slacks and a teal tank with a pullover sweater and black flats. Am I too casual? As I pull into the harbour, I wonder how I missed this area on my bike rides. Ms. Glimmer and I visited the harbour homes many times on our afternoon sojourns and yet missed this tucked away jewel. I find Dock R easily and notice that indeed Adam has the best slip on this stretch. Slip15 looks out on a little patch of green, grassy park with a picnic table, barbeque, and an interesting twisted tree with branches so low they make a convenient bench. It's a tranquil setting. Adam is waiting on his deck and as I approach he comes up the dock and unlocks the gate for me.

"Welcome. No trouble finding it?"

"None at all. I rode my bike all over here, but missed this."

"Yes, we're quite hidden. I like the privacy."

"It's so serene here."

"Well, let me show you around. Watch your step as you climb aboard the *Mer Sea*."

"Mer Sea?" I repeat as I read the words in script on the side of Adam's boat.

"Merci means 'thank you' in French. And Mer is also 'sea' in French."

"So it's redundant then? Sea sea?"

"Yes, and also about gratitude."

"Oh, I get it. Clever."

"I thought so." He winks. Damn, he's so cute. Thankfully, he's also dressed casual in jeans and a forest green pullover.

"Do you speak French?" I ask.

"Just a little. I have a fondness for the language and country. Let me show you around."

"Okay," I tell him as I tuck a stray strand of hair behind my ear.

"She, the *Mer Sea*, has a central salon, galley, dining room, back deck, and upper deck. There are two bedrooms and two bathrooms," he proudly announces as he shows me around.

As I peer into the master bathroom, I take notice on how small the shower is and how you have to step over a wall to get inside.

"Hmm, doesn't seem to be room for two people to get cozy." Oops, did I just say that out loud? My face feels flushed with embarrassment. I back out of there quickly. "So the living room has a fireplace too?" I ask quickly to change the subject.

"The living room is called a salon and the fireplace is electric, more for ambiance." Adam looks at me and winks. Oh, now he's teasing me since he knows how flustered I get around him.

I stand in the galley to put a little distance between me and him. Is it getting hot in here? On the counter I notice there is a large bowl with three ripe pears.

"Want one? I bought them from the farmers market." He gestures towards the bowl of pears.

"Uh, no thank you." That's the last thing I need. I'm already feeling ready to jump Adam's bones, an orgasmic bite of a pear will send me over the edge and God knows he has already witnessed too much weirdness from me.

"Don't like pears?"

"No, actually I love them. . . . just . . . uh . . . saving my appetite for dinner." I give a partial truth.

"That's understandable. Make yourself comfortable. I thought we would head to Long Beach's Rainbow Harbor. There is a great steakhouse there overlooking the water. I hope you like steak?"

"Yes, that sounds great." I take the opportunity to soak in the details of his boat and the peacefulness. Adam has it decorated with nautical decorations and art—old maps and boat drawings—definitely the décor of a single man.

Adam handles the boat with ease, backing it out of the slip, heading through Anaheim Bay and entering the open ocean. I climb out on the front deck carefully, using the rails for support, grateful that I wore flats as the boat rocks in the swell. On the bow, I watch the waves as they split in the center and splash up the sides. Sea spray makes my lips salty. I quickly tie my hair up as the wind threatens to whip it around my face. White clouds lightly dot the skies, breaking up the monotony. I move towards the back to follow the waves that have run down the sides of the boat. Here the water is churning and appears confused as to which direction to go and so it dips down and disappears as it flows away from us. I think I like this end better—watching the water recede from the boat and find new boats to crash into. Maybe I should have brought a coat. Out on the open water feels much cooler than on the docks.

"Hey, are you getting cold? I have extra jackets, or you can stay warm inside," he yells out to me.

"Okay," I yell back. Is he psychic? I carefully make my way back inside where it is warm and comfortable.

"Gets cold fast, huh?"

"Yeah, how did you know?"

"Just been doing this long enough."

The sky darkens as the sun drops lower. I'm bundled up in Adam's coat watching how the sun dances on the sea. The water takes on an eerie, inky appearance. As the last bit of sun dissolves into the ocean just a little north of Catalina Island, Adam enters the breakwater of Rainbow Harbor and slows his speed considerably. The sea park is lit up with twinkling white lights, activity, live music, and families and couples enjoying a pleasant evening. Adam skillfully docks his boat along one of the visitor slips. He jumps onto the dock and ties up the *Mer Sea,* then reaches up a hand to help me down. I grab my *Pear Wear* bag and jump down as gracefully as I can manage. My hand reaches in my bag for a brush. I undo my hair and comb out the windblown tangles.

"Interesting bag," he comments.

"Like it? I made it."

"Looks a little like a backpack, but different."

"Yes. It can be used as a backpack or as a basket liner for a bicycle."

"I see that."

"I just started making them and have already received orders for more. In fact, next weekend I'm selling them at the farmers market by my home."

"Do you call them anything—your bike bags?"

"*Pear Wear.* I call them *Pear Wear!*"

"*Pear Wear* . . . I like it. Hungry?"

"Starving."

"Great. The restaurant is right over there." He grabs my hand and leads the way.

The restaurant looks like a lighthouse and is situated at the tip of the sea park with views on three sides of the harbor. The hostess leads us to a small table outside on the patio that is protected from the wind by glass walls. There is a heat lamp close to the table to keep us cozy. There are comfortable couches to lounge on by a fire pit. Adam sits down at my left.

"Would you like any drinks?" Our young female server, dressed in all black, asks us.

"I would like a lemon-drop martini, please," I answer quickly. Adam laughs at my drink choice and orders dark ale for himself.

"What? I've always wanted to try one."

"You'll love it; they're potent. Shall we get you two?"

"You're not trying to get me drunk and take advantage of me?"

"Never." He squeezes my hand, causing my heart to race again.

We both order steak with baked potatoes and sautéed vegetables. After dinner and conversation we sit enjoying the night over coffee and a shared tiramisu. Everything was delicious, adding to the perfection of the evening. While I watch the white lights flicker on the water and feel the martini spread through my blood stream, I'm lulled into a hypnotic state. Adam's hand rests on mine. The alcohol, the lights, the warmth of his hand transports me to an experience that I struggle to decipher—a daydream, a past life, or a fantasy? I decide to see where it takes me. *Kiss me again. I lift up to greet his lips. His hands warm on my body, the grass beneath is soft and damp. Kiss me again, please.*

"Mmm," I murmur out loud.

"What?" Adam asks and snaps me out of my daydream.

"Oh, nothing, just thinking how nice this evening is."

"Well, the night is still young. Do you want to stretch your legs before sailing back? It's a pleasant area to walk."

"Yes, that sounds perfect."

Around the sea park, we pass an old steamboat, many boat rentals, the aquarium, vendors, and families with young children. There are also a few lovers, tenderly kissing and holding each other. I wonder where our night will lead. Will we be kissing too? I blush at the thought and that familiar pulling in my lower abdomen makes itself known. Need to come back to earth . . .

"Adam, I don't know too much about you. Where did you grow up?" I come up with a benign topic to quell my libido.

"Not much to tell. I was raised in Los Angeles."

"College?"

"I graduated from UCLA and started teaching."

"Did you ever marry?"

"I was married, but divorced years ago, no children. And have been single since. Claire, my ex-wife, got the house."

"Oh, that must've been tough. How did you meet?"

"We met in college. She's a biologist—consumed with work. After the divorce, I bought the boat and spent time sailing, teaching, and writing. A peaceful, simple life. And then I met you . . ."

"Me?" I question.

"Yes, you. Life was under control, predictable, easy. And then you showed up in my workshop and I haven't been thinking clearly since."

Well, so much for benign topics. My stomach flips, threatening to upset all the contents from dinner. I'm at a loss for words. Do I tell him that he's been on my mind since we met, too? Oh, why does it have to be so complicated? I had one clear path in mind—look for J. And then Adam comes into my life and completely confounds my plans. Naomi tells me to enjoy myself. Maybe she's right. All I know is that I want to kiss him terribly.

I stop walking and take his hands. They are beautiful, masculine, very much like my vision at the restaurant.

"Adam . . ."

"Yes."

"Kiss me," I beg.

He turns towards me and takes my face in his hands, gently brushing the hair back from my face. I look deep into his eyes, not noticing the people milling about, and lift my face towards his. Adam leans in and to the left and firmly places his mouth over mine. I gasp. His mouth possesses me and I willingly surrender to the kiss. We stay locked in this kiss for what seems a timeless moment, until it appears that Adam becomes aware that we are in a public setting and releases me, teasingly biting my lower lip before letting me up for air. Wow, what a kiss! I actually feel lightheaded. Who knew that one kiss could do that?

"Come, let's head back to the *Mer Sea*," he suggests.

He doesn't need to convince me; I'm already starting in that direction. My thoughts are only of ripping off his clothes with my teeth. I'm thinking things I never thought and don't care to censor myself tonight. Well-controlled Tess is checked out and I don't give a damn!

As we climb back on the boat he prepares to sail back to Huntington Harbour. Not going to have sex now? I'm disappointed. He senses my frustration and leans in to whisper in my ear, causing shivers up and down my body.

"When we get back to the harbour, I'm going to start kissing here." He reaches down and gently touches the back of my ankle. "Then continue all the way up to your head and then start on the front of your body all the way back to your feet."

"Ahhh." It's all I can say. I'm breathless. Can't this boat go any faster?

I'm silent the entire trip back, my mind is taking a vacation and my body is on full alert, senses heightened. As we pull back into the harbour, I'm feeling more nervous. Am I excited or nervous? It's been so long since I've had sex. Please don't let me disappoint him. I head to the small bathroom off the salon to freshen up. I brush my teeth with the toothbrush I keep in my bag, brush my hair, and stare closely in the mirror.

"Tess, you want this man. At least for tonight, you want him. Enjoy," I whisper to my reflection. The floats squeak against the slip as Adam eases the boat into its space. One more deep breath—ready. I exit the bathroom.

Chapter 29

Adam is turning off the engine as I approach. His hair is windblown, tempting me to straighten it with my fingers. He reaches out and caresses my cheek with his fingertips.

"Come," he whispers, taking me by the hand and leading me down the four steps to his bedroom. Dim light filters in from the salon above, creating a warm glow. Adam stands in front of me and slowly undresses me, peeling off layers of clothing: jacket, pullover, blouse, and leaving me in my black bra. Next his fingers work to pull down my zipper. My breath catches as his hand brushes my belly.

I wiggle my hips out of my slacks and kick off my shoes, then work my feet out of the pant legs. I shiver as I stand exposed in only a bra and panties in front of a fully dressed Adam. Humph.

"I love your hair." He grabs a handful of it and playfully gives it a little tug.

He eases me on the bed and stands with an admiring smile—taking in the scene. My mouth has gone dry. I lick my lips . . . waiting.

"Turn over," he says.

"Huh?"

"Don't you remember what I told you I was going to do to you? I don't go back on my promises."

Although I'm hesitant, I turn over. Somehow laying on my belly, with him at my feet, multiplies the vulnerable feelings I have. I take a deep breath and try to relax. Then it starts . . . oh . . . soft, wet kisses are placed first on my ankle, lingering over my pear tattoo, then on the back of my legs, now moving upward ever so slowly . . . my, oh, my . . . my brain has completely gone to mush . . . at the point where my leg meets my panties . . . can't take it . . . ah, now on my lower back . . . moving up . . . anticipating where the next kiss will be . . . shoulder blades . . . excruciating slow he moves up the back of my head . . . sending shivers down my spine.

"Turn over," he orders and I comply immediately. Now I can see him. He takes off his sweater and shirt. I long to help him out of his clothes and reach up to him. He backs inches out of reach.

"No, you just enjoy the experience," he tells me. Arghh.

Adam stands back for a moment, giving me a chance to take in his beauty. I notice the small patch of hair in the center of his tan and toned chest. I want to nuzzle it and drink in his scent, but for now I'm content to see what he has planned next. He comes close and continues his trail of kisses. This time starting on my forehead, making me feel cared for. Then moving down to my eyelids, ever so gently . . . my cheeks, the tip of my nose . . . completely skipping my mouth that longs for a deep kiss . . . down to my neck, making me moan slightly . . . to my chest, again skipping the area where my bra is and moving down to my belly that craves him so since we first met . . . ahhh . . . now down to my thighs after he conspicuously avoids the area covered by panties . . . kissing my knees . . . shins and finally my feet, ending at the tip of my big toe.

Wow. Never, I mean never, have I had an experience like that. Where in the world did he pick that up? I need to ask him one day. I roll my head from side to side basking in the leftover burn from where his lips touched my skin. As I roll my head back to the left, I notice he is undoing his pants. Oh God, this is really happening.

Adam removes his pants and leaves them in a bunch on the floor with all of the other garments. He removes his socks quickly, leaving his briefs in place and climbs on the bed next to me. Not being able to resist any longer I hungrily kiss him, tasting him, exploring his mouth with my tongue. He responds in kind, greedily consuming me. Breaking away for air, I throw my head back as he starts kissing my left ear lobe, pulling it gently with his teeth, then moving down to my neck as his fingers slide the bra strap off my shoulder. My hands take advantage of the freedom to caress his chest, shoulders, and firm triceps. He maneuvers his position and straddles me. I lift up and undo my bra, letting my breasts free from the confines of the satin material.

"Ohhh," he sighs, causing me to be secretly pleased. Adam takes my right breast gently up in his hand and lays kisses all around, avoiding my nipple, saving it for last. Finally he takes my nipple in his mouth, once again using his teeth to tug it towards him. This time I moan, not from pain, but from a pleasure stirring deep down in my groin. My body arches in response. As if on cue, Adam lifts off me for a moment to help me out of my panties as I struggle to free him from his underwear. He is erect, circumcised, and at the ready as I notice a wet glistening on the tip of his penis. He pulls out a condom from one of the drawers in his headboard and deftly rolls it on himself. I await his entrance.

Adam straddles me once again, looks me deep in the eyes and plunges into me, causing me to cry out in pleasure. My back arches as I rise to kiss him. We move in unison, riding each other as the rhythm of the rocking boat accompanies us in our lovemaking. An intuitive sense comes over me as I anticipate and match his rhythm. This feels oh so familiar and at the same time exhilaratingly new and fresh. I'm having these two simultaneous and opposite feelings course through me. It's reminiscent of a déjà vu experience.

In one quick and seamless move we roll as one and now I'm straddling Adam, taking my time to roll to my own rhythm. Adam's hands are freed up to explore my breasts as I continue my rocking. Finally we both cannot take it, tiny moans of pleasure escape from Adam alerting me that he is near orgasm. His vocalizations push me over the edge and I begin to come. It wells up in me from my belly, shoots down to my feet, and then moves up my legs, causing my calves to tighten. Back up to my belly, it rushes throughout the rest of my body and out the top of my head. I'm tingling from head to toe as my body continues to pulsate. Adam cries out in release as he witnesses my orgasm.

I carefully lift myself off him and lie on the bed next to him. With my head on his damp chest I listen to his heartbeat return to a normal rate. Adam gently fingers my necklace that rests against his chest.

"It was Jared's," I explain.

"Ah. That's a nice gesture. Keeps him close to you."

"Yes. I've been wearing it almost continuously since he died. I found it in his room hanging on the bedpost. He got it when we went to Hawaii on vacation as kids."

"Thank you for sharing your memory with me."

"Thank you, Adam, for listening." My body has not felt this relaxed in months. I close my eyes and give into the feeling as Adam strokes my hair.

"Stay the night," says Adam. "Let me get you something to sleep in." He eases out from under me. Adam pulls out a pair of his pajama bottoms and a t-shirt from a drawer under the bed.

"Okay."

Prince should be okay for one night. There is plenty of food and water left out. As I dress I take in the details of the bedroom. The bed is bigger than I thought could fit on a boat, king size! And the ceiling is high, too. No worries about me bumping my head as I straddle Adam. Then I notice the little window hidden behind the head of the bed. I have to check it out. It has two slated wooden doors that slide open. Peering out I see that we are right about at the water level. The moonlight is playing on the water surface. This is magical.

I take in the rest of the bedroom. There is a great attention to detail. The headboard is curved wood with abundant storage. There is a small table next to me and the cabinet above the table is filled with books. I pull out one of Adam's books.

"That was my first published book," he explains. Wow, I hope I can say that one day. I go back to peering out the little window and watching the light play . . . it lulls me to a dreamy state. Adam lies next to me, playing with my hair. The boat rocks gently; I drift off into a deep slumber.

"You know that first feeling of confusion when you wake up in a strange place? Yeah, me too. Most of the time it hasn't been like this though. Most of the time, I'm disappointed. Like when I slept the first time in my apartment after leaving Richard. Those initial few minutes when all is forgotten and then realization seeps back into consciousness. One of those, 'Oh yeah, my life sucks' moments. Or staying in a really crappy motel. For a second I'm dreaming that I'm in some luxury suite and then I awaken to stare at stained walls and my foot touches some bunched-up cloth under the blanket. I reach down to retrieve the offending bunchiness to discover someone else's black socks. Then it becomes painfully obvious that the housekeeping staff did *not* change the sheets after the last customer. I thought the sheets smelled stale. No lying—that really happened to me. I think I'm scarred for life," I tell Jared in my mind.

Well, this morning is nothing like that. The first thing I notice, coming out of my sleepy haze, is that the ceiling looks awfully close. How can this be? Did the roof cave in? Where am I? After a moment of confused panic, it dawns on me. I remember. Oh, I didn't imagine it. I turn my head to the side. He is here too. He's real. Last night was real—not a dream. Now that's the best feeling.

I didn't know I could sleep that well. The rocking of the boat provided a comforting rhythm to sleep to. Am I really here with this gorgeous, mysterious man? He's already awake and it appears he's been watching me sleep, making me feel a little bashful. He seems perfect for me. We match so well. How can he not be the one? Adam Ormand, not J. Wait . . . what if his middle name starts with a J? That must be it.

"Adam?"

"Mmm hmm," he responds.

"What's your middle name?"

"Reid. Adam Reid Ormand. Why do you ask?"

Releasing the breath I was unknowingly holding, I respond, "Oh, just curious."

"Tess, you are a puzzle."

"You don't know the half of it." I hop out of his bed, adding lightheartedly, "Hey, let me make you some breakfast."

"Okay. Sure, sounds good."

After using the bathroom and slipping back into my clothes from last night I pad to the galley to see what I can make. In the tiny refrigerator I find eggs, cheese, and mushrooms and set out to make a scramble and coffee.

"Okay, now it's official. He's not the one I was searching for, but why does my heart want him so. I'm going to talk to Naomi about it." I tuck Jared's necklace back inside my shirt.

I finish the last touches on the breakfast plates, including fresh pear slices as garnish. "I know what you're thinking, Jared. They're only for decoration. I will pass on them, feigning fullness." Adam climbs the stairs looking delicious in loose sweats and a t-shirt. His hair is tousled from sleep.

"Good morning, bright eyes," he says.

"Good morning. Breakfast is served."

"Smells and looks delicious. Shall we eat up on the deck?"

"Okay, that sounds fun."

"I eat most of my meals out there."

We take our plates and coffee to the back of the boat. He has a small table and chairs set up with a picture perfect view of the harbour. The serenity of this time of morning envelops me and calms my uneasiness regarding J. Adam heartily engulfs his plate of food including his pear slices.

"You gonna eat those?" he asks, pointing to my untouched pears.

"No. Too full. Help yourself."

"Don't mind if I do." He reaches, but I grab one and feed it to him. As his mouth closes over the succulent pear, juices run down his chin, causing that familiar pulling in my groin. I want so badly to lick the juice off his chin, but resist.

"Mmm, they're absolutely delicious. Pears just happen to be my favorite fruit, ever since I was a kid," he tells me.

"Wow. Me too."

"Really. What a coincidence."

"Yeah . . . coincidence . . ." My voice trails off. What could it mean? Is there more going on here than I realize?

Adam leans in for another bite of pear. I oblige and feed him.

"Kiss me," he whispers.

"Ahh. Well, now wouldn't that be interesting." I consider for a moment and then . . .

"What would be intere . . ." He doesn't finish his sentence. I plant my lips firmly on his and push my tongue deep into his mouth, tasting pear juice. Instantly the world fades away once more and I'm transported to my otherworldly state . . . *"Feed me another piece," I beg him as he teases me with the pears, dripping juice on my bare breasts and licking it off ever so slowly and sensuously. The soft grass beneath me provides a perfect bed for our outdoor lovemaking. The pears are so ripe and hang low on the tree we rest under.* "Feed me another piece . . ."

"Tess." Adam is shaking me.

"I'm fine. I'm fine. Just give me a moment." I pull away and take some deep breaths to clear my head.

"What the heck was that? You looked like you were in a trance. Am I that good of a kisser?" Adam jokes to lighten the mood.

"It's kinda hard to explain . . ."

"Try. I'm a good listener." Adam rests his chin on his thumb and his crooked forefinger across his upper lip in a contemplative pose.

"It's pears."

"Uh huh . . . go on."

"They seem to affect me. I don't know why. They seem to . . . uh . . . transport me." I look down, afraid of the strange looks I imagine him giving me.

"Okay. So let me understand this. You eat pears and you are . . . what did you call it? Transported?"

"Uh huh."

"To where? And does this happen a lot?"

"I don't know *where* and only if I eat pears so I try to avoid it, but you were looking so sexy and you were making me horny with those lips and pear juice on your chin and the pulling in my groin and for a minute I didn't give a damn. I wanted you and so I went for it." I've said too much and suddenly feel flushed.

"I was looking sexy, huh, and you wanted me? Now I understand why you call your bike bags *Pear Wear*. Why not forget about the pears for a while, what do you say? Let's go back to the 'me looking sexy' part." He gets up and takes my hand, leading me back to his bed.

Chapter 30

"So how was the sex?" Naomi says as she answers the phone.

"Hey, not so much as a hello? And, by the way, what makes you think we had sex?"

"It's not rocket science. You didn't call me last night which means you must have been with Adam all night."

"I could've left early because the date was a disaster."

"Nope, you would've called me."

"Darn, you know me too well."

"Well, you haven't answered my question."

"It was . . . it was . . . Oh, Naomi." I sigh.

"Wow. That good, huh?"

"In a word—incredible."

"I'm so happy for you."

"Thank you. I really need to talk to you, though."

"A problem?"

"More like concerns or confusion. Do you want it in alphabetical order or in order of priority?" I try to lighten it up.

"Whichever way. Shoot."

"Okay, first of all, he's definitely not J."

"I thought we already knew that."

"Yeah, but then I got to thinking maybe his middle name starts with a J. So I asked him."

"And?"

"Reid."

"Yeah, that's not a J. What else?"

"Well, he loves pears too. Weird, huh? And I ended up having another pear incident in front of him?"

"You didn't. And he didn't run the other way? What happened?"

"Never mind. Suffice it to say it was an interesting scene."

"I bet."

"So, what do you think?"

"Have you considered that you may have known him in a past life?"

"Like a soul mate? Can you have more than one?"

"I think you should make an appointment with your regressionist again or talk to Dr. Feinberg from the women's conference. Or you can talk to my psychic friend again."

"I don't know. Let me think about it."

"Okay. But for now, enjoy yourself with Adam."

"I will." We both start giggling.

"Bye sweetie. Talk to you soon."

Prince is demanding his breakfast as I end my call. "Okay. Okay. Hold on. I'm sorry I'm late. I had the most wonderful time, Prince. But now I need to get back to making more bags for the farmers market next weekend. Gonna help?" Prince conspicuously ignores me.

On the back covered deck of Adam's boat I rest. I feel like I must be directly in the pelican flight path. They pass right by me, gliding close to the surface. I swear the tips of their wings touch the water. It's breathtaking to watch. Terns and cormorants also keep company here, diving for their breakfast. And occasionally the California gull squawks his announcements to the group. It always sounds as if they have been wound up by a tiny key in their back. I love to hear them winding down. Over the last few weeks, I've gotten accustomed to this comfortable routine. Adam has educated me on the local water birds and boat life.

"You really get to know yourself, your likes and dislikes, living on a boat," Adam tells me. "There is only so much space to store your belongings so you only take what is essential or valuable to you—valuable to your interests and preferences. All other items must be discarded. I found it very difficult in the beginning, but soon realized I didn't need all that I thought I did. I learned to live sparsely and it fits my life well. If you want a book, other boat owners lend out and we relend. We only use what we need."

Hmm. I wonder if I could scale down like that if I ever lived on this boat. I like playing with the idea of life on the water. My mind wanders there frequently. I need to get some closure regarding J and Adam, but I don't want anything to burst my little fantasy life I've been living these past few weeks. I've been having too much fun and my *Pear Wear* bags have been taking off. I sold all but three at the first farmers market and have been close to selling out each week since. Between biking, journaling, sewing, and spending time with Adam, my days are filled. In fact, Adam asked me to make some bags for kids to sell at the craft fair at his school next month.

". . . so that's why working as a school teacher suits me. I have the summer off to sail and write. During the school year I plan where I want to visit. It's ideal, sailing and writing in different ports with varied scenery for inspiration . . . I was wondering if you would like to accompany me on my next short writing trip over the winter break? I plan to go to Catalina Island for scene inspiration." Adam's question breaks my musing.

"Huh?" I shake off my dreamy state. "Yes, I would love to go."

"Great. Maybe you'll be inspired to write also."

"Uh, maybe."

"Don't say maybe. Make a promise to yourself to write something every day. You owe that to yourself. Even if you never show it to anyone, it will enrich your life."

"You know, you're right. I will. Thanks." I lean over and kiss him, only meaning to give him a peck, but quickly it becomes more. He seems to hold some power over me.

Chapter 31

With Christmas coming up, I'm at a loss for what to get Wade. I realize I don't even know him anymore. Richard and Wade have gone on without me. It's almost as if I died, or was erased from the snapshots of their lives. They no longer need me, that's very apparent. I suppose it's the same for me. I've gone on with my life—my new life in Belmont Shore, Prince, and this confusing relationship with Adam that I still haven't sorted out.

Richard, hope u and Wade r well. Can u give me idea of what Wade would like 4 Xmas? I text.

New smart phone.

Ok. Thx. How r u?

No response. I stare at the phone for another five minutes trying to decide to let it go or text again when another text comes through. Oh good.

Been invited to an awards dinner Friday for OC writers. Please be my date?

What? At first I'm confused as to why Richard would be asking me out or interested in writing. Looking closer, I see it's from Adam and my heart speeds up.

Yes

Pick you up at 6:30.

Ok

Richard's unanswered text has left a lingering sourness on me. I push it out of mind, like I'm so good at. Focus on my date with Adam.

"An awards dinner? Sounds fun." Naomi is picking at her Chinese tofu salad. Our table at a little Bohemian cafe she loves is covered with hand-painted art: curlicues, hearts, and peace signs—so very Naomi. I wonder if her wedding will be like this. I could see her doing a Renaissance Faire wedding with flowing fabric and bright colors, all the bridesmaids singing and dancing around the maypole. Yup, my eclectic friend.

"Yeah, I guess. I'm a little uneasy. A lot of his writing friends will be there. What the heck do I wear to something like that?"

"I'll help you find something fabulous. Sounds like Adam's getting serious."

My stomach flips and somehow my appetite has taken leave; my tortilla soup goes cold.

"I don't know. You really think so?"

"Duh. Tess. So did you make a decision on what to do about this J issue or are you going to let it go? I mean you have someone right there in the flesh. You don't really need to know, right?"

"Yeah, maybe you're right. Maybe I'll let it go."

"Finished?" She points to my half-eaten soup.

"Yeah, somehow I'm not hungry anymore."

"Well, let's go shopping and find you a knockout dress!" She jumps up, pays for both of us and bounds out of the restaurant.

"Wait up." I leave a generous tip and trail behind Naomi's flyaway, red hair.

Everyone appears comfortable in their attire, schmoozing and sipping champagne. I'm glad Naomi helped pick out my dress. Without her expertise I wouldn't have fit in at all. Adam looks absolutely dashing in his tuxedo, complete with bow tie and maroon cummerbund. He takes my breath away and from the way he looks at me, I think I do the same. I'm wearing a floor length, soft crème satin material with tiny rhinestones accenting the plunging neckline. It has a halter tie around my neck, leaving my back completely bare. I feel sexy and stylish. Good choice, Naomi.

"You're the sexiest woman here," he whispers in my ear, sending chills down my spine and causing goosebumps to rise on my arms.

"Stop, you're giving me goosebumps," I scold.

"Good." He smirks and lifts my hand, softly planting a kiss on the back of it.

"Henry, Madeline, good to see you," Adam announces as an attractive couple approaches us.

"Adam, good to see you too. What has it been, six months?" says the greying man in the blue pinstripe suit. A middle-aged woman with a bob, wearing a simple black dress, holds on to the man's arm.

"More like a year. It was the annual writing society holiday party."

"Oh right, now I remember, you read a portion of your work during the open mike. And now you get an award for that wonderful piece. I can say, 'I knew you back when.'" They both chuckle.

An award? He didn't tell me he was getting an award. I smile nervously at Madeline, who is staring at me with a puzzled look as if to say, "And you are?"

As if Adam read Madeline's mind, he says, "Oh, please forgive my manners. Madeline, Henry, I would like to introduce you to my girlfriend, Tess Whitaker. Tess, these are my dear friends from the O.C. Writing Society."

Girlfriend?! Did he call me his girlfriend? Naomi was right. My mouth feels dry.

"Good to meet you both," I manage to get out.

"So, Tess, are you an author, too?" Madeline asks.

"Uh, not really. I've written a couple of articles on fitness."

"Oh, she will be," Adam chimes in. "She's also a talented seamstress."

"I wouldn't say that. I only make bags."

"Bags?" asks Madeline as she wrinkles her nose slightly.

"I sell bike bags that double as a backpack/purse."

"Yes, they are in high demand. Tess is quite creative."

"No doubt," Henry adds.

"Well, dear, we really should mingle," Madeline tells Henry.

"Of course. See you around, Adam. Congratulations on your award. So nice meeting you, Tess. I'm glad to see Adam looking so happy."

"Nice meeting you both," I add. After they are out of earshot I turn to Adam. "Why didn't you tell me you were getting an award?"

"I didn't want to make a big deal of it. It's only a token recognition for the novel I wrote. What did you think of my friends?"

"Henry seems very nice, but I'm not sure Madeline approves of me." I look down. Maybe I'm not good enough for Adam.

"Oh Madeline, don't worry about her. She and Claire were good friends. I don't think she's moved on yet, even though the rest of the world has." We both laugh as he pulls me in close.

"Girlfriend, huh?"

"Oh, yeah, you caught that? I know I haven't asked you. I hope you didn't mind back there. Let me ask you properly now." He pauses to look into my eyes. "Tess, will you be my girlfriend?"

And right here, among fancy hors d'oeuvres, champagne, and uppity-up people in their sparkly attire, I'm faced with answering a question which I don't even have the answer to. For a moment, the world slows down, giving me a chance to think. Okay, it's probably that my mind sped up, but I swear I glanced up and people were moving in slow motion. The list-making part of my mind kicks into high gear:

- He's sexy, cute, and smart
- He's not your soul mate
- How do I know that? Maybe I have more than one. Naomi mentioned that
- And what if J is out there looking for you?
- And what if he's not?
- How can you commit when you still have unanswered questions about J?
- But . . . I love him

I love him? Wow. I do. I didn't know that until now. In an instant the world goes back to normal speed.

"Yes. I would love to be your girlfr . . ." Before I can finish the sentence, Adam scoops me in a tight hug, lifting me off the ground. "Put me down," I shrill.

"Come, let me introduce you to all the rest of my friends, girlfriend." He beams.

Late into the early morning hours, I'm still awake in his bed staring at the award displayed on his shelf. The moonlight bounces off his *Quill and Ink* award, creating a star pattern that dances on the boat ceiling. The evening was more than I could've asked for, delicious cuisine and attentive service. Adam's friends seemed genuinely pleased with me, well, except for Madeline. The pride I felt when Adam accepted his award went down to my core. And most pleasing of all was when he asked me to be his girlfriend. A perfect evening, even though unanswered questions still float into my mind from time to time. I continue to watch the light play on the ceiling until sleep takes over.

I can't go on like this anymore. Without Thomas I am nothing. The world is so full of suffering. Many of my friends and loved ones have died. Many good soldiers have met their death too. Everything is dark: our moods, our clothing, our lives. I can't go on . . . "Thomas . . . Thomas," I cry.

"Tess. Wake up. You're having a bad dream." Adam shakes me.

I open my eyes and notice my cheeks are wet from tears. "Oh," is all I can manage.

"Are you okay? You were crying out for someone named Thomas. Who is he?"

"I don't know. Just some crazy dream," I lie.

"Seemed pretty upsetting to you. Are you sure you're okay?"

"I'm fine. Let's forget it. I already have." I get up and head to the bathroom. Behind the locked door, I grasp the sink for stability. My eyes are bloodshot and cheeks tearstained. My God. Now these blasted dreams are bleeding into my life with Adam. This has got to stop. I splash water on my face, brush my teeth, and dress quickly. Applying my smile as I would lipstick, I unlock the door to enjoy the morning with Adam.

Chapter 32

"It was almost a catastrophe, Naomi. He heard me calling Thomas' name. I mean, it's not like I can really explain the truth to him." I sit next to her, both cross-legged on her couch, making napkin holders for her wedding.

"I think you really need to have another regression. I've been thinking about it and I have a theory."

"Go on."

"Okay. The reason you continue to have these past life memories come out as dreams is that you have yet to resolve some trauma or issue from the past. I think the only way you'll be able to move on and have peace is if you go back and deal with that past life."

"So what you're saying is that in order for me to move forward with Adam, I need to resolve the past life issue with Kathleen and Thomas?"

"Yes, exactly. Something must have happened there that you haven't dealt with because the dreams still continue and they're becoming more intense."

"What if I can't deal with whatever it is that happened to them?"

"You? Come on, Tess. You're one of the strongest people I know. I have complete faith in you and whatever it is I'm here to help you through it. I want nothing more than for you to be happy and I'm sorry, but I think you might have to walk through this fire to get to the other side."

"I was afraid you were going to say that." I look down at the napkin holder that I inadvertently mangled. "Sorry," I say as I hand her my disastrous handiwork.

I finally feel ready to go back and find out what happened to Kathleen and Thomas, I think. Last time I was so emotional that I couldn't finish recalling their life. I hope I'm ready this time.

Barbara instructs me as she did previously and I relax easily. I cross over the bridge as I have before and find myself back in the year 1918.

"I'm despondent. I received notice that Thomas died fighting for our country. I don't want to live. I don't eat. I just sit. I don't have the energy to tend to my children. Life is bleak in the streets. So many have died from the war and the influenza. People don't walk outside often. They're afraid of becoming ill. We hide away hoping the darkness will subside, but it goes on and on. It's too much for me to bear."

I stop because the pain of this memory is palpable. Tears are streaming down my face. I lost the love of my life.

"Go on. If this is too painful, pull up out of Kathleen's body and watch the scene from above as if you are watching a movie."

I rise out of Kathleen's body and view the scene from above, briefly. For a moment I hover, but then I'm jolted back into her body. Is it that I'm not ready to leave her, or vice versa? Some part of me, I guess, must realize that I need to experience this again with new eyes, the eyes of Tess. It may be the only way to close this chapter of my life. My hands tremble. I start again.

"I'm sitting in a chair in my home and staring at . . . empty space. God is punishing me for participating in Margaret's séance, and rightly so . . ."

"Continue. What are you doing now?"

"My color is sallow. I'm unable to stomach any nourishment. I don't fill out my clothes anymore. My eyes are sunken and stare into the distance of nothing."

How long I've been sitting here, I don't know. Far away, I hear something like a child crying. Not far off, I realize. I lower my head toward the sound. Robert's head is lying on my lap. He cries out again and again, "Mama. Mama."

I don't have the will to live. There is no life left in me. I'm dried up. Even Robert's tears are unable to reconstitute me.

Thomas Jr. pulls Robert away from me. To where I don't know. My children are learning to fend for themselves. I'm unable to care for them or myself anymore. I'm no use to them. I get up from the chair, wearing only the dressing gown that

I've worn for days on end. When is the last time I washed? I run my hand through my disheveled, dirty hair. I once wore my luminous hair with pride. How long ago was that? How long since Thomas and I danced together?

"I want to die. I can't go on without him," I cry.

With resolution I stand up. I walk with purpose to the kitchen and start a fire to heat water. After placing the metal bathing tub on the floor, I empty the heated water into it. I continue to fill the tub, and then fetch Thomas' straight razor. My fingers maneuver with difficulty to untie my gown. It falls to the floor and I stand naked, my ribs protruding obscenely. I test the water with my toe and then ease into the tub. My eyes close. For a moment I relish the silence and peace. The warm water is inviting.

"I want to sink away into this quiet water," I say aloud to no one.

Oh . . . I take a deep breath. Thomas' razor feels good in my hand. Its mirror-like surface mesmerizes me for a brief interlude. I watch the light from the window reflect in the blade. Without another thought, I slice my left arm from my hand to elbow. I follow with my right and then my thighs. I gasp at the searing pain. A scream is stifled. The agony is almost a relief. At least now I'm feeling something. I let all my pain flow into the water. The water turns from clear to pink to red.

I stop again. I'm heartbroken and shocked. My tears are flowing freely and my sentences are coming in short bursts between my sobs.

Barbara instructs me, "You can remain detached from the emotion of this scene as if you were a reporter. Taking a deep breath you will find yourself at peace. You are merely reporting on a scene with calm detachment."

I take a deep breath and feel at once peaceful again, but continue to stay in Kathleen's body despite Barbara's kind instructions.

I'm getting sleepy. My mind drifts as I sink further into the water. Life drains from me. Wait . . . I hear a faint tune.

"What is that music?" I say. "It sounds vaguely familiar."

I realize it's in my mind. It's the song Thomas sang to me many years ago. I can hear the words now, "I love you as I never loved before . . ."

I'm now lost in a world within my mind. In my vision I'm dancing happily with my dashing Thomas. With this scene playing in my mind, I take my last breath.

"Tell me what happens next," Barbara suggests.

I'm quiet for a few minutes, experiencing the sensation of leaving Kathleen's body. Finally, a picture emerges. "I see it now. My oldest son found me. Thomas Jr. never told Robert that I killed myself, to save him from the pain. Robert assumed that I died of influenza, like so many had."

"And what happened to your children?"

"They went to live with an aunt. They lived to be in their forties. Both of them had a hard time of it. I caused them so much grief."

"You can now understand and get clarity from your higher perspective."

"I'm rising high. I feel expansive. There's overflowing peace here. I feel free and connected and feel so much love. I can feel Thomas' love."

"Do you recognize anyone from that lifetime in your current life as Tess? Go back and look into their eyes. You will know them by their eyes. Look at Thomas Jr. and Robert."

I scan their eyes and gasp.

"Oh my God. Thomas Jr. is Wade, my son today. And . . . oh my . . . Robert is Richard, my ex-husband." I'm flabbergasted and, quite honestly, freaked out. "How can this be? I married my own son."

"From another time period, Tess."

"Yes, I know it was from another lifetime, but really, this is a lot to take in."

"Take a deep breath, you feel very much at peace. You can now integrate this new understanding into your current life and help heal family dynamics that have been strained. You will remember everything and now that you have been able to recall this past life trauma, no longer will it plague you in this lifetime. You can now heal and move ahead with your life."

Barbara brings me out of hypnosis and I'm silent. I don't know what to say. I'm saddened for Kathleen and Thomas. I'm saddened for Thomas Jr. and Robert. I feel guilty and depressed. I really need to sit with this for a while. I thank Barbara for her skillfulness and leave the office with my handful of tissues. My eyes feel strained and puffy from all the tears I shed.

I walk down to the ocean. I don't feel up to driving at the moment. I'm reeling. As I reach the beach, I find a place in the sand and shuck my

flip-flops. There is much to think about. I start to tick them off one by one. Let me see:
- I killed myself. Now I understand why I cried out, "I can't go on without him" after my meltdown a while back.
- If I killed myself back then, do I have the risk of doing it again in this life?
- My death left my children abandoned, which is basically what I did once more when I left Richard and Wade to move to Belmont Shore. I feel a lot of guilt on behalf of Kathleen and myself today.
- If Thomas Jr. is Wade today, then it completely makes sense why he is so angry with me in this lifetime and doesn't even know why. He's the one that found me dead and knows how I did it.
- And if Robert is Richard today, then it also makes sense why he seems childlike and dependent on me and why Wade tends to act like the adult around him.
- Lastly, but most importantly, I need to find a way to heal this so we don't repeat it again and again in future lifetimes.

I sit on the beach until the cold forces me to get back up and head home.

Back at my apartment, I feel horrible. What kind of monster am I? Any peace and rational thinking I found on the beach, I left there too. I press the tips of Jared's necklace into my breastbone. I feel nothing. All I had is gone, I fear.

Guilt is crushing me. My chest, my lungs, and mostly my heart are being crushed by some unseen force. I wonder if the force will win and smash me to smithereens. I don't see any other way around it. I may allow the guilt to win. At least then this pain will stop. Inches inside my front door I collapse into a fetal position and gasp for air. Prince is wary. He's smart enough to stay away from something this far gone. Like when an old lion leaves the pride to die, the younger animals know better than to follow. And so Prince keeps his distance. I don't blame him. I don't want to be near my wretched self either. I disgust myself. I would spit on myself if I had the strength. But, I don't.

It takes all my energy merely to breathe. Maybe I should stop. I forcibly empty my lungs with one great exhale and wait. Silent now, I wait for the "now what?" Part of me is praying for it all to end, and yet . . . my eyelids shut for a moment . . . "Aaaaagh," I cry out in despair as a gulp of air rushes in. I can't even do that right.

I lay in that heap most of the night, ignoring the cell phone ringing at first light. Nothing resolved. Nothing better. I still live and still feel like crap. What a piece of shit I am. Not only did I kill myself and abandon my two children in turbulent times, but I abandoned them once again in this life. Great job, Tess, let's see how much damage you can do. I wish I could make it right.

No, I'm going to make it right. I sit up too fast, causing my head to spin. Back down I lay to stop the vertigo. Ohhh. Take it slow. This time I ease up gently, using the wall to steady myself. How the hell am I going to make it right? Tell Richard and Wade what I did to them and beg their forgiveness? No way. They'll think I'm nuts.

I make it over to the toilet and sit, head in hands, mulling it over and emptying my very full bladder. What to do. What to do. I start repeating my new mantra. What to do. What to do. What to do. All the way to the kitchen. What to do. Making tea. What to do. On the balcony. What to do.

I don't even deserve this nice apartment, my *Pear Wear*, Prince, Ms. Glimmer . . . Adam. I don't deserve any of it. I should have never left Richard. I should have been a devoted wife and mother. Not the selfish bitch I am. Always looking for my "Knight in Shining Armor." He doesn't exist. Get that through your thick head, Tess!

If I never left Richard and Wade then maybe I would have corrected the wrong I did as Kathleen. Maybe that's why we're together again, so I can devote myself to them. It makes sense that I never found Thomas/J again. He is obviously repulsed by me and my weakness. My stomach lurches.

Time must have passed sitting out here on the balcony. My only measurement is not that my tea has disappeared from my cup, but that my tea is cold now. I dump the tepid brew into the potted succulents and go back to my mantra . . . what to do. Breathing that mantra in and out, in and out, something dawns on me . . . slowly the thought emerges; a voice is heard—*make a correction.* Make a correction?

Wait . . . I jump up and start pacing three steps west, three steps east, back and forth. Could it be that easy? If I go back to Richard and Wade now and completely devote my life to making them happy, would it undo my past damage? Maybe if I dedicate my life to them this time then in my future life I can find love. That's it. I'll give up my Belmont Shore life. Go back to Richard. My mother will be happy. Wade will have a full-time mom. Richard will have his wife back. I can go back to personal training. All will be happy, except me, but that's my fault.

I expect Richard and Wade will be angry for a while, but after some time they'll fall into a comfortable routine. Okay, now I have something to do. I can work with that:

- Call June and give notice
- Say goodbye to Esther
- Cancel my booth at the farmers market (will lose deposit)
- Let Naomi know of change of address for her wedding invitation
- Tell Adam I can't see him anymore
- See if Richard and Wade would be willing to have Prince live with them
- Oh . . . and, most importantly, beg Richard and Wade to let me back into their lives

There goes my stomach again—lurching. Shit, I'm going to be sick. I run to the bathroom and grab hold of the toilet rim. Dry heaves, my favorite, nothing in the stomach to come up anyway, not even tea. The cold bathroom floor becomes my temporary refuge. I use the shower door as support for my throbbing head and await the next wave of nausea to hit.

My cell phone is going off again. Do I want to talk to anyone? Nope. Hasn't whomever it is figured that out already? It has been ringing all morning. Just give me a moment to digest my new truth (or un-digest as the case may be) before I have to face the rest of the world. Why do I feel like I have been handed a life sentence? Oh, wait, that's because it is.

Again with the phone—probably Adam. I can't talk to him right now. This time I listen to the voice message.

"*Tess, what is going on? I have been trying to reach you. Did I say something to upset you? Please call me back.*"

Oh god, now he thinks it's something he did, not that I'm some kind of abomination. I wipe away my tears on the back of my sleeve and dial his number.

"Adam." The vomiting irritated my throat, making my voice sound raspy.

"Tess. What is going on? I've been worried sick." His voice is edged with strain.

"Please. I need a little time."

"Is it something that I did?"

"No. It's not you. It's something else. I don't really want to discuss it."

"No Tess, that's not an option. We have something special and you cannot close up on me like this!"

"I can't Frédéric, please don't."

"Frédéric! Who the hell is Frédéric? First you're calling out for Thomas in your sleep and now calling me Frédéric? Look, maybe you need to take some time and straighten out all your men. Let me know when you have it figured out!" His voice is harsher than I can deal with.

"Wait. No, Adam . . ." but he hung up on me. Frédéric, who is Frédéric? Maybe I *am* crazy! God help me. I lean over the toilet and throw up.

Chapter 33

"Tess! Open the door. Tess. Do you hear me? Open the door, dammit! . . . You're really scaring me . . . Dammit . . . Dammit. If you don't open this damn door I'm going to call the police . . . Why won't you answer the phone or the door?" Naomi calls out.

I can hear the desperation in her voice and slowly I make my way to the door, but instead of opening it I find myself easing down to the floor and resting my back against the solid wood. I hear sobbing coming from the other side. My heart breaks.

"Tess . . . please open the door . . ."

"I'm here . . . don't cry."

"Dammit, you're making me so mad. Please let me in . . . Tess . . . please."

"God, you're relentless." I stand and unbolt the door. She rushes at me as I recoil in shame.

Where am I? A heavy fog in my brain confuses the situation. The smell of unfamiliar sheets, the softness of an unknown pillow, causes me alarm and I bolt upright.

"Shhh. Lay down. You're safe," Naomi tells me as she places her hand on my arm.

"Oh, my head." The room spins, convincing me to lie back down. Glimpses and snippets of memory flash in my mind. *The hushed and panicked voices, calls made on the phone, Raj coming over, Naomi handing Prince to Valerie. Raj scooping me up and placing me in his car. And Naomi . . . oh yes.*

Naomi bathing me and dressing me in clean pajamas and helping me to her bed . . . dear, dear Naomi.

"I still think we need to call a doctor or take her to the hospital," Raj insists as he stands in the doorway of her bedroom.

"No Raj. I told you this is not something a doctor can help with."

"Well, what do you suggest? She's a mess. Look at her."

"Shh, I think I know what she needs. Sit with her, please." She gets up to leave the room.

"No. Don't leave me," I croak out as panic threatens to take over.

"Hush, rest now. I'll be right back. Raj will be here." Naomi lays her hand on my forehead before retreating to another room.

Raj stands a good few feet away from me as if I have something contagious. That's fine with me. I feel repugnant anyway. I turn away and fall back asleep.

"Tess . . . Tess . . . Let's get up, okay?" Naomi is once again sitting on the bed. This time she has a tray with some crackers, cheese, grapes, and a large mug of chamomile tea. "Try and eat something," she pleads. I raise myself to a sitting position. "Slowly, move slowly this time."

"I really don't feel like eating. My stomach is still sick."

"A few crackers then, and tea, okay?" She hands me a cracker. "I'll feed you if I have to."

"Fine, I'll take a few bites." I take the round water cracker from her hands.

"You ready to talk to me?"

"In private." My eyes dart to Raj, once again standing like a sentry in the doorway.

"Raj, could you go over to Tess' apartment and pack an overnight bag for her? She'll be staying here for a few days."

"Wait. What about Prince?" I start.

"Valerie has offered to watch him. He'll be well taken care of, which is what you need right now. Don't argue." Naomi squeezes my hand.

"I'll be back in a couple of hours. Tess, get some rest," Raj adds.

"Hold on." Naomi gets up and hugs Raj. I can barely make out their whisperings.

"I hope you know what you are doing," Raj whispers to Naomi.

"It'll be fine. Now please give us some time. Thank you for understanding." Naomi kisses him on the cheek and then comes back to me. The sound of the front door closing, signaling Raj's departure, causes me to stiffen up. It's time to confess.

I feel cried out, exhausted after rehashing the whole regression, my graphic past life suicide and the shocking revelation that Richard and Wade were my abandoned children from a past life. Naomi cried with me, held me, and encouraged me to go on when I was too disgusted to say the next word.

When my tale was told we sat holding hands quietly. "Come lie down with me for a while. I'm so tired," I ask her. She obliges and crawls into bed. I lay my damp cheek on her chest and instantly fall into a deep slumber.

"*I love this tune,*" *Kathleen tells Thomas as he sings in her ear. They are dancing and happy once more. Swirling and twirling.*

"*This is our last dance, you know,*" *he whispers.*

"*But, why?*" *Kathleen asks.*

"*That's the way it is. Time for us to have other experiences. You understand?*" *he asks.*

"*I don't know if I can,*" *she answers.*

"*You are strong. Let it go. Let it go.*"

When I open my eyes, Naomi is still holding me, stroking my hair. "You're awake. Sleep okay?" she asks.

"I had another Thomas/Kathleen dream. Different though. Thomas, in his own way, was telling Kathleen to move on."

"Sounds like he may be on to something."

"I don't know. Do you think so?"

"I do. Let's get up and get some fresh air. Take a walk, what do you say?"

"I don't know. Not sure I'm up to it."

"Sure you are. Now get up, get cleaned up. Raj brought you a bag. It's in the bathroom."

I make my way to the bathroom with care, not trusting my balance. Actually I'm steadier than I thought I would be. Sure enough, Raj and Naomi thought of everything: comfortable clothes, toiletries—all laid out for me. I shower, washing off the grittiness of the last day, or it is two; time has escaped me. I dry off and dress in sweats and a tank top, then comb out my hair and skip the makeup. No point.

"Well, there you are and looking so much better. Doesn't she look better, Raj?"

"Much," he says and heads back to the living room.

"Come, let's take a walk on the strand." She grabs my hand.

She's right. The fresh air does make me feel better. More grounded in the present. The rhythm of the waves, a light breeze, people living their lives all around me, no one taking any notice of the two of us, makes me feel one hundred percent better.

"Thank you," I tell her.

"You're welcome."

Guess now is as good a time as any. I approach Naomi with my plan for my future. "You know, after my regression I heard an inner voice telling me to 'make a correction.'"

"Okay." She pauses to let me continue.

"The only solution I came up with to make this correction is to go back to Richard and Wade, and be the best wife and mother I can be . . ." I feel my eyes prickling again.

"No. Take a step back for a moment."

"I don't see another way to rectify the situation. This way I can break the cycle and we all can heal."

"And what about Adam?"

My heart sinks when I hear his name. "I don't know." I dab my eyes with tissue that Naomi hands me from her bag.

"You know, you've had too much trauma to figure this all out right now. Let's enjoy the beach. We can plan your future later. Deal?"

"Deal."

"How about some hot chocolate?"

"Ok." I smile. She always knows what creature comforts work on me.

Chapter 34

Outside Naomi's window the winter trees are barren. I reflect on the year since leaving my old life behind. It feels like a whirlwind of emotions and events. Having some time away at Naomi's place has been healing. She has provided me peace and quiet for meditation and introspection. I haven't had to lift a finger or do anything except work on me.

"You're looking pretty serene," she announces as she hands me a plate of fruit for a snack. She's been doting on me for the last few days. "I want to talk to you about your idea of going back to Richard. I've been thinking about it."

"All right. I guess it's time to talk about it," I admit.

"Staying with someone out of guilt will only keep you all in bondage. You have to set yourself and them free, even if it's painful. It will be more painful if you don't. I believe when your voice told you to make a correction it was more of inner correction—a releasing of guilt and forgiving yourself. You have never forgiven yourself for taking your life. That's why the dreams plagued you. Forgive yourself and let Richard live his life."

I'm quiet for a moment to let her words penetrate my stubborn mind. "Let me sit with it for a while, okay?"

"Sure," she tells me and leaves the room for me to work it out.

I hadn't thought of it that way and wondered why. Since no other ideas have popped into my mind, I figure I might as well sit with this one, as Doug taught me. The idea drops into my consciousness and I breathe it in. It circulates and percolates. Does it resonate truth?

I follow my breath in and out for most of the afternoon until something . . . something starts deep in my belly. Something around my belly button, first a spark, a soft, glowing ember appears. I give all my attention to this ember, breathing life into it like coaxing a fire to start. It grows, spreading out to my solar plexus and abdomen. The glow grows and strengthens with each breath. It takes form in the shape of . . . oh, a raven.

My raven has come back to visit, but this time it's gold in color. My gold raven takes flight throughout my body and I travel with him, entering my lungs, heart, and blood vessels. Each brush of the raven's wings illuminates my body with golden light. The raven dives and soars and continues his flight through me. Once my inner body is illuminated, the raven dives low and turns suddenly to start his ascent towards the top of my head. Higher and higher he flies until it pierces the top of my head, causing me to cry out from the impact. The raven shatters into a million golden fragments and rains down on my outer body and down on the floor. I feel as if I am sitting in a golden puddle of liquid light.

I pant from the energy expelled and soak in this puddle of truth. A deep peace that I've never experienced comes over me. I search my heart, but can no longer find the burden of guilt I had carried for so many years, even another lifetime. It's gone and I'm free.

When I open my eyes, I'm surprised to be greeted by evening. How long have I been sitting? I rise to find the source of the chatter I hear. Naomi and Raj are putting the last touches on the dinner meal. The table is decorated with candles and fresh flowers.

"It's beautiful," I exclaim.

"There you are." Naomi turns around as she hears me. "My goodness, you look radiant! You found the peace you were seeking. I can see it." She rushes to hug me.

"Wow, amazing. You look so much better," Raj says. "Naomi did know what you needed."

"Did you ever doubt me?" Naomi teases. "Come, let's eat."

"Good. I'm starving," I tell her as I pull up a chair at the end of the table.

"That's my girl," she says as she sits to my left. Raj takes a chair across from Naomi, grabbing a bowl of pasta and serving us both. Wine flowing, candles flickering, laughter abounding, we fill the evening with love and, most comforting of all, I have a peace that feels lasting.

Chapter 35

The next morning I wake to find the peace I discovered yesterday still abundant. I take an internal inventory to look for any hidden guilt and find none. A deep breath of relief escapes and I quickly wash up and pack. Time to go home.

"Hey there. See you slept well. Ready for breakfast?" Naomi asks over her morning coffee, sitting with her leg casually draped on Raj's lap.

"I think I'm going to wear out my welcome. I feel ready to go home. I have some things to tend to, namely Richard and Adam."

"I understand. Are you sure you feel up to it? Oh, what am I saying, I can see you are by the look in your eyes."

"Naomi, I can't express to you how grateful I am to you and Raj. You saved me."

"Don't mention it." She gets up to hug me.

"Thank you, my dearest friend. I love you." I hug her tightly.

"I love you, too. Go take care of business. Call me later." She releases me and opens the door. "Raj can you drop her off?"

"No problem. Glad you're doing better. You had me pretty scared," Raj adds.

"I'm sorry about that, really." I give Raj a quick peck on the cheek. We head back to my home.

Please pick up, please, please, I silently beg as Adam's cell phone rings.
"Hello."
"Adam . . ." I'm suddenly out of breath.

"Yes." He sounds hesitant.
"Can we talk?" I get out.
"Of course. Can you come by the boat?"
"Now okay?" I hold my breath.
"I'll be waiting."

I end the call, again that giddy feeling bubbles through my body. I freshen up in record time, kiss Prince on his head as he pulls his ears back in annoyance, run down the stairs, and jump in the car. My heart is fluttering, keeping time with the song on the mp3 blasting on the car speakers. "Good, good, good, good vibrations," I sing aloud. Naomi would love it.

The harbour parking lot is still empty—only a few cars and trucks. I pull in by Dock R, Slip15. It's quiet this morning. No noise except for the squawking of egrets nesting in the tree above me. I quickly scan the boat. No sign of him. What if he's not here? I notice a pulling, sort of a magnetic attraction, to my right. I feel him. I can actually sense him, or his energy. I turn toward the direction of the tugging and there, behind me, he is sitting on a bench in the picnic area. He's sporting a smile that warms my heart.

I rush at him as he stands and opens his arms. Never have arms felt so good, warm, and accepting.

"Adam. Oh Adam," I cry.

"God, I've missed you," he whispers into my hair. I nuzzle his neck, drinking up his scent. Finally I pull away as I know I need to talk to him.

"Can we sit?" I say.

We sit on the bench facing each other, examining and stroking each other's hands as if we rediscovered a treasure, which indeed we have.

"Tess, before you start, I want to say I'm sorry for my outburst previously. You were going through something and I wasn't supportive."

"No. No, you had every right to be upset and concerned. I don't know if I would've been as patient. Without going into specifics, I had some parts of my past that I needed to work through and heal before I felt I could commit to a new relationship. My feelings for you are very deep and I knew it wouldn't be fair if I hadn't cleared my past first. I hope you can find it in your heart to forgive me for my odd behavior and the pain I've caused you."

"Of course. Thank you for telling me. Maybe someday you'll feel comfortable enough to tell me the whole story."

"I would like to . . . someday," I say as I look into the warmth in his eyes and feel the deep pulling.

"Kiss me, Tess."

Rain in southern California seems to take me by surprise. From my window table in a café in Santa Monica I watch the puddles form while I wait for Richard to show up. We agreed to meet halfway. At first he was hesitant, but I told him I really wanted to talk to him. I take a couple of deep breaths and scan for any tension or doubt, but find none. He approaches cautiously, like a rabbit concerned about dining with a wolf.

"Hello Richard." I stand up and greet him with a hug. He stiffens.

"Tess," he answers, still unsure.

"Sit. Let me get you lunch." I hand him a menu.

"What's this about?" He sits down, but doesn't look at the menu even as the server approaches.

"Have you decided or do you need a little more time?" A male server asks.

"Uh, I'd like the turkey club? You, Richard?" I ask.

"Yeah, that's fine," he says. At least he's planning on staying to eat.

After the server takes the order, I start. "Thank you for meeting me. The reason I wanted to meet you is that I want to apologize."

"Okay," he says through tight lips.

"Richard." I take a breath. "I've done horrendous things. I felt a lot of guilt. I left you and Wade to fend on your own."

"Yes."

"I know that I can't take it back. But I hope someday you and Wade will find it in your hearts to forgive me. I love you both. I've done a lot of soul searching and wanted to tell you this . . ."

"Okay."

"I only want you and Wade to have so much happiness and love. If you both stay angry with me, I'll completely understand."

"You do seem different. I don't know . . . more assured?" He softens.

"I've done a lot of thinking."

"Apparently . . . well, I can't speak for Wade. You know how stubborn he is." We both chuckle. "But, you do appear sincere. I'll work on letting go too. Thank you for your apology."

"No, thank you, Richard," I say as I place my hand on his. Our food arrives and we eat in a shared silence. Outside, the rain has stopped and the sun is poking his head out.

*

"Okay Tess. So if I understand correctly, you are interested in finding out if you knew Adam in a previous lifetime. Am I correct?" says Barbara as I, for the fourth time, settle into the chair.

"Yes. Can that be done?"

"Yes. I have many clients that come in searching for people they know or once knew. Sometimes a loved one has died and the client hopes to find their loved one in a previous life. This gives them peace—that they find each other over and over. Sometimes the client comes in not due to grief, but simply curious."

"Curious. Yeah, I guess that would be me. I admit, though, that after my last experience, I feel a bit hesitant to try this again."

"Not all lifetimes are that tragic. Many are peaceful. I cannot guarantee that the lifetime you are searching for will be peaceful, but even if it's not, you're strong enough now to handle it. You have grown so much since your last session. If, however, the session is stressful for you we will simply leave that scene and bring you back to a place of serenity. Okay?"

"Okay. Let's do this." I recline in the chair and mentally relax my muscles. I take a few deep breaths and release the tension I didn't know I was holding.

"Tess. Since you're now accustomed to hypnosis, as you listen to my voice your eyelids will feel heavy and your breathing will stay deep and regular; you are already feeling a deep sense of peace and tranquility. With each breath you take you go deeper and deeper into a deep state of hypnosis. That's right. Go now to your safe haven where your body can rest and rejuvenate while your mind is free to travel—to travel to other places and other times, in lifetimes before this one . . . Now picture Adam in your mind's eye . . . Take a look at his facial features, the contour of his jaw, his nose, mouth, and now picture his eyes. Look deep into his eyes. As you look into his eyes, they will take you back to another lifetime in which you were together . . . Go there now. Tell me what you see."

"I don't see anything . . . wait . . . the scene is blurry, but clearing now . . . ah . . . I see rolling green hills and orchards . . . I can't tell what type of fruit trees they are . . . oh . . . they belong to me, I mean us."

"Go on. Who is us?"

"Um . . . mon mari et moi."

"Good. You're speaking French, but you can speak English for me. Are you in France?"

"Oui, uh, yes. My husband, his brother Nicolas, and I own an orchard here."

"Do you get a sense of a date?"

"1839."

"Go on."

"We're very happy, very much in love. My husband's name is Frédéric and I'm Brigitte. We're doing well. Our orchard yields a good harvest for us."

"What do you grow?"

"Pears. Mostly d'anjou, but we have something special. We have a few Nashi pear trees. You see, most pears are not good eaten straight from the tree. Usually you pick them green and let them ripen. If they ripen on the tree they are gritty and mushy. But the Nashi pear ripens on the tree. It is a rounder pear that is very juicy. They are in high demand out here."

"And where is here?"

"We are near a small village called Estagel in France."

"Go on."

"Oh my . . . Nicolas, Frédéric's brother, is Jared. I see it now . . . Nicolas is forever a jokester, making us laugh or causing us angst. At times he teases me mercilessly. Mostly he adds more life to our simple home. Nicolas is bright. In fact it was his idea for our Nashi pear. The brothers traveled far into the Orient to bring back the young saplings."

"Okay. Let's go to the next significant event with Frédéric in that lifetime."

I take a deep breath and let the image of Nicolas/Jared fade. Tree branches come into view. I can feel the sunshine, from the memory, on my shoulders.

"The sun is warm. I have spread out our lunch under one of our prized Nashi trees. Frédéric has other ideas in mind besides lunch. He picks a large ripe pear off our tree and places it beside him. Frédéric leans in and slowly pulls the ties of my chemise, revealing my bosom . . . I lay back on the soft green grass as Frédéric cuts a slice of pear and drips the juice on my bare breasts . . . ah, he bends down and slowly licks off the juices that have run down my breast and on to my belly . . ."

Frédéric has cut up small pieces of pear and arranges them on my bare belly. Ever so slowly he eats a piece, then feeds me some. My breath is halting. My hips rise whenever his mouth lowers to taste another bit of pear warming on my skin. Oh . . . he teases me so. I plead with him to stop this pleasurable torture and make sweet love to me. With a smirk he unties his tunic, giving me a moment to appreciate his beautiful toned torso. The sun is high in the sky and his face is partially backlit, yet I can still make out his chiseled features, full mouth, and loving eyes. He obliges my wishes and positions himself over me, his strong hands caressing my breasts, his lips tasting of pears and wine. He takes me . . .

"Tess, if you're ready, it's now time to move forward in time."

My mind leaves the pear orchard, the scene blurs, and new images slowly come into focus.

"We are elderly now; our children are grown and have taken over the farm. We're sitting and watching the sunset, holding hands. Life has been good to us."

"Go on to the death scene, if comfortable."

Once again the scene I'm experiencing recedes and is replaced with a new image.

"I'm old, my family is around me. Frédéric passed on in his sleep a few months back. It's my time to join him. I've had a good life. I'm ready."

"Is there anything you learned from this life?"

"I'm grateful for a life of simple pleasures and hard work, but filled with love and family. It was truly rewarding."

"Okay, at the count of three you'll be wide awake, alert and refreshed. One, two, three."

"Mmmm." I open my eyes and stretch.

"Welcome back."

"That was amazing. Was I really speaking French?"

"Yes. It's called xenoglossy. It happens sometimes."

"So many things make sense now. It was wonderful finding Jared again. And then there are my feelings of familiarity with Adam: speaking French when I never learned it in this life, Adam's boat being named a French name, and my crazy obsession with pears. My God. No wonder pears have that effect on me. Adam has been sexy for at least two lifetimes."

"Well, it appears that some of your questions were answered."

"Yes. This was absolutely incredible. I feel a big weight lifted off me. Thank you so much, Barbara."

"You're very welcome, although you did all the work. I was simply a guide. I'm always available if you want to better understand other relationships in your life."

"I'll keep that in mind. Right now I feel content. Thanks again."

Chapter 36

With my journal in hand, I sit on the back of Adam's boat staring into the quiet water. I notice there are many nice locations to write on the boat. I'm not sure which spot is my favorite. I try out the back deck and when I get too cool I go up to the top covered patio and stretch out on the black and grey striped upholstered benches. With a pillow behind my back, I can stretch out and stay comfortable and warm while still being able to take in all the sights around me. Yes, this is the perfect spot. There is much more swaying up here than down below. It feels soothing. I can see why Adam likes writing on the boat. The ambiance helps to stimulate the muse.

I'm ready to write my story down now. Many questions in my life have been resolved. I found happiness, love, and a deeper peace. There are some areas where I still haven't found resolution, like my issues with my mother. It must be past life related, but I will tackle that another time. My yearning for J ceased. Now it's more of a curiosity. Maybe I will find him in a future life. I have more faith in the process now. Doug helped me with learning to trust the process of the universe. I think he was trying to teach me that part of having an intuitive sense is not about changing outcomes but changing my reaction. Still, something keeps pinching in my mind, like a splinter. On a couple of occasions Jesse behaved like he didn't know who Doug was. Is Jesse mistaken, or did I imagine it all? Nah, that's not possible. Is it?

"Anyway, Jared, I plan to tell my story as a tale of fiction. I mean, come on, who would believe it otherwise. It's quite unbelievable even to me. I doubt anyone would take it seriously if I wrote it as a memoir. Of course I will change some of the names and facts to protect the identity of the people involved."

I look up from my journal to watch my man for a moment.

Adam is busying himself with his "semi-annual boat maintenance" as he calls it. I'm not kidding—he has checklists and goes over every inch of the boat with a fine-tooth comb. He's extremely focused, which I find quite sexy. But I also realize it's better to keep out of his way when he's going over his checklists. He has tunnel vision like he has horse blinders on.

"This gives me a good excuse to take my leave and head over to the coffeehouse to write. First to swing by the apartment and pick up my mail which tends to pile up when I spend extended time on the boat—really, can you blame me, Jared?"

I quickly plant a kiss on the back of his neck. "Going to go write, be back later this afternoon. Love you," I tell him as I climb off the boat onto the dock.

"Okay, sweet pear, see you later," Adam calls back. My heart swells when he calls me that. How did I get so lucky?

On the drive back to the apartment, I reminisce on Adam's proposition for me to live on the boat. It was one of the flawless evenings where the sky glows a soft orange off the clouds and the red wine in our glasses complemented the scene. Adam and I were admiring the beauty of the sunset and sipping some good wine. *El Roy*, I think he called it. It was delicious is all I remember as I swirled it around my mouth. I never have been a wine expert, but this wine was exquisite. I was sitting thinking there couldn't be a more perfect evening and glanced over at Adam. He was partially silhouetted by the setting sun and yet I could still make out his features. He was absolutely beautiful and took my breath away. I smiled and he smiled back one of his drop-dead gorgeous smiles that can make me swoon every time. Actually, I think he knows this and uses it to his advantage. Anyway, as I was thinking how much I love being here with him he bursts out with, "I love you, Tess. I want you to come live with me on the boat. Say yes."

I mean, how could I say no after that? There was no hesitation, but a bold strong proclamation of his desire, his desire for me. No one had ever been that direct with me before. I was bowled over. At the time, however, I hadn't considered what to do with all my stuff. Not that I have a lot of stuff. In fact most of it is still packed away and stored in my garage.

I guess a storage unit is next on my list of things to arrange. I won't be too sad to say, "Adios" to my landlady, June. And Prince seems to enjoy being a proper shipmate on Adam's boat. Who would have thought my life would turn out so well? I sure didn't.

The mailbox is full of mail I've neglected. I toss the letters into one of my latest *Pear Wear* design bags and pop into the apartment to water the hydrangea on the balcony. Yeah, part of me will miss this place, the high-beamed ceilings, the neighborhood, Buddy, and, of course, my eccentric neighbor, Valerie. There is also a part of me that feels ready to move on, too.

"Valerie, you decent?" I call through her open screen door.

"Oh sure, honey. Even if I had no clothes on I'd still be decent."

"Okay, now that's just TMI."

"Come on in," she tells me.

"Hey, I wanted to tell you thank you for being a good neighbor and friend."

"So you really going to live on a boat? Don't think you'll get all claustrophobic?"

"I don't think so. It's roomier than I originally thought. I'm really excited. This move is much more fun than my last."

"Your last move wasn't all bad. Hey, you freakin' met me."

"Very true. You're really something, Valerie. Maybe that's why I like you so much."

"Probably. But seriously, don't go forgetting all your old friends. Keep in touch, okay?"

"I'm only twenty minutes away. I'll be around."

"Hey, if you need a honeymoon trip booked, I'm your girl."

"Whoa, slow down. We're living together, not getting married. By the way, how's it going with you and Jim?"

"Completely fabulous. So glad I needed tile work. He's a real catch."

"I'm so happy for you. Well, talk to you soon, gotta jet. Going to go write."

"Good for you. Take care of yourself. You deserve to be happy too."

We hug briefly before she retreats back into her apartment.

On one of my bike discovery tours months ago, I came across a unique coffeehouse nearby. Maybe I can write my book here. *The Den* is filled with plush couches and chairs. The walls are old bricks. This looks to be a very old building. Against the walls are bookshelves filled with books. It's unnervingly quiet in here. Not even any music playing overhead. This is very different from the coffeehouses I usually frequent. Everyone whispers here just like, well, a library. A blond woman to my right, sitting with her friends, starts laughing. I half expect a matronly librarian to shush them.

I order a butterscotch latte with soy milk, to save on calories, and choose a table by the window. The lighting is dim in here. Dim lights tend to make me sleepy. I'm here to write, not sleep. It is, however, a nice change of scenery from the apartment or the coffeehouse up the street from me. I wonder if all the quiet will make me sleepy though. Somehow the constant chatter at the other cafés acts like white noise and keeps me focused. It's warm in here too. I have already shed my jacket and wish I could shed my shirt. I have a sports bra on under my shirt. It can't be too much different than a bathing suit, right? Okay, maybe it is, but it shouldn't be:

- Warm
- Quiet
- Dim lighting
- Plush couch

Hmm. This sounds like a recipe for a nap, not a brilliant writing session, and I recently ate lunch, too. Well, at least I got an extra shot of espresso in my latte. I pull out my computer, set it up, and dig into my bag for my headphones. I grope inside the bag and my hand is met with all my mail. Hmm, bills, ads. Wait . . . Naomi's wedding invitation. I take this one out. It's elegant and simple, in crème and black, with gold embossing. I tear open the envelope.

Rajit Chandra Singh
and
Naomi Justine Hall
Request the Honour of your Presence

In the Joining of their Love.
Saturday the ninth of February
At the home of Mr. Singh
Rancho Palos Verdes Estates
Dinner Reception Following

What! I read it again. Naomi *Justine* Hall. How did I never know her middle name? Oh my God, of course. With my eyes closed, I breathe it in and my heart swells.

Okay, so how do I begin? I guess I'll start from my apartment. I take a deep breath and close my eyes to attempt to capture the mood and feeling of that day when I first moved into my apartment. I begin typing:

Chapter 1

Broken. More broken plates and cups, or worse . . . Damn, there goes the champagne wedding flutes. I curse under my breath and gather myself and the delicate crystal pieces that spill from the overturned box. Shards of china fall between the open steps and rain down on unsuspecting insects living in the grass below.

The End.

About the Author

Heather S. Rivera, R.N., J.D., Ph.D. lives in Huntington Beach, California with her husband, Mark. Her best friends consist of Kala (a Puggle), Kiki (a neurotic Chihuahua), and Danzy (a black cat who believes he helps her write). When not writing, Heather works in the institute that she founded with Mark and speaks on past life research.

Heather is the author of *Healing the Present from the Past: The Personal Journey of a Past Life Researcher*. To find out more about PLR Institute and the work they are doing please visit: www.plrinstitute.org www.heatherrivera.com

Made in the USA
San Bernardino, CA
31 March 2014